HARD CASE

A CAT MARSALA MYSTERY

◆   ◆   ◆

Barbara D'Amato

CHARLES SCRIBNER'S SONS

NEW YORK LONDON TORONTO SYDNEY TOKYO SINGAPORE

Charles Scribner's Sons
Rockefeller Center
1230 Avenue of the Americas
New York, NY 10020

Manufactured in the United States of America

1 3 5 7 9 10 8 6 4 2

Library of Congress Cataloging-in-Publication Data
D'Amato, Barbara.
Hard case: a Cat Marsala mystery /Barbara D'Amato.
p.   cm.
1. Marsala, Cat (Fictitious character)—Fiction. 2. Private
investigators—Illinois—Chicago—Fiction. 3. Women
detectives—Illinois—Chicago—Fiction. 4. Chicago
(Ill.)—Fiction.
I. Title.
PS3554.A4674H33   1994
813'.54—dc20   94-13858

ISBN 0-684-19686-7

For Tony

ACKNOWLEDGMENTS

My thanks to Dr. Liz Orsay, Professor of Emergency Medicine at the University of Illinois, who graciously let me shadow everybody in the Emergency Department and answered hundreds of questions patiently. And to Sharon, Molly, Roy, and all the people at U of I who took time to tell me stories. Also, thanks to the staff of the surgical wing at the Grand Haven Hospital, Grand Haven, Michigan, where I worked many years ago. None of the unfortunate events in this book could have happened in their units.

Special thanks to David Strecker, R.N.,M.S., and Joanne Strecker, R.N., B.S., who took time out of their busy schedules to read a draft and offer advice and corrections.

HARD CASE

◇ 1 ◇

You've heard of a Michigan roll? To make one you take a whole lot of one-dollar bills, roll them up, and then roll your lone twenty or fifty around the outside. Then when you pay for your drinks, you whip out the roll, peel a couple of ones from inside and pay, but it looks like you have a serious roll of serious money, and men admire you, and women all want to hang on your arm and gaze into your eyes.

In Chicago, this might not be smart. I have what I think of as a Chicago roll. Actually, it's in my wallet, but the principle's the same. I put on one side any twenties or fifties I am lucky enough to have. Freelance reporting is not a way to get rich. My more numerous singles go on the other side, the side that I naturally open when I take out my wallet, so when I pay for anything, all anybody standing behind me would see is a lot of ones.

If you're female, slight of build, and out on the streets a lot like I am, things like this can be important. It's not that I particularly worry about being attacked. But certain safe-city behaviors become automatic.

So when I was paying for the jacket, I shielded the wallet as I took out the two twenties. I was in a secondhand store, and some of the people around me looked like their second hand was the one they used to pick pockets. Secondhand stores are good. In fact, they're great places to shop in the north Loop, because this is mostly a rich area, the part near Lake Michigan especially, and it's full of people who think if you've worn it twice, it's worn out. Secondhand places are fine, but some of the people who hang around them are not fine.

In any case, I now owned a nearly new gray linen jacket in almost-my-size. I would need it this afternoon when I went to the University Hospital complex—known as U-Hosp by the cognoscenti—to watch their trauma center at work.

Hal Briskman at *Chicago Today* had called me yesterday, July 22, which was a Sunday, but in all the time I've known him, I've called him at work absolutely any day of the week, and always found him there.

"I got this great assignment for you," he said.

Since Hal is quite often the person responsible for my being able to pay my rent, I said, "Excellent! What do you want me to do?"

"Well, see, we are heading into major health-care reform. It's going to be the biggest revolution in health care in decades, and in some sense the biggest ever. Now, you know everybody is concerned about the costs of health care. But in this country we are also proud of the things we've achieved in medicine. One of the proudest achievements is the specialized trauma unit. You take somebody who has been, let's put this brutally, essentially reduced to hamburger in a traffic accident, zip him to a trauma unit, and they have all the equipment and personnel right there to jump into action. Hook him to a respirator, heart-lung machine, whatever, sew up the damage, put in bionic parts, whatever else, and wowie! It's like things you would have seen in movies twenty years ago.".

"Yes, I can imagine."

"However! However, as of ten years ago we had ten level ne trauma units in Chicago. Then there were nine. Then there were eight. You follow me?"

"Perfectly."

"The University of Chicago trauma unit, Michael Reese Hospital, Weiss Memorial. All closed. Now there are six, and two of them are shaky. The unit at Northside Methodist closed *this week*. We now have exactly six trauma units in the whole metropolitan area. Why? The money crunch. The hospitals that have trauma units lose yea amounts of money on them. So they close. This may be very bad news for the people of Chicago, not just the rich and not just the poor. *Anybody* can be in a traffic accident, even a pedestrian crossing the street. I want you to go in there and find out whether trauma units are worth the cost."

"Yes. Fine. But Hal, I'm not an accountant."

"I know you're not."

"And even if I interview accountants on the costs of trauma care, it's gonna be a deadly dull article."

"No kidding. That's not what I want you to do at all. I want you to spend five days in a level one trauma center and tell about what you see—the people who work there and the people whose lives are saved there, and how they're saved. The human angle. Your personal touch."

"Oh."

"I want a medium-sized piece—say six thousand words. Your underlying question should be: Are trauma centers worth it? I've set up an appointment for you for tomorrow with Dr. Hannah Grant. She'll get you in and introduce you."

"Does she know what my 'underlying question' is?"

"Yes. And it's one she cares a lot about."

"All right. What time?"

"The three to eleven shift. Get there at ten of three."

.

"You knew I'd do this?"

"Well, sure. You need work, don't you?"

I ground my teeth. And quit rather swiftly, too. The last thing I needed was dental bills on top of food, clothing, and shelter bills. "Yes, Hal. I always need work."

The point of my gray jacket was to look somewhat professional. A white jacket would be wrong. It would be deceptive, as if I were trying to palm myself off as a doctor. I have no general objection to palming myself off as anything that will work in getting a story, but in this case all the trauma center personnel would know I wasn't a doctor. And why fool the patients? They might ask me to suture a slash and then where would we all be?

And, of course, my usual garb of Levi's and a sweatshirt weren't quite right, either. Actually, my guess was the Levi's would be okay, but not the sweatshirt. I'd wear the jeans with a white turtleneck and the jacket and be just fine.

Most of the time, when I get an assignment, it takes me a while to decide how to handle it. How to give it a form or a flavor that is consistent and interesting. "Do something on why a trauma center is valuable" is pretty vague. What's different about a trauma center, different from an emergency room? Why do we need them?

When a case comes in to a trauma department, several people—different ethnicities, genders, and professional levels—swing instantly into action to save a life. In uniform they might look like cogs in a well-oiled motor; underneath they'd be different people with different personalities and outside lives. Many different individuals working as a precision team, like people in an orchestra all playing different instruments. Why do they do it and what are they like? That was part of the answer.

Then I'd segue into the lives saved. Why do we need trauma centers?—if we do? What's so special?

At quarter to three on a hot and humid July afternoon, I was parking in the visitors' lot. This is a multistory garage as big as most high-rise apartment buildings. A blue stripe on the pavement showed me the way out of the lot. A signpost at the lot exit pointed to various buildings, the whole complex covering several city blocks. It was so big that many of the buildings were out of sight behind other buildings. Cardiac Care. The Grumann Pavilion. Hecker Women's Hospital. Orthopedics, with two subheads: Ambulatory Care and Prosthetics. Loeschner Neurologic Services. Outpatient Surgery. Major Surgery. Beale-Parkins Cancer Center.

Lord, all of them were places I didn't want to be!

And on a separate red signpost, Emergency Care and Motriss/Beale Trauma Center.

Labeled yellow stripes on the pavement went to all the other hospital buildings and units. A red stripe led off to the emergency and trauma building.

I had done enough ambulance following in my days as a reporter before I went freelance to know that emergency departments and trauma units were not the same things. In a way, they were the same medical specialty, but level one trauma centers handle high-risk, usually critical cases, victims of disaster, crime, or accident. Which is not to say that critical patients don't wind up in emergency units or that noncritical patients don't wander into trauma centers. But if you are a person who thinks he might be having a heart attack, you should go to the nearest emergency room, not the trauma center.

Chicago has hundreds of hospitals, and most of them have emergency rooms. These emergency departments are tied into a radio communications system so that patients can be sent to whichever unit is able to handle them. In the event of a large-scale disaster, one center far from the disaster serves as the dispatching link and distributes cases to the nearest appropriate ERs and trauma centers. But there are only six level one trauma centers. They are special. They are specifically designated units, carefully spaced geographically, with a trauma surgeon on the premises twenty-four hours a day, an anesthesiologist twenty-four hours a day, certain designated specialists available on call within a fifteen-minute drive, and extremely high tech equipment. The designated trauma center system makes it possible to concentrate expensive equipment and top medical skills in specific places, instead of having partial systems scattered here and there.

I wanted to enter my trauma center the first time by the same route a patient entered, so I followed the red stripe across asphalt that radiated visible waves of heat in the July sun, past the visitors' entrance, and around the back until I found the ambulance ramp. There was an ambulance pulling away, and I smelled the odors of hot automobile metal and oil. No other ambulances were arriving right now. It seemed there was no major disaster in the works.

I walked up the ramp. Two wide glass doors on tracks pulled back automatically when I got close. A bell rang twice as the doors opened. I hesitated. I was intimidated. The staff here would be highly professional people doing a highly skilled job. Things would happen fast and bloody. Would I be in the way? Would they detest having me here, watching but useless? Would I be underfoot at the wrong second and would somebody die because of it? Would I make an idiot of myself—faint or cry or something?

When you feel this way, there's nothing to do but put on your professional face—I was a professional, too, after all— and your firm stride, and forge ahead.

I took a deep breath and walked in.

◇ 2 ◇

Inside, the air was wonderfully cool. I was in a large lobby, and I faced a central, crescent-shaped desk. To the left of the desk were two small offices and to the right of the desk another two. All four offices had glass windows with horizontal blinds on the inside. The rooms on the left were labeled POLICE and PRESS, and on the right TRIAGE NURSE and EMERGENCY MEDICAL TECHNICIANS. The triage blinds were angled so that you couldn't see in, but a shadow moved against them. All three of the other offices were empty. All the signs were written in both English and Spanish. The red stripe continued past the desk, but I stopped.

I said to the woman behind the desk, "I'm Cat Marsala. To see Dr. Hannah Grant. She's expecting me."

"Through there. Follow the red stripe as far as it goes, then take a left and go down the corridor. You'll see her name on the door."

The stripe led through a wide arch into a very large lozenge-shaped room, a huge, bright rectangle with rounded corners. The stripe ended just inside. The center of the room contained another island, this one twenty feet across and horseshoe-shaped. Half a dozen people in white coats, two in blue coats, and one in a pink coat sat at computerized workstations or stood making notes. One sat at a terminal, speaking into what I assumed was the direct radio hookup to emergency medical technicians in the field. She said, ". . . patient coming to you as his desired and closest." A foot away from the terminal was an EKG machine receiving incoming signals and printing them out on a strip of paper.

It was like the interior of an intergalactic starship. Everything that wasn't stainless steel was white. The walls were glossy white, the sheets were white cotton, the ceiling was white sound-absorbent tile, the floor was white, matte-finished tile.

Against the walls on two sides of this huge room were ranks of examining tables making up eight or so treatment bays. They were separated by white curtains on tracks. There were two plastic chairs near the place where each curtain bunched up when it was pulled back. On the far wall were doors leading into maybe six walled rooms, one of which looked like a fully equipped operating room with a scrub room attached. There was only one patient in the unit, in a treatment bay, surrounded by four people speaking softly and urgently. To my right there was a wide steel double door, closed and unlabeled. To my left, at the end of one wall of treatment bays, a corridor led off. On the wall behind me, near the door I'd just come through, was a six-foot-wide, shiny white board showing a diagram of the rotunda and blocked, numbered spaces for all the treatment bays and the operating room. There were wipe-off markers and an eraser on a shelf next to it. Space seven had "Martin, closed head injury" written in. Space five said "Morchumb" with an arrow labeled "X-ray." Obviously the staff wrote down each case when it came in, then updated it according to how the case was handled.

Several staff members glanced at me, then dismissed me and then went back to whatever they were doing. So much for being self-conscious.

As in most emergency rooms, each examining table had its own set of shelves with supplies, a steel chest with bottles of antiseptic and fixative, slides, tongue depressors, gauze squares, and swabs, and a group of outlets and connectors on the wall. I sidled past one and saw MED GAS SYSTEMS over a bank of outlets reading NITROGEN, NITROUS OXIDE, OXYGEN, VACUUM, and AIR. I supposed one electrical outlet was for a defibrillator. The trauma center had much more electrical equipment ranged along the walls than most emergency rooms. Some of it looked like what you'd need if you wanted to launch an ICBM.

Other than the stunningly high-tech look, the most striking difference between this and the emergency rooms I was used to was the lack of crowds. Waiting rooms in busy emergency departments are filled night and day with people holding bloody heads, people holding their stomachs, people moaning, people crying, people bleeding, people holding onto their sick relatives, babies throwing up, people who just wandered in because they didn't feel well and didn't have a personal doctor. Most emergency rooms look like a way station on the retreat from Da Nang. This was quieter. And much scarier. I had the feeling that here Death stood invisible near the big white case board, watching the entries as they were brought in and occasionally stretching out a long finger: "You. And you. And *you.*"

I hung a left as instructed and entered the corridor. All along it on my left were doors. All along it on the right were lockers. It was a blind corridor, with rest rooms at the far end. I didn't go all the way to the end. The fourth door I passed was labeled DR. HANNAH GRANT, DIRECTOR OF TRAUMA SERVICES.

Hannah Grant was a slender woman with short dark hair shot with gray. The hair had been cut in an efficient, blunt bob, but apparently wanted to curve forward on its own, giving her the look of a person who valued and aimed for efficiency but might burst out into impulsiveness if she had a spare moment. Her clothing was the same: a knee-length white coat over green scrub pants and scrub top, and around her neck a stethoscope and a necklace of baked clay animals, mostly pink and purple elephants, that had to have been made by a child. Her child? Her grandchild? She was at that forty-fivish age when it was hard to guess which.

Her office was tiny, and absolutely crammed with books. I introduced myself.

"Cat Marsala? Good to have you here. I read your article on the Lottery."

"Oh. Uh—really?"

"Very clear."

"Oh. Well, thank you."

"It's not easy to explain long odds to people."

In her line of work, probably she often had to try. I said, "Hal explained to you the sort of article he wants—"

"The value of trauma units."

"Uh—" I wondered whether he had really made it clear that I could be pro or con on the question. While I was still thinking this over, she smiled and added, "I should have said, 'the value of trauma units, yes or no.' Well, don't expect me to be unbiased." She stood. "I'll show you around."

"Thanks." This was a no-nonsense person.

"These are the senior staff offices—the attending physicians, chief resident, and so on, lockers for everybody, including med students and residents. There are no interns anymore. We call them first-year residents," she said, gesturing as we walked back down the hall. There was a man in green scrubs coming out of an office, carrying a bunch of paper. "This is Dr. Sam Davidian," Grant said. Davidian held out his hand and I shook it.

"Dr. Davidian," Hannah Grant said, "is a trauma surgeon. Trauma surgery is an advanced specialty. Sam, this is Cat Marsala." There was a tone in Dr. Grant's voice that I filed away for future analysis.

"Dr. Davidian," I said. "Nice of you people to allow me here."

Dr. Grant said, "You understand that you must not talk with the patients. You must *not* ask them any questions."

"I won't—"

"And you must not use their names in anything you write. I think you'd better not write down any of their names in the first place. Their anonymity is to be maintained at all times. Patients have the right of complete confidentiality."

"I understand. I don't intend to talk about specific cases—"

"I'm sure she won't," Dr. Davidian said, smiling at me.

"And you must not," Grant said in an even firmer voice, "get in the way."

I was firm on this one myself. "I'm *very* good at being un-obtrusive. And I understand that you don't need to be distracted when you're working."

Together we walked into the big trauma room. "This is the treatment rotunda," Dr. Davidian said.

"Dr. Jacob Coyne, Cat Marsala," Dr. Hannah Grant said, gesturing at a tall, bony man of about thirty who was the staff member nearest us. He was leaning against the wall, writing on a clipboard. He just nodded at us.

A janitor, an elderly white man, was mopping the floor. "This is Lester Smalley," Dr. Grant said. "Cat Marsala."

I held out a hand to shake hands, but he raised his, palms

forward, showing that he wore plastic gloves. "Welcome to our humble premises," he said, with a courtly nod.

I said thanks. He had a large wagon on wheels, on which was a big bin for waste and a smaller square bucket with wash water. There were also dispensers for two sizes of plastic bags, rags, towels, half a dozen spray bottles of various chemical cleaners, a dust pan, a dust mop, broom, yellow sandwich boards that said CAUTION WET FLOOR, and a heavy wringer attached above the water container. Blood on the floor must be a constant problem. The water smelled of bleach. I had heard that bleach kills the AIDS virus. As I thought of this, I realized I had been seeing red waste containers all around the room with the word BIOHAZARD on a background of linked black rings on an orange label.

In one of the treatment bays, a young woman pulled a sheet off the table, then wiped down the sides with a cleaning cloth.

"This unit was built to order," Dr. Grant said. "See how the staff in the center of the rotunda can keep an eye directly on *all* the patients at once?"

"Yes. I see."

"Even in the OR nobody's out of sight. There's a window. See? A lot of hospitals have to make do with units that have been converted from old-style hospital corridors. You know, where there's a row of rooms along both walls? The patients are in closed-off rooms. Then they squeeze staff desks in wherever they can, usually at the ends of halls, and the staff can't really see what's going on. Also, we have almost everything we need right here, built into the space." She gestured at one corner. "Mini-lab." She gestured at another corner. "Cast room. Medications." She looked around with a smile. "This is a very satisfactory space."

It was now about three-ten and noticeably quiet in the trauma center. I would always afterward remember that that was the very moment the tempo changed.

The woman at the radio console said, "They're about four minutes out."

At the same moment, a young man emerged from the back of the area, from the one treatment bay that was busy. He crossed to the central island. "Call radiology and set up a CAT scan," he said, and a woman all in white swiveled to a speakerphone.

A second or so later, the outer doors opened. I recognized the ding-ding-ding that announced somebody coming through. Three staff members moved into position.

The woman who entered was a few steps ahead of two EMTs pushing a large gurney on which a tiny blond child lay shrieking. The woman was not more than twenty-eight, but she was a heart attack looking for a slightly later decade to happen. Very overweight, with a bright pink face, she had meaty arms with blemishes on the skin. The blemishes seemed to be lots of tiny broken blood vessels. I have a friend who is hefty but carries it healthily. This woman didn't. Her arms had as much muscle tone as risen bread dough. Her hair was the color of brown paper bags and hung limply down to the bra straps that leaned out from the sleeveless tank top she wore. Her other garments were jade green stretch pants and green-and-white running shoes. At least she was color coordinated. She came running in, gasping for breath, flesh bouncing.

The little girl was folded up in a fetal position, except for one arm that had been secured to the gurney rail. An IV line ran into the arm. The child couldn't have been more than two, and when I say she shrieked I don't mean she was screaming. She emitted a thin, bladelike, keening wail. She would stop just long enough to suck in a breath and then shriek again.

That shriek made the back of my neck prickle.

The tiny girl was dressed, if you could call it that, in a washed-out chenille bathrobe made for a six- or seven-year-old.

A nurse whose nametag read FERN BUTLER, R.N., gestured the EMTs to one of the examining bays. Dr. Grant followed the gurney and I followed Dr. Grant, with my hands clasped behind my back.

Grant mumbled to me, "Triage should have sent this case to the burn unit."

Fern was shooting questions at the woman.

"What is your name?"

"Ooooh. Oh, Lord."

"Name?"

"Oh. Tanya Williams."

"What is the child's name?"

"DeeDee."

"Is DeeDee your daughter?"

"Yeah."

"How old is DeeDee?" Fern asked.

"She just fell in. She fell in," Tanya said.

Fern Butler was medium height and middle aged, with a round pink face, a face that seemed broader than it was high, as if she'd been taken by the ears and stretched a little sideways. It was a pleasant face, and she looked like she could be cheerful under other circumstances. Right now she was grim. She repeated herself, firmly. "How old is DeeDee?" The mother whimpered.

I couldn't take my eyes from that little body. The child was bright red down one side. The right side of her face was red.

So was what I could see of her right shoulder and arm, her chest, and part of her abdomen.

A young black man, maybe twenty-eight and slender, whose nametag read WILLIAM MICHELSON, M.D. was examining DeeDee while Fern asked questions. Dr. Grant stayed back and watched them.

"How old is she?" Fern said, louder.

"Nine—nineteen months."

"Does she have any medical conditions we should know about?"

"What?"

"Does she have any medical problems?"

"No. No, she never gets sick."

"Any allergies?"

"No."

"What happened?"

"She fell—I was filling the tub to bathe her, and she just fell in."

"The water was that hot?"

"I put in the hot first. I hadn't put in any cold yet."

DeeDee shrieked. Dr. Michelson tried to look in her eyes and ears and listen to her heart. She refused to let him touch her. Her hands and arms were drawn up tight against her chest. Fern moved over and smoothed the child's forehead. Dr. Grant said to the child, "That's right, DeeDee. It's all right to be scared. But you're okay, now, hear?"

DeeDee didn't stop shrieking, but she looked at Dr. Grant. Dr. Grant said, "You can have one, too," and handed DeeDee Dr. Michelson's stethoscope. Michelson blinked but didn't object. "Here, you hang on to this, DeeDee. Now we each have one. It will make you feel better."

DeeDee loosened her fists just long enough to take hold of

the stethoscope and clutch it to her chest. Grant gently lifted the bathrobe away. The child's right thigh was red, too.

"Now you hold your toy and I'll hold mine. Want to listen to my heart? No? You can, if you want." She placed the business end of her stethoscope on the unburned part of the little girl's chest. The child whimpered, but at least she had stopped the terrifying shrieking. She sobbed a couple of times and made sounds, none of them words.

Fern said to the mother, "She fell in?"

"I went to get some soap. And she was climbing on the tub, and she must've fell in."

Gently, Dr. Grant took DeeDee's elbow and drew the arm just a little way away from the chest. The part of the chest under the arm was a normal pinkish white, not red. Dr. Grant and Fern Butler exchanged a glance.

I stood in the corner of the room, keeping my hands clasped behind my back.

Michelson said, "Tetanus," to a young white woman, whose nametag read BELINDA FOWLER. She left immediately and I brilliantly deduced she was going to get a tetanus booster. Two other staff members stood nearby. The nametag on one read DR. ZOE PETERS on the other DR. SONALI BACHAAN. Both were so young they had to be first-year residents.

Michelson took the child's blood pressure with a small cuff, talking to the child all the while. So far, he was keeping her calm. When he tried to draw blood, though, the child shrieked again, and not even Fern's cooing helped at all. The mother shifted from foot to foot but did not try to soothe her child.

Fern and Michelson had to hold the child down to draw blood. Then Michelson stepped back, looking drained and grim. For good reason. Already the child's skin looked like it was loosening on her thigh and back. She wouldn't come out of this unscarred.

Dr. Grant folded her arms and snapped at Dr. Michelson, "What should you be doing now, Dr. Michelson?"

"Uh—my Lund and Browder chart."

"Then get to it."

"Right," he said, pulling out a small pad of white paper.

Faintly I heard the double bell that announced the opening of the doors. Fern immediately handed the clipboard and an attached pen to a younger woman standing behind her. Fern mumbled something to her, pointed at the bottom of the page, and moved swiftly toward the incoming group. Dr. Grant and I followed her.

Maybe this was the emergency that had been "four minutes out." A gurney arrived with two EMTs, one on each side, one steadying a plastic bag of stuff running into an IV, the second holding something on the patient's chest with one gloved hand.

Dr. Davidian fell into step behind the gurney, saying to the EMT, "Is this the pneumothorax?"

"Yeah, we've got a left chest, obviously—" said the EMT, as I caught a glimpse of two Chicago police officers joining the parade.

Dr. Grant said to them, "Keep back if you want to stay."

The plumper one said, "Sure thing," in an easy rumble, like he'd played this scene many times before.

"Dr. Davidian will let you know when you can interview the patient," Grant said.

Davidian and the EMTs marched toward one of the treatment bays, trailed by two nurses, two cops, and me. I jammed my hands into my pockets and sauntered over next to the two cops, at the outside corner of the bay.

The patient was a young white boy. He was about fourteen. This was an event that, unfortunately, I had seen too much of back when I was a reporter.

"A drive-by?" I said to the cops.

"Yeah. Just outside Parson High School," the chubby cop said.

"Gang member?"

"Not this kid. Well, he may or may not be. But the kid they were shooting at was a seventeen-year-old on the sidewalk. This kid was shooting baskets on the playfield."

"Fifty feet behind the target," the other cop said.

Davidian and a nurse whose nametag said MARVELINE KRUSE took over for the EMTs. Davidian said, "Hi. I'm Sam." There was a bandage on the boy's chest, but it had come loose. Underneath was hole in the chest. The hole sucked in air, and then a few seconds later it breathed out a bubbly froth of blood. Nurse Kruse swabbed around it and Davidian placed a fresh bandage over it. "So you play basketball?" he said, while he flashed his penlight in the kid's eyes.

"Well, not much," the kid said in a whisper. He was terrified. I would be, too.

"Football? Parson has quite a team."

"No. I'm not big enough."

"What're you interested in?" Davidian asked. He discovered that the boy was interested in baseball. Davidian kept him talking and focused on something other than his wound. At the same time, he said to Marveline Kruse, "Get the chest surgeon, and we need the OR stat."

"Okay."

"And tell the police they'll have to talk with him in the morning."

I looked around, realizing I had lost track of Dr. Grant.

She was in the central part of the rotunda, standing with her arms folded, watching the medical students, nursing

students, and residents crossing to and from the center island
to the patients and to the supplies cabinets. An orderly
wheeled the patient who needed the CAT scan out of the
room in back, through double doors opposite the office corridor. So, I thought—that door goes to the rest of the hospital.
Michelson worked on the little burned girl. An anesthesiologist and the chest surgeon arrived, and Davidian and the
surgeon scrubbed and began surgery on the boy with the
bullet wound in the chest. Dr. Bachaan both assisted and ob-
served. Lester Smalley washed, then dried, his way across
the far side of the floor. He was the only one whose job I
fully understood. The tempo in the room was faster now.
Even as I watched, a buzzer on the desk sounded. Fern
Butler leaned into the radio console, listened, and said to
EMTs in the field somewhere, "How far out are you?"

"Are you busy?" I asked Dr. Grant. "Can I ask you some
things?"

"Sure. I'm just"—she smiled briefly—"supervising."

"About the little girl. What did you mean when you questioned Michelson about a Lund and Browder chart?"

"You have to come up with a BSA. BSA just means the
percent of body surface area that was burned. And then
you have to judge the severity of the burns. In water burns
that's hard to do at first, because you don't have any charring
and sometimes no blistering. First-degree burns are the
shallowest, and they don't have blisters. Second-degree
burns usually blister. Third-degree burns usually don't blister, because they're too deep. They go all the way down
through all the layers of the skin. They're so deep they don't
even hurt; even the nerves are killed. Unless they cover a
very small area, they won't heal without skin grafts."

"What do you think the child's burns are?"

"Second and maybe some third degree, I think."

"From bath water?"

"Well, we'll see." She changed the topic. "The Lund and Browder chart tells you how to judge body areas. With adults, when we figure how much body area was burned, we use the rule of nine. The head and neck is nine percent of the body, each hand and arm is nine percent, each foot and leg is eighteen. But children are different. Their heads are large in proportion to their bodies, and their arms and legs are smaller. And it changes as they grow. So you use Lund and Browder, which gives you percents by age. The area burned tells you a lot about how serious it's going to be. I was making sure the resident knew what he was doing."

"What else will you do for her?"

"She's on Ringer's lactate to keep her body fluids up. She's had a tetanus booster. She'll be watched for hypothermia and we'll catheterize her to keep track of how much urine she's putting out."

"It's that serious?"

"She's burned, I would guess, over about thirty percent of her body. That is very serious. Even if some of it is first-degree burns, she could go into shock with no warning. The good news is she wasn't in a combustion fire, so we don't have to worry about her lungs. She wouldn't have inhaled smoke or superheated air."

"I see."

Behind us we heard the buzzer, then the stutter of a radio, breaking up and then coming clearer. Dr. Grant cocked her head. "Automobile accident. It sounds like four injuries."

"Do you have to get ready?"

"We *are* ready. We're always ready. Of course, we have a certain limit to our capacity. When we're full we give the emergency medical system what we call a 'bypass' and patients go to other trauma centers. Are you getting along okay—finding out what you need?"

"Starting to. This is still confusing to me. It's like a kaleidoscope. I still can't remember even who most of the staff are."

"It'll get clearer." In the distance we could hear ambulance sirens. Dr. Grant gestured at Marveline Kruse. Marveline moved toward the entry.

Fern Butler at the radio console said loudly, to the room, "Listen up, gang! Expect four from this accident." She moved toward the door and Fowler took her place at the desk.

"Is the trauma center always like today, quiet for a while, and then *wham*!?"

"It can be. Mondays are the busiest days."

"You'd think it would be Friday. Or Saturday night."

"I know. But it's the same, Monday, all over the country. After three-thirty it tends to get busier and busier until about seven. That gunshot wound, for instance—most of the gang violence is right after school. Then there's the rush-hour automobile accidents."

"And then it quiets down?"

"Well, domestic violence is more an evening thing. And drunk driving peaks, oh, maybe around eleven P.M."

"Oh."

She smiled, more softly this time. "Some evenings I feel like we're picking up the pieces, straightening out what we can, and then kind of putting the city to bed for the night. Silly, I guess."

That instant the doors burst open with another gurney. On it was an elderly black woman, moaning. Her hands and face were covered with blood. Dr. Zoe Peters, the resident, and

Fern, the nurse, met her gurney. In the distance I heard other sirens.

Keeping back and keeping my hands in my pockets, I watched the ballet as personnel separated themselves, three going to take care of the new case. Over half of the staff was now tied up with patients. In a minute more cases would hit.

I found Dr. Grant at my side. She was watching the doors.

"I meant to tell you, you've done what I asked. Kept out of the way," she said. "That's very professional of you."

"Well, thanks."

"You take our job seriously, not just your own job. I like that in a person."

I smiled. This was an odd, perfectionistic woman, but I liked her. If I were injured, I'd just as soon have a perfectionist doctor take my case.

In less than a minute, the doors opened again. How would it be to work in a place where every time the doors opened they brought a new challenge and a new threat of somebody dying?

Dr. Grant left me abruptly. She and the bony young man, Dr. Jacob Coyne, approached the gurney.

A middle-aged black man with gray in his hair lay on his back. His entire chest was crushed—even I could see that. He was still alive, and the EMTs were pushing air into his lungs with a bag that fitted onto a tube that entered his throat. I could see his chest sink down between breaths.

Dr. Grant gestured the gurney to one of the treatment bays, then gave one of the EMTs a small shake of her head. She didn't believe the man would live. The EMTs and Dr. Coyne trotted fast into the treatment bay. At the same instant, the doors beeped again and another gurney came right behind this. It was a young black man, with a head injury, who kept saying, "I can't see! I can't see! Oh, my God!"

Dr. Grant and Dr. Bachaan followed this one.

I trailed after them. As I left the entryway, two other gurneys came in, one with a thirtyish black woman, one with a small child, probably her son. As the EMTs pushed them into separate treatment bays, the woman said, "I want him with me!" Dr. Michelson, who must have left the little burned girl in the care of a nurse, went to the woman.

One of the EMTs said, "Ma'am, please don't move! You have a back injury."

The other EMT said, "We thought there were four in the car, but then we found the kid on the floor in the backseat."

The student nurses rushed to the treatment tables with supplies. Obviously, some of them were roving gofers, responding to calls from any of the treatment bays. Dr. Coyne shouted for a suction machine. Dr. Michelson yelled for more sponges and the portable X-ray. Dr. Peters yelled for a portable X-ray. Dr. Bachaan sent for an eye specialist. Literally every human being in the unit was occupied except me.

I stayed a couple of minutes with Dr. Grant, Dr. Bachaan, and the young man who couldn't see. "Now, I know you're frightened," Dr. Grant said, "but we don't want you to worry too much. These things very often seem worse than they are. Now, we don't have your name. Please tell me."

The man just made fists out of his hands and tried not to scream.

"We're going to take good care of you. Your sight problem may be just temporary, and we're going to need your help here."

"I'm Antoine Holyrood," he said. His voice was ragged with fear. As Dr. Grant talked, she watched the progress of Dr. Bachaan's examination. She wasn't obvious about it, but she didn't miss a move the younger woman made. From the way Grant hung over Bachaan, I felt confirmed in my belief that the young woman was a first-year resident.

Finally, I toured the unit. Every last person was tied up, and there were clearly not enough senior attending physicians to go around. Coyne was working over the man with the crushed chest. Fern and Dr. Zoe Peters dealt with the elderly woman. Dr. Grant and Dr. Bachaan bent over the young man who couldn't see, encouraging him. Dr. Michelson was treating the young woman. Her little son waited, sitting on an examination table nearby, guarded by Marveline Kruse, who spoke to the child in soothing tones. The child had a small cut on his chin. There was a whole lot of soothing going on. Then Dr. Davidian came out of the OR, said, "The pneumothorax is going to recovery," and hurried off down the office corridor. Bathroom break, maybe?

The elderly woman moaned. Dr. Peters said, "Where's that damn suture cart?" Fern was already totally occupied cleaning the blood from the woman's face and hands. Dr. Peters said, "I'll be right back."

Like everybody here, Fern wore gloves. "Roll over just halfway, ma'am, on your side," she said. I stopped to watch for a second, keeping my distance. Fern took a look at the pads the EMTs had placed over a couple of the cuts on the woman's back. She started to clean them.

"You had some accident there," she said.

"I don't understand what happened. I was in the car just riding, and then I was on the street on my back."

Fern, wearing gloves, cleaned some of the back wounds, covered them with gauze, and then said, "Lie back down. The doctor will stitch those." She started rubbing a little salve on the woman's chest. "You just relax," she said, adding salve and rubbing some more. The woman seemed to be

calmer. There was a bump on her forehead, but the most sur-
prising thing was a huge swelling on her hip, about the size
of half a basketball. The skin over it was distended and shiny.
"I know this looks like a lot of blood," Fern said soothingly to
the woman as she threw away blood-soaked gauze. "But a little blood looks like a lot. You have children?"

"Two boys. My Charles was in the car with me."

Charles must be the patient with the crushed chest. Fern
wisely did not respond to that. "Well, then, you know how
when a child is cut, it looks like a lot of blood but it isn't. I
think we're gonna get you fixed up just fine."

Dr. Peters arrived. "I don't know why they don't stockpile
a whole day's set of kits," she grumbled.

Fern stopped rubbing salve and said, "Several lacerations
on the back."

Pointing at the swelling, Dr. Peters said, "I'd like to talk
with Grant about this hip later."

"I'll tell her," Fern said.

"And we need an ortho consult." Dr. Peters said to the
woman, "Are you on any medication?"

"Blood pressure. Hydro—" She was too dazed to go on.

"Hydrochlorothiazide?"

"That's right."

Peters said to Fern, "BP?"

"One-ten over seventy."

Dr. Peters had swung a metal table into place. Now she
pulled on gloves. "Fern, pass me the local anesthetic," Dr.
Peters said. They set to work.

I saw Dr. Grant approaching, and she looked into our bay,
stopped a few seconds, and then went on.

One of the EMTs stood at the desk, finishing his paperwork. "How'd the accident happen?" I said.

"Truck driver fell asleep on the Eisenhower. Crossed the

median. Head on into this car with dad, mom, granny, teenager, little kid."

"How's the truck driver?"

"Walked away."

Again, I toured the rotunda.

Dr. Coyne turned away from the middle-aged man with the crushed chest. He pulled off his gloves and threw them into the biohazard bin with a loud flap. A nurse pulled a sheet over the man's head.

Coyne made notes on a form, stuck it into a vertical file on the central desk, washed his hands, and moved immediately to help Sonali Bachaan with the young man who couldn't see.

I felt strongly ambivalent—admiration for the swift competence here, and at the same time sorrow at the desperate condition of the patients. The man with the chest injury who had died was discreetly wheeled out. They had covered him with a sheet, pulled the curtains around the treatment bays nearest him, and then wheeled him through the door that led to the rest of the hospital. Not long after that, as Dr. Peters was sitting her up to turn her over, the older woman gasped and collapsed.

Fern stepped toward the cardiac monitor, which showed a flat line. Then she hit a code button that set off a light and an alarm, and yelled, "Staff! Code!"

She handed Dr. Peters a laryngoscope and an endotracheal tube to keep an airway open, and slid a board under the woman's chest.

By now Sam was there, and they started CPR. He climbed on the gurney and pumped the woman's chest, the board underneath providing rigidity, while Peters squeezed air into her lungs with an AMBU bag. At Davidian's orders, Fern filled syringes and injected the IV line with a sequence of drugs.

CPR didn't work, and Davidian asked for the defibrillator. He tried to jump-start her heart, which caused her to lurch as if alive. He tried again. And again. But there was still only a flat line on the screen. "Let's crack the chest," Sam said. "Get me a tray."

But Grant said. "Nothing's ever going to bring this lady back." She and Davidian looked at the clock.

"You're right," he agreed, reluctantly.

The relatives of the family, the Holyroods, arrived. The white teenager with the gunshot wound had been taken to recovery after Davidian removed the bullet from his lung, and nobody could trace his parents anywhere. The little burned girl, trailed by her mother, an orderly, and a medical student named Brunniger, left for the burn unit.

For the next several minutes I walked around the room unobtrusively and watched. The bustle, the people moving back and forth, the calls to the central operator for a neurosurgeon, the calls upstairs for an eye surgeon or to central meds for special medications they didn't stock, the shift of a nurse from one case to the next to the next—it all looked confusing, but I was beginning to see the well-oiled machine it really was. Eventually, once I recognized all the individuals and the part each played, I thought that I would focus the opening of my article on the kinds of people who worked here. All these different people, various genders, ethnicities, ages, backgrounds, all merging into a quietly functioning unit.

I was pleased about that.

There was a trail of blood on the floor, and Lester Smalley kept mopping, mopping, mopping.

The tempo slowed. I noticed some of the staff disappear and come back with candy or coffee. Dr. Coyne left and re-

turned with a candy bar. A resident named Qualley came
back from a cafeteria break and went to help Michelson. Dr.
Michelson went out and came back with nothing, so I
guessed he'd been to the men's room. The student nurses
and first-year residents tended to stay with their patients. Dr.
Coyne, Dr. Davidian, Dr. Peters, Dr. Bachaan, and Dr.
Michelson wrote up directives or filled out forms. Charge
nurse Fern Butler wrote up the nursing notes. An army may
travel on its stomach, but a trauma center, like police departments and other such things, travels on its paperwork.

Sam Davidian started down the corridor to the rest rooms
and offices, but was beeped by Fern to take a look at the little
boy. He found the child trying to make a race car out of the
wheeled suture cart.

"What do you have there?" Davidian asked. "A cut chin?"

"Mmm. Yeah."

"Look, let's sit you up here again, and not crash the cart
into the wall. Lie back, tiger."

"You gonna stick me with a needle?"

"Well, yes. But only with some brand-new cybernetic-age
stuff that will numb the hurt."

Sam had the loaded syringe in his right hand, out of the
child's sight. When the little boy said, "What's new about it?"
Sam brought his hand up and injected the local anesthetic
before the child could jump.

"Now that didn't really hurt, did it?"

"Not much."

"Once more and we're all done."

"What's so great about it?"

"This is new. It's called Tegucaine, and the FDA has just
approved it for patient use."

"Why?"

Watching, I realized that Sam was talking with the child as if he were an adult, and the child really responded to it.

Sam said, "It's supposed to wear off faster after you use it."

"Why's that good? I'm better off if it keeps the thing all numb."

"No, you might hurt yourself. There's a reason we human beings need pain. It's to keep us from hurting ourselves. Has your dentist ever used anesthetic in your mouth?"

"Yeah. I had this big cavity filled once."

"And didn't it make your tongue numb? And didn't they warn you about biting your tongue while you couldn't feel it?"

"Yeah!" He giggled. "And I ate a sandwich anyway, and I bit my tongue and bled all over the sandwich."

"Well, see? The faster it wears off the better. And while we're on the subject of speed, I'm done here. You only needed two stitches, my man."

I was surprised when people took breaks in the middle of treatment and another staffer took over. But I shouldn't have been. I had to remind myself that we were not in a crisis situation here. This was not a disaster. It just looked like one to me. These people did this job, exactly this job, day after day, five days a week.

The young man with the eye injury turned out to have a head injury as well. Dr. Coyne and Dr. Bachaan talked with the eye surgeon and put in a call to a neurosurgeon. The family stood by, too upset to speak, the young man's aunt holding his hand and stroking it. They had been told of the other two deaths and appeared to attach themselves to the young man as the one family member they could help. Dr. Coyne happened to pause near me, and I asked, "How serious is it?"

"Very," he said.

I needed to get away. Just for two minutes, maybe, but out of here.

I wasn't going to be sick or anything like that. I'd seen accidents before. I was *exhausted*. Just suddenly completely drained. I had to have a break. Thinking of a reasonable excuse to leave, I said to a student nurse who was passing by with a box of syringes, "Where is the rest room?"

"That way. Just past the lounge." I entered the corridor. Yes, a bit beyond Grant's and Davidian's offices and short of the lounge was a sign that said REST ROOMS, protruding perpendicularly from the wall.

I walked toward it.

The hall was as brightly lighted as the rest of the building. Dr. Grant's office door stood open. So did Dr. Davidian's. There were half a dozen staff offices with the doors closed, probably some other "attendings" from other shifts, whom I hadn't met.

The corridor dead-ended at the two rest rooms, WOMEN and MEN. Just short of there, past the last office, a sign protruding from the wall read STAFF LOUNGE. I could see vending machines. So this was where people had been getting their coffee. Maybe I'd go in there instead. There's nothing like caffeine or chocolate to bring a person out of a low.

As I entered, I could see feet. Somebody was so tired they were napping.

On the floor.

It was Dr. Hannah Grant. She lay on her side, half-turned away from me. Her tongue was sticking out. The tongue was quite long. And tan. How very odd—a long tan tongue. For a second I almost giggled, it was so inappropriate, so bizarre. I moved closer. No, it wasn't her tongue. It was a tongue depressor.

"Help!" I yelled out the door. As a couple of people in the trauma center rotunda turned to look, I yelled "Help!" again, louder.

They were coming, but seconds might count. I turned her on her back and then saw that the tongue depressor had been under her cheek, not inside her mouth. I held her nose, and blew a quick breath into her lungs.

Except that it wouldn't go in. I couldn't give her any air.

◆ 3 ◆

"You were the only person who got a look at the murder scene before they trampled all over it," Det. Sgt. Robert Hightower said.

I said, "They didn't trample. They were trying to save her."

"Why are you defending them?" His manner was a combination of "I'm in a hurry because I'm important" and "Why do I have to deal with civilians?"

"I'm not defending them. I'm just describing them. That's what they do. They try to save lives. They wanted to resuscitate her."

"Are they friends of yours?"

"No. I'd never met any of them before today."

"Mmm." It was now five P.M. Hightower had taken over Dr. Grant's office as a command post and was questioning me there. He'd been told I was not a staff member, so he probably hoped to get an outside view of things. "So what is this research you're doing?"

"Research? I'm not doing any research. What gave you that idea?"

"Dr. Davidian said you were working on a paper."

"I'm not working *on* a paper. I'm working *for* a paper. I'm a reporter. I'm doing a story on the trauma center for *Chicago Today*."

"Oh." Something shifted in his mind. His set of ideas about me changed; so did his manner. Suddenly he found he had time to be courteous.

"A trained observer, then. Great. Describe the scene as you saw it."

I gave him full marks for keeping the sneer out of his voice. Trained observer! He figured I was born Sunday and came here on Monday?

I thought I might as well stun him with my visual recall.

"I left the central rotunda to take a break. It was four twenty-five. I was heading for the rest rooms, but when I spotted the lounge, and the machines, coffee seemed like a good idea. When I entered the lounge, I saw Dr. Grant's feet, though I didn't know whose feet they were then. They were just visible around the L shape of the room. The lounge has a short entry and then the lounge itself is around to the left. It's built that way to allow for a supplies cupboard in the corridor outside."

"We know that," Hightower said.

"Good. In the corridor, on the floor near the entry door, I noticed a smear of reddish brown, probably blood from somebody's shoe. Inside the room, Dr. Grant was lying near the table. There was a plastic cup near the body, what looked like spilled coffee near the cup, coffee with cream, by the way, judging from the color. There was a half-full cup, no cream, on the table. There was a dropped clipboard, and a quarter. The quarter was under the table near the table leg. The coffee may have been on the table when it spilled, because there was spilled coffee with cream on the tabletop as well. Dr. Grant was lying on her left side but facing mostly down, with her knees drawn up toward her chest. Both hands were near her neck but not touching it. Her cheek was scratched. There was a tongue depressor lying just under her left cheek." Nothing on Earth would get me to admit that when I first saw it I thought it was her tongue.

"Her hair was somewhat ruffled, but her clothes were intact, not like they were later, after the resuscitation efforts. There was no one else in the room. All the lounge lights were on, as I gather they always are. Also on the only table were a few magazines and, I think, one newspaper. There was nothing on the sofa or the chairs. I didn't check the wastebasket. It's located near the soft drink machine."

Sergeant Hightower smiled wryly. "You happy now?"

He was making fun of my trying to wow him with my detailed description. But I wasn't going to give him the satisfaction of reacting. "Not really," I said, deliberately misunderstanding. "Dr. Grant was kind to me. Her permission allowed me to come here. I knew her less than two hours, but she treated me like a professional"—I hesitated, not quite adding "unlike some people"—"and I'm sorry she's dead. This isn't a happy moment."

"Mmmp. Tell me what they did to her next."

"Dr. Sam Davidian and Dr. Jacob Coyne and a nurse, Marveline Kruse, came running into the lounge when I yelled for help. Not because they were the only people worried, but because they were free for a moment from whatever they were doing."

"All right, then what?"

"When I found her, I tried to blow a breath into her lungs, but it didn't seem to work. The nurse, Kruse, took one look and tried to start breathing into Dr. Grant's lungs, too. She blew, then blew harder, and nothing happened. Dr. Davidian had arrived a little after her and he said, 'Stop that! If you don't see the chest rise immediately, don't *ever force it!* You can force some object down into the bronchi!'

"Dr. Davidian tried the Heimlich maneuver to loosen

whatever Grant had inhaled, but it didn't work. The crime scene was getting messed up; I can't deny that. Dr. Davidian yelled, 'Get an airway!' Kruse ran to get the airway. Coyne gave Dr. Grant another sharp blow just up under the rib cage. They tried the Heimlich maneuver again. I think they tried it three more times—without any success whatever."

"You think? I'm surprised you aren't certain."

I ignored that. "Kruse came in with an angled thing made of plastic. It's about this long," I made a seven-inch space with my two index fingers. "I understand you put it down a person's throat to keep an open airway."

"Yes, and—?"

"Dr. Grant was blue. She had been bluish when I found her. Her fingers were blue, her fingernails were blue, her face was purplish blue. Dr. Davidian shoved two fingers into Dr. Grant's throat, feeling for whatever it was, and suddenly said to Coyne, 'Don't bother with the airway. Get a forceps or a hemostat or whatever's closest.' Coyne ran out.

"Davidian listened to Dr. Grant's heart and shook his head. He lifted her eyelid and shined a light across the eye a couple of times. Coyne came back with forceps. He angled Grant's head back and held a flashlight. Davidian plunged the forceps into Dr. Grant's throat—" His decisiveness had made me wince, but he had no time to waste.

"He pulled out a wet, wadded-up piece of white stuff that looked like Kleenex. He tossed it and the forceps behind him, and immediately started blowing air into Dr. Grant's lungs."

The wet white thing had landed with a plop. "I went to look at what they had pulled out, but I didn't touch it. It was what they call a sponge. You've seen it, of course."

Sponges are really squares made of multilayered gauze.

They are used to mop up blood, or wash an area of skin with antiseptic, that kind of thing. Emergency rooms and trauma centers like this use thousands a day. However friendly these sponges are when used the way they were intended, when Davidian pulled this one out, it was suddenly a thing of horror.

It must have been jammed down her throat with the tongue depressor.

I told Sergeant Hightower the rest of it.

I told him that several other staff people, getting themselves free from patients for a minute, came running in. Dr. Zoe Peters had wheeled in a defibrillator. Staff jammed into the lounge. Dr. Sonali Bachaan stood at the edge of the group, wringing her hands and saying "Ba-cho! Great heavens!" They were used to death, but this time it was their friend and fellow worker, after all, who was dead or dying.

And actually, very obviously, dead. Zoe Peters angrily demanded that somebody use the defibrillator. Coyne growled at her. "The pupils are fixed and dilated. What do you expect us to do, rouse the dead?"

As personnel went soberly back to the central area, I had asked, "Did anybody call the police?" I looked around. Several of the faces were surprised.

Dr. Davidian, however, said, "I did."

I thought, Thank goodness somebody around here was playing with a full deck.

I studied the lounge. The plastic airway had been kicked under the sofa. The spilled coffee cup was cracked into a dozen polystyrene fragments and the coffee that had spilled from it was tracked around the floor. The quarter was invisible, but had to be someplace. Nobody would pick up a quarter at a time like this. Dr. Grant's shirt was open. The piece of gauze, the "sponge," lay on the floor, but now was flattened. I explained all this to Hightower.

"Somebody had *stepped* on it," Hightower said. "I knew it. It looked like it. They stepped on the murder weapon!"

Actually, I felt some sympathy for him.

By five-thirty or so, word of the murder was out to the Chicago media. Channels 2, 3, 5, 7, 32, WGN radio, and a lot of other media people swarmed in the paved area outside the trauma center entrance. U-Hosp security let them into the press room, the one in the outer lobby near the triage nurse and the police room, but they did not get inside the unit. U-Hosp security was very efficient. They barred the press from stepping onto the red stripe that led to the entry doors, insisting that emergency vehicles had to have room to enter. This statement was reinforced by the fact that ambulances continued to arrive. The hospital issued a statement that it was horrified and saddened. Hightower issued a statement including most of the bare facts and assuring the public that detectives were on the scene and a full investigation was in progress. These statements were read to the press outdoors fifty yards from the entrance, so that there was no bunch of people to block the doors.

I didn't make any effort to report on the murder. I'm not in breaking news anyway, anymore, and the media had the basic facts already.

Besides not allowing any media into the unit through the trauma unit entrance, security had stationed two large uniformed men to block the door from the rest of the hospital into the trauma center and to check the ID of anybody wanting to get in from that side of the rotunda. Security was very experienced at this kind of thing, Dr. Davidian told me, because they received a lot of high-profile patients here—politicians, movie stars, whatever. Since there were only six level one trauma centers in Chicago, and this was the most central with best access to the Loop, big names were likely to be brought here if they were seriously injured.

The press had been kept out of the unit, but not the police, of course. The invasion of the police—the uniforms first, then the detectives—had been an odd clash of cultures. The trauma center staff was very much accustomed to dealing with police officers. Cops came in with accident victims. Cops often accompanied the EMTs. Cops were here practically all the time, "sitting on the suspect," as they put it, from some gang shoot-out. Cops came in with people they had shot, and cops came in with cops who had been shot. There had been cops here this afternoon for a while with the teenager who had been shot, trying to get a statement from him before he went into surgery.

So the staff was used to the police. They knew many of the First and Eighteenth District officers by name. What they were used to, though, was the police taking instructions from the medical staff. Things like "You can't question him right now, he's sedated." Or "Please wait right over there: the doctor is probing for the bullet and we'll have it for you shortly." The staff was totally unaccustomed to being the subjects of the investigation.

This time, they were all suspects.

The uniforms took over the staff lounge and most of the hall, and then the detectives arrived and wanted to take over the whole unit. At that point the staff was still working on two of the automobile accident victims, and the body of the elderly woman, the second death, was just about to be unobtrusively wheeled away. A stabbing victim came in on a

gurney, trailing EMTs and blood. The cops got in the way
and they started ordering the staff around. At that point Dr.
Sam Davidian finally lost his temper.

"Hold it!" he shouted, standing in the middle of the rotunda. "You are not in charge here, and you are *not* going
to endanger my patients!"

Hightower said, "This is a homicide scene, Doctor."

"In there," Davidian said, pointing toward the lounge, "is
a homicide scene. In here"—he pointed to the treatment
bays—"is a trauma center. We work here. You go in there, do
your work, and you *keep out of our way!*"

It was probably his finest hour.

Of course, in fairness to the detectives, they were under-
standably upset that the crime scene and the body had been
completely messed up by the resuscitation efforts. One of
them—not Hightower, who seemed a politic, if supercilious,
person—said to Davidian, "Didn't you *know* she was dead?
You're the experts."

Dr. Davidian said, "People can be revived. And it's our job
to try."

"But she wasn't revived. Couldn't you tell—"

"The answer is yes, she looked dead, and no, you don't always know until you try. And yes, we're the experts. And
because we're the experts, we know we have to try."

While the cops went on doing their thing, which involved
detectives interviewing all the staff that had been on the
floor, evidence technicians fingerprinting the lounge (where
everybody and his brother had already been), evidence techs
going over the lounge floor with a hand-vacuum to pick up
hair and fiber and other traces, and finally the detectives
taking over Dr. Grant's office as well, the rest of the trauma
center went on with its work. One new automobile accident
victim had been brought in while I was being interviewed.

He turned out to have a fractured thoracic vertebra, probably from being hit in the back of the chest by some lumber he had been transporting in his pickup truck when he rammed into a small van that had braked suddenly for a dog. Dr. Davidian was pretty sure there were fragments of bone cutting into the spinal cord. But they needed more sophisticated X-ray studies than they could perform here in the unit. I went over to the central desk to watch the sequence of events. He spoke into the hospital intercom about myelography and T-8. Within a few minutes, a nurse from radiology and two orderlies were there to transport the patient.

I was still confused about who was who and what was what in the trauma center. So much of it was unfamiliar. There were machines around the walls, but their purpose was a mystery us to me. Much of the equipment near the examining tables was mysterious, too. Even the staff was mostly unfamiliar—I didn't know the names of half of them yet. Everything had happened too fast to assimilate.

Plus, it was dawning on me that one of the elements I wanted to fit into my story might not work either. I'd been thinking of opening the article with the different sorts of people who worked here fitting together into perfect teamwork—the staff as a well-oiled machine.

In reality, somebody hated Dr. Grant enough to kill her. For all I knew, the trauma center staff was a seething mass of mutual resentment and anger. The one time I actually go in on a story thinking I had a hook—no problem, easy stuff— and look what happens!

Having sent his patient to radiology, Dr. Davidian leaned back against the wall and sighed. He was just a couple of feet away from me, so I glanced over at him. Late thirties, early forties maybe, nice face. He was a craggy man, the sort that looks like he ought to be doing something with horses. He also looked very tired.

"Long day?" I asked.

"Long in a way. I've only been here"—he checked the wall clock and found it was six-fifteen P.M.—"three and a quarter hours, and it seems like ten."

"Were you a friend of Dr. Grant?"

"A friend? Not exactly. She didn't go in much for friends on the unit."

"A colleague, then."

"Colleague sounds good." He sighed again. "I suppose we can't go into the lounge to get coffee?"

"No. I don't think you can." I wasn't going to let him off the Grant question so easily. "Did Grant irritate the staff? She seemed very perfectionistic."

"Not irritate, exactly."

"What then?"

"Oh, nothing very important. She actually hadn't been on the staff very long."

"Oh?"

"The hospital board wanted to put somebody in to 'tighten up the unit.' They got Dr. Grant in from Stevens Memorial a little over a month ago to act as a kind of whip to get us into line."

"And she was resented?"

"No. Not a whole lot, for sure. The rest of us were used to working together, that was all. She was a good doctor, very good, very professional. She knew her stuff. And with a teaching hospital like this, you have fresh, untrained medical students and student nurses rotating through all the time. A whole new batch every five weeks. You really do have to ride herd on them every single minute. Some of them want to do more than they're trained to do, and you certainly can't allow that. And some of them are scared of doing the things they're supposed to do and you have to push them. Not everybody wants that kind of job. I respected her."

"But nevertheless, she was somewhat resented."

"You have to understand how it was. She might have been the very person we would have picked for the job, if we'd been asked. It's just that the regular staff people here felt they should have been consulted first. She was just rammed down our throats."

He stopped cold when he realized how Dr. Grant had died.

"Oh, my God! I wish I hadn't said that."

◆ 4 ◆

Fern came by and said to Dr. Davidian, "We've got a kitchen fire coming in. This is the second today. Somebody had better talk to triage."

Sam sighed. "I'll do it."

The doors beeped. The gurney and the EMTs entered. A different pair of EMTs, a different case, the same urgency.

By "kitchen fire," she meant, of course, victim of a kitchen fire. The woman's arm and one side of her face was burned. As the gurney went past me, I smelled the odor of cooked meat. The cooked meat was her.

As my stomach lurched, I consoled myself with the knowledge that she was not burned over a large body surface area. BSA. I was learning things. Dr. Grant had taught me that.

Out of nowhere, I became aware of a welling up in me of anger about Dr. Grant. She was a valuable person. There aren't all that many people in the world who do their jobs well, hold you to doing yours well, and can acknowledge it when you do. I hardly knew her, but I knew her enough to be truly angry she was dead. I wanted the killer caught and punished. I wanted justice.

It struck me how very unlikely it was that the killer would be caught and punished. Somebody might confess, I suppose, but other than that, where would they ever get any proof?

Suppose they found, say, fingerprints of Sam Davidian in the lounge? He probably went in there half a dozen times a day. Suppose they found hairs from Fern's head? She probably ran a comb through her hair before going back to work after a coffee break. Suppose they found Dr. Bachaan's lipstick? Could have been left behind anytime. Dr. Coyne's prescription pad? Likewise. Fowler's comb? Likewise.

Okay, so evidence of the killer having been on the scene wouldn't be helpful. Well, what about opportunity? Maybe somebody saw the killer come out of the lounge, and would remember and tell.

Except how would you know which person was the killer? Say Dr. A tells Hightower that he was in the lounge when Dr. Grant went in. Dr. A says Grant was alive when he left. Then say that Dr. B tells Hightower that he saw Dr. A coming out, went in and saw Grant dead. You wouldn't know which to believe, even then. If B is telling the truth, then A would be the killer. But B might be lying and might be the killer himself.

Come to think of it, it wouldn't be definite even if I had seen Dr. B myself, leaving the lounge just as I started down the hall, and if I then went directly into the lounge and found Dr. Grant dead. Even then, Dr. B could say he found Dr. Grant dead and was just too frightened to give the alarm. Who could prove different? It would be suspicious, but it wouldn't prove guilt.

Add to this the fact that I *didn't* see anybody leaving the lounge before I went in. I hadn't even seen anybody heading toward any of the offices along the corridor, or anybody leaving the rest rooms.

And as far as seeing anybody in the corridor, that wouldn't

prove a thing. The rest rooms were next to the lounge. So if someone had been seen going into the corridor, he only had to say he was heading for the bathroom and never went into the lounge at all.

Plus, it was my impression that Dr. Grant had been attacked more than just a minute or so before I got there. She was blue when I arrived. So she had probably lain there for several minutes. It was perfectly possible one or two people could have gone along to the rest rooms in that time.

This was hopeless.

Certainly, it wouldn't hurt to get a schedule of who had been in and out. We might find out who was the last person who'd admit to being there. But it was not going to tell us whether he was the killer or some silent person who came after.

All right, forget opportunity; let's ask this: Was the murder planned, or did it just happen? I thought somewhere in my head was a fact that could tell me this much.

Something about the room . . .

I put everything else out of my mind and focused on the lounge. The actual, physical space. Some fact about it needed to be noticed, in the sense that I had to get it to the conscious level of my mind. What was unusual about this particular room?

I wandered down the corridor to take a look at it. However, even though the evidence techs had been there and gone, Hightower had assigned someone to make an X of yellow barrier tape across the door. I couldn't go in. Craning my neck, I could see a bit more than half the room before the corner cut off my view. I could see the food machines but not the table and sofa I knew were farther back, behind the L. Still, I knew what was back there. That was where I had found the body.

There were several food machines. There was a machine that dispensed chocolate bars, hard candy in little bags, bags of peanuts, corn chips, and potato chips. There was a hot drinks machine that dispensed coffee four ways: black, with cream, with cream and sugar, and with only sugar. It dispensed tea and cocoa, too. All of these drinks came in Styrofoam cups. There was a sandwich machine that dispensed limp sandwiches—ham and cheese, turkey, tuna salad, and ham salad—in triangular plastic packages. And, of course, there was a soda pop machine. Coke, both classic and cherry, diet 7-Up, Mello Yello, ginger ale, and Jolt.

There was also a fruit machine. Not a very wide selection, though. All stuff that wouldn't spoil very fast. Of six little display doors, three contained apples, two oranges, and one a can of fruit cocktail.

That was it for the machines. Other than that, the room had one central table, six chairs, two of which had arms but were not particularly comfortable, and a long plastic-covered sofa, which I couldn't see from where I stood. I remembered that a brown rug covered a very small percentage of the floor, and was placed in front of the sofa. The sofa was against the back wall; the chairs were irregularly bunched around the table. There were two windows side by side with blue-and-white-striped curtains at their outer edges. The curtains could not be pulled or moved in any way. There were two pictures on the walls, one of them over the sofa and one of them on the bare wall near the door. They depicted mountain lakes and were framed by thin strips of brown wood. No glass. In the ceiling were fluorescent light fixtures and air ducts. Along the floor under the windows was a baseboard heating unit. There was a wastebasket—plastic, an unfortunate aqua color, round, about fourteen inches in diameter and maybe two feet high. A small refrigerator where employees could store food brought from home. I had noticed the handwritten sign on it: "Food only. NO SPECIMENS!" There was an automatic coffeemaker with a glass pot. Oh, and a microwave to heat stuff you brought from home.

As far as I could remember, that was every single thing that the room contained. So what did that tell me?

Aha! Yes!

There were no potential weapons in the room! The ashtray was too light, the pictures were too flimsy, the food machines were far too heavy to pick up and brain somebody with. The killer might have tried to hit Dr. Grant over the head with a chair, but it would be a very uncertain method. Or the killer might have tried to stun her with a pop can, but they weren't very heavy either, and would be likely to burst, softening the blow. The glass coffeepot would shatter.

Most rooms have something that can be used as a weapon, things like heavy ashtrays, pokers, hammers, knives, fat books, or even heavy lamps. The treatment rotunda, for instance, was full of potential weapons.

So the killer, if he or she had planned ahead to kill Dr. Grant, knew the weapon had to be brought in.

If he had *not* planned to kill Dr. Grant, he either had the weapon with him accidentally or had to go out and get it and bring it back. A tongue depressor and a piece of gauze-pad "sponge"—how likely was it that somebody would just happen to be carrying them around? Not at all likely. Close to zero. The tongue depressors were in jars on the stands in every treatment bay. There was no need to carry them around. Used depressors were immediately thrown in waste cans, not stuck in somebody's pocket. The same was true of the gauze pads. They were dispensed in their thousands in paper wrapping for sterility. After they were used they were thrown away. The ones used during surgery came in large sterilized packs. Nobody ever kept used sponges in their pockets. Not these days of AIDS. Used supplies went in the biohazard bins.

So whoever killed Dr. Grant must have planned ahead and brought the weapons intentionally. Either they brought the weapons to the meeting in the first place, or they met with her, found out that she was a threat, and went out, got the weapons, and came back to kill her.

Premeditated murder.

Okay. I thought that was solid reasoning. Now what about the killer's choice of this specific weapon? After all, there were a lot of other lethal items in the rotunda—a scalpel, for instance, or a syringe filled with an overdose of practically any drug in the medical formulary.

Might a scalpel or a drug be traced? I wasn't familiar enough with the systems here to be sure. A scalpel might be missed from a particular set. As for a syringe, somebody might have noticed the killer taking it and the drug out of a drug storage cabinet. I'd have to find out what sort of track they kept of drugs, but my impression was that opiates and abusable drugs—narcotics, mostly—were kept under lock and key. Other meds less so. Certainly nobody kept track of sponges and tongue depressors. The staff used them like water. You'd have to steal hundreds before anybody would ever notice.

But that may not have been the most important reason. The very ordinariness of the murder instruments meant that nobody would have been alarmed if they'd noticed the killer picking them up. And while ordinarily nobody would carry them around in a pocket, it wouldn't look totally bizarre to absentmindedly *put* one in a pocket. It would look very odd to drop a scalpel into a pocket.

Smart.

And smart in another way. Somehow the killer had to lull Dr. Grant into feeling she was not in danger. She would not simply have held still for a scalpel or a syringe, but a sponge or tongue depressor would have looked harmless, for a split second at least. By the time her brain registered she was in real danger, it would be too late.

So—we had weapons that were untraceable, items no one would remember the killer taking. We had a murder scene that would yield traces of everybody on the staff and therefore incriminate nobody.

I thought about going to Hightower and telling him why I was sure the killing had been premeditated, but somehow I couldn't imagine him being very appreciative. He wasn't going to solve this, unless the killer was very stupid. To judge from the crime scene, the killer was smart as hell.

As far as I could tell, there was no reason in the world why this wouldn't turn out to be a perfect crime.

· 5 ·

To get out of everybody's way while I thought, I stood back in a gap between two machines and under a sign that was headed EMPLOYEE NEEDLE STICK PROCEDURES. Lester Smalley mopped his way past, inclined his head at me, and said, "How are you?"

I said, "Okay, how are you?"

"Deeply saddened. Dr. Grant was a fine woman. A fine woman."

After a couple of minutes, Marveline Kruse came along the row of bays, pushing the trauma center's portable X-ray toward the gap where I was standing. The machine lives there during its down time. My resting spot was no longer mine. Marveline was the student nurse who had tried to breathe air into Dr. Grant's lungs, and to judge by Davidian's reaction, had only pushed the sponge farther in. I had had the impression earlier this afternoon that Dr. Grant intimidated her.

"Hi," she said.

"Hi. My name is Cat Marsala."

"I'm Marveline Kruse."

"You're a nurse?" I was ninety-nine percent sure she was a student. She didn't wear the full white uniform; she was in white with a blue shirt, but better err on the side of complimenting people.

"In four months I will be, if everything goes okay. I'm a third-year student."

"Maybe you can clear something up for me. What's a T-eight?"

"What? When was the term used?"

"Dr. Davidian over there in bay four was saying T-eight."

"Oh, the spinal injury. Eighth thoracic vertebra."

"Thanks. Where're you from?" There are at least a dozen Chicago accents, let alone the many foreign accents in this city. Hers wasn't any of them.

"I'm from Carbondale. Well, not exactly Carbondale. I'm really from a little place called Grimsby, Illinois." She giggled.

"Where's that?"

"It's about ten miles outside Carbondale. You know, west of Carbondale. In the Turkey Bayou/Oakwood Bottoms Recreation Area. I'm not even from Grimsby, really. We live near the Big Muddy River."

"That's a long distance from here."

"In more ways than one." She giggled again, pushing a piece of wispy hair behind her ear.

"Isn't it scary for you here? Chicago is so extremely urban."

"Well, see, I needed to get away. Back home it isn't very— it's not an easy place to make a living. Of course there's some people who do pretty well, where I live. Some big farmers. Couple of restaurants. I mean, it's not all *poor*. But mostly— you know, after the country stopped burning soft coal, it was just real hard living for a lot of people."

"So you came here."

"Yeah. Once I'm an R.N., I'll have a profession I can use anyplace. I can get work wherever I go."

Not too many people outside Illinois realize that southern Illinois is really in some sense a southern state, utterly different from the northern part. Carbondale is three hundred and thirty miles south of Chicago, and a world away. Towns like Carbondale and Cairo are geographically farther south than Louisville, Kentucky. Cairo, at the southern tip of Illinois, is farther south than Richmond, Virginia. As a matter of fact, not too many people in northern Illinois realize this either. Marveline was telling me she came from the southern coal mining area, one of the most depressed places in the United States. Marveline had come to Chicago to better herself. She'd come here to get away from her family and be trained in a profession.

She was at most twenty years old, very pretty, with green eyes, pink cheeks, and wispy, curly hair the color of light Lake Michigan beach sand.

"You left your family? And your friends?"

"Well . . ." She let it hang. "Mmm-mm. You know. Sometimes you have to start over."

"Oh."

She saw what kind of impression that remark had made on me and hastened to correct it.

"There's a lot of real nice people in Grimsby. I don't mean there aren't. It's just, like, sometimes you need to start over."

Somebody'd hurt her, and it was more probable that family had hurt her than neighbors or strangers. She was trying to be fair, and I liked that.

The PA system said, "Patient pickup in X-ray."

I said to Marveline, "I feel so sorry about Dr. Grant."

"Oh, God! Isn't it terrible? I mean, I've seen some pretty terrible things since I've been training here, but they weren't anybody I knew. I don't mean that makes it okay, but what I mean to say is Dr. Grant was somebody I knew. And she was nice."

"Nice?" I asked. That wasn't the impression I'd received

about most of the staff's attitude to Grant. Capable, yes; exacting, yes; nice, no.

"Well, like, I was just *petrified* of her at first. You know? I guess I was still scared of her, really. But what I found out was she was really fair."

"Fair how?"

"Well, she didn't snap at you just because she felt like being crabby. She watched. And if you did the right thing, she'd nod. She'd only snap at you if you did the wrong thing."

"That can still be hard on you when you're learning."

"Well, see, the other thing is, she never asked you to do anything you hadn't already been told how to do. You know? She was really fair."

"Yeah. Actually, I agree. She was firm about what I could and couldn't do while I was here. But when I stuck to what she'd said, she acknowledged it."

"That's Dr. Grant exactly."

I had arrived here today for the three to eleven P.M. shift. It was now seven P.M. The amazing thing was, despite the murder of their colleague, and despite four hours of exhausting, blood-soaked, death-shadowed work, the staff went right on coping. Like cops, they took staggered lunch breaks. Since this was the evening shift, "lunch" was at seven P.M. for some of the staff, seven-thirty for others, and eight for the rest.

Fern, Coyne, Michelson, and I went to the hospital cafeteria together. The three of them carried beepers and would go right back if they were called.

"Ordinarily, we'd get sandwiches or the special and bring it back to the lounge," Fern said, as she picked up a plate of fried chicken and french fries. She didn't have to specify why we weren't going to do that today.

Michelson opted for a tuna melt, and Coyne got a double cheeseburger, then, as if trying to make amends for the cholesterol, picked up an apple. Fern got tea. I hesitated, looking at the fruit plate with low-fat cottage cheese without enthusiasm, then took a cheeseburger and a piece of chocolate cake.

The cafeteria was immense. U-Hosp is a major teaching hospital, and this cafeteria served all the doctors, nurses, administrative staff, orderlies, cleaning staff, electricians, plumbers, everybody who worked in the complex, which included two dozen small and large buildings. It was a little city all by itself. As we loaded food onto the trays, I caught glimpses of the cavernous kitchens, stretching far back into the belly of the building.

We sat at a table against the wall. Fern said, "Maybe nobody will recognize us. I hope."

I said, "What do you mean you hope?"

"Well, it's out on the news. Dr. Grant. People are gonna be curious. I just surely and purely don't want to answer any more questions right now."

Dr. Michelson said, "You got *that* right!" very emphatically.

Dr. Coyne shook his head.

They might not want to answer questions, but I certainly had a lot to ask. However, you don't do political reporting in Cook County as long as I have without developing some subtlety.

"You've got to excuse me if I don't understand who everybody is yet," I said. "Dr. Michelson, you're a resident?" Michelson was a broad-shouldered black man, not too tall. He gave the impression of being a very methodical person, and was even now cutting his tuna melt into bite-size pieces with his knife and eating them with his fork, instead of picking it up in his hands and taking the chance of getting grease on his fingers.

"Fourth-year resident," he said.

"What does that mean?"

"Well, basically it means I've finished four years of medical school, got my M.D., and entered my residency, and now I've decided to specialize. In emergency medicine. So I'm doing rotation in the trauma center. By the time you're in your fourth year of residency, you're pretty senior. I'm generally in charge of the residents and medical students on their rotation here."

"A fourth-year resident is a pretty big deal," Fern told me.

That could mean if there was something wrong going on in the unit, he might be blamed. If Dr. Grant had been brought in to whip things into shape, was it Dr. Michelson, among others, who needed shaping up?

I studied Dr. Jacob Coyne, under cover of taking a bite of burger. He was eating his own cheeseburger in an avid sort of way, taking a bite, then another half bite before putting the thing down and chewing. Coyne was not overweight by any means—in fact, he was bony, with large joints. But there was just a suggestion of plumpness around the jowls and a smoothness or softness to his arms and neck, as if under his skin was a thin layer of fat.

"Dr. Coyne, you're a—a full physician—or a—I don't know what you call yourself."

"I'm a specialist in emergency medicine. I finished my residency two years ago at Northwestern Medical School."

"I see." That meant he was senior to Michelson in the pecking order here. He, too, would be responsible for problems in the unit. He might have reason to be afraid of Dr. Grant. I turned to Fern and smiled. "But I'll bet the real boss on the unit is the chief nurse. Isn't that you?"

"I'm what we call the charge nurse. And I'm in charge,

all right." She laughed. "When I say jump, they jump."

All three of them laughed. Fern Butler was plump, of medium height, and pink faced. She had the kind of eyes that became half-circles when she laughed. Walt Disney cartoon-child eyes. Jolly eyes. It was obvious that the two men both liked her.

"We've got a good staff here," Fern said.

For just a moment I thought of turning the conversation to the murder to see what they'd say. I thought of telling them that one of their good staff killed Dr. Grant. But even if I didn't say it in an accusing way, it was still too confrontation-al. It would be better to observe them.

I was about to mention their stamina, the way they kept going from case to awful case, when Fern said, "What will you do now?"

"About what?"

"You mean you're going to go on with your—your writing whatever it was?"

"Well, of course. What did you think?"

"I thought the murder would put you off."

"Does it put you off treating the next patient who comes in?"

"Of course not. This is what we *do*. Oh, okay, okay. I see what you mean."

"It's my job."

"Yes. I see that."

"In fact, the article I'm going to write is all about that very thing. About the kind of people who are willing to do this kind of work. And how they manage to do it."

Michelson said cautiously, "What do you mean?"

"Look, every day that you come to work, you're under fire. You're subjected to a constant barrage of desperately injured people. And in the nature of things, a lot of them die. How do

you stand it? Why do you do it? Why would you want to subject yourselves to that? In other words, what kind of people
are you?"

"Yes, I see what you're after," he said.

"But we're not all identical," Coyne said.

"Exactly! What I'd like to do is find out a little bit about
each of you. Go to your homes, if you'd let me. Profile you as
individuals."

"I don't know," Michelson said. "You mean print this in a
newspaper?"

"I'd let you read it first. I don't do exposés. I'm not a muck-
raker. My job is to explain people to my readers. I'm into trying to understand."

Coyne said, "I suppose if I could read it first."

"Plus, if you want, I'll give you a fictional name."

"That seems fair," Michelson said.

Coyne said, "Yeah, I guess."

And Fern said, "Actually, it sounds like fun."

Bingo! Gotcha!

The rest of the shift was like the first, except there was no
murder. We had a window washer who had fallen from a
third-floor scaffold, not when he was washing windows, but
when he was equipping the thing for the next day. He survived. He said if he'd been actually washing windows, it
wouldn't have happened. "I have a routine. I always follow
my safety routine when I'm working. The reason I fell was I
wasn't thinking of myself as working."

Which is very true about routine work. You don't necessarily remember that you've dotted the i's and crossed the t's,
because you always do.

This was a principle that I should be able to apply to the

staff work in the trauma center. Only one person had seriously veered away from procedure that day. The killer.
Which should mean that I could place everyone else, if I
worked at it.

We had a child thrown through the windshield of a car. He
wasn't wearing a seat belt. He may survive.

We had a man slashed by his wife in a fight over which
television channel to watch. He survived.

We had a head-on collision with three people in one car
and two in the other. Three survived.

We had a young man who had been on a motorcycle, flee-
ing some gang members, and crashed through the plate-glass
window of a storefront, slashing his forehead, forearm, and
leg badly and losing a lot of blood.

The shift was drawing to a close. Up to that point I was doing fine. It came over me quite suddenly. One instant I was
watching Dr. Davidian sew the muscles on the young man's
thigh. Michelson was assisting, holding the retractors.
Belinda Fowler was sponging out blood occasionally, with
sponges exactly like the one that had strangled Dr. Grant.
Every once in a while Michelson would say "over here on
the left" to her, trying to get oozing blood out of Davidian's
way so he could sew more accurately. Davidian was using
prethreaded needles. These were not like sewing needles, but
instead were curved, like eyelashes. He held them in
a clamp-ended tool, and the crescent shape of the needle
made it possible for him to grab through a piece of the muscle
on one side of the cut, bring the thread partway through and
then grab hold of a piece of muscle on the other side. Then by
tying the thread, he pulled the sides of the wound together.
He finished the muscle and started work on the skin.

Davidian said to me, "We'll be done here in a couple of
minutes."

As I say, I was dealing perfectly well with this. And then suddenly I wasn't.

I am *not* squeamish. In fact, my earlier newspaper experience tells me that most people are not as squeamish as fiction would lead you to believe. In the goriest accidents you find people helping each other, not freaking out. Also, I had spent my first five reportorial years covering traffic accidents, among other rookie-employee things. So the sight of blood is not by itself new to me.

Now, I felt my head and hands growing cold. The sounds in the room became distant. Apparently there was still enough circulation to my brain for some of the neurons to keep firing, because I turned and walked out of the treatment bay. Although I didn't bend over and put my head between my knees, because I would have felt too humiliated and nonmacho if I did, I hiked as fast as I could to the women's rest room.

The bathroom was functional. Period. No benches. No chairs to sit in. I opened one of the stall doors and went in and sat there.

It wasn't really the sight of blood that had done it to me. It was everything at once, I suppose. The death of Dr. Grant, a woman who had been helpful and welcoming to me, was bad enough. That she had been killed by one of a group of people I admired was bad, too. On top of that, the injured and dying kept coming into the unit, and coming into the unit, and coming into the unit. And something else about the whole trauma center experience bothered me, too, but it hung just at the back of my mind, out of reach.

I sat, breathing slowly, then finally started rubbing my head all over, which sometimes has the effect of clearing my brain. After quite some time, I looked at my watch. It was quarter to eleven. The new shift would be arriving, and some of the people from this shift would no doubt come in here to "freshen up" before going home. I got up and went to the mirror over the sink. My hair looked like the coat of a black poodle that had just stepped on a live wire. I combed it and walked out of the rest room.

Dr. Sam Davidian was standing there with his arms crossed, waiting for me.

"You need to be taken out for a beer," he said.

"Well, I was thinking more of going home." This was not a very gracious response, but I was peeved that he had noticed my weakness. He didn't seem to mind.

"And a hot pastrami," he said.

"Oh. A hot pastrami? Well, yes, you may be right."

"The Indigo isn't the most authentic blues club in the city," Sam said. I was calling him Sam now instead of Dr. Davidian.

"No?"

"No. It's not exactly 'living' blues. The singers do a lot of retrospectives. But it's the only one I can think of that's still serving real food at eleven-thirty at night."

The singer was caressing a song in a Leadbelly sequence. The lights were blue and purple, except on the singer, where a pin spot picked him out, sitting on a wooden stool, cradling a silver guitar.

The beer was icy cold and the pastrami was warm. The knots and kinks in my muscles were letting loose one by one. I extended both legs, then folded them, then extended them again. Having fixed that, I leaned my back to the left, the right, the left, the right. Then I rotated my neck.

Sam said, "Tired?"

"Too much tension. This job must tie you up in knots sometimes."

"Not really. I suppose I'm used to it."

"But how do you stand the sadness and the—the unpleasantness? Day after day."

He said seriously, "Because I help. I make a difference."

"The stress must be enormous."

"You don't understand the satisfaction. I don't save everybody I treat. But just imagine a job where you get to battle death. Actually go right in there and fight death! The patient would literally be dead in minutes if you don't do the right thing."

"Yes, I can understand that. Still, there's something about the whole trauma unit experience that makes me uneasy."

"What?"

"I don't know."

"It's not usually like today. Today was unprecedented. The job's not like that."

"Oh, I know. That's not what I mean. Poor Dr. Grant. I liked her. Sam, who killed her?"

"Can't you relax, even for a little while?"

"I would think you'd be more anxious to find out than I am. You work with these people. They're your colleagues."

"And my friends. I don't think any of them could have done it."

"Sam, you certainly don't believe some crazed killer came in the back way, from the corridor that goes to the rest of the hospital?"

"It's possible."

"It may be possible, but it's highly unlikely. You people might not notice each other, because you're used to seeing each other move around and go back and forth for coffee or go to the rest rooms. But I was watching, and you always look up when the corridor door opens."

"Well, you look up if you're there. Nearby. But what if nobody was nearby?"

"No, the place was full of patients. There was staff on that side. Plus, whoever it was would have to cross the whole treatment rotunda to get to the office corridor."

He sighed. "Yes, okay. I suppose we would notice. Probably several of us would notice."

"So you're going to have to face it. One of you killed Dr. Grant."

He sighed again and drank some beer.

"What sort of person was Hannah Grant?"

"Skillful, a good teacher, too."

"Was she sympathetic?"

"What exactly do you mean?"

"Sam, in cases where somebody is intentionally killed— I mean, like this one, not like a drive-by shooting that hits the wrong person—it's important what the victim was like. For instance, was she harsh? Would she give a second chance to a person who made a mistake?"

"There's a limit to how many second chances you can give people when you're dealing with the lives of patients."

"Of course. But everybody makes an occasional mistake. And different people in positions of power have different ways of exercising their power. Some people snarl at the person who makes a mistake. Some people threaten and scare the guy so much he gets all tense and makes twice as many mistakes. Some people take the person aside, show him where he went wrong, and have him go over and over what he was supposed to do so he won't make that mistake again. So what was Dr. Grant like?"

"To be honest, she was more on the strict side than the sympathetic side."

"I had that impression. She thanked me for following her instructions."

"But that's a point, too. She always said something nice when somebody did a good job."

"Fair, then?"

"Definitely fair."

"Fair but unforgiving?" He frowned at that, so I said, "Fair but unyielding?"

"That's about right."

"Sam, what are the people on the staff like? They all look so efficient in uniform, but I'm already picking up on underlying personalities. Grant seemed to be riding the black resident—Michelson—about a burn chart. Questioning him as if he were a student."

"He's not a student. A resident has graduated and he's a full-fledged doctor."

"I know that. Now. But he's still in training. Right?"

"Yes. For a specialty. Like, Michelson is specializing in emergency medicine."

"So was she picking on him?"

"No. You have it all wrong, Cat. Grant's job is training. She has twenty years' experience in this stuff. She's training him. Was."

"Oh."

"Michelson is very capable. He's tense, I know. He wants to be perfect."

"And he can't?"

"No human being is perfect. Michelson lives in terror of making a mistake."

"Maybe he should. He has people's lives in his hands."

"No. All that kind of tension does is cripple you up and make you hesitate. Sometimes you have to make a hard choice fast. And you might be wrong."

"If Grant *seemed to him* to be riding him, could he have snapped and killed her?"

"Lord, no, Cat! Michelson is a mature guy—he's put up with pressure before. Lots of pressure in med school, and on rotation as a resident. No way."

"Well, who, then? You know Marveline Kruse, the young white woman from downstate? Student nurse?"

"Sure I know her."

"I think she badly needs to succeed in Chicago and stay away from her hometown. And she seems worried about whether she's going to make it through."

"Worrying about whether they're going to make it through is endemic here. It's what training is all about."

"But if Dr. Grant said Marveline wasn't making the grade, she wouldn't make it, would she?"

"No. You're absolutely right that Hannah Grant could make life-or-death decisions about anybody in training."

"And that's a reason to kill."

"Not for Marveline. She's entirely too meek."

I thought about the staff, as far as I knew them. Dr. Coyne—he was young but not a resident. He was now a full-fledged doctor. Self-contained and buttoned up. I wondered why. The nurse, Fern, was pleasant and hard-working, but who knew what her private motives might be? Who knew what the private motives of *any* of them might be? Dr. Zoe Peters. Angry about something, but not necessarily about Dr. Grant. Dr. Sonali Bachaan. A trauma surgery fellow from India, I had been told. Faces swirled around. They all seemed so helpful, wearing their white coats or green scrubs, their stethoscopes around their necks. And one of them was a killer. I said to Sam, "Who, then?"

"Will you please relax and eat your pastrami sandwich."

I took a bite of the sandwich. It was very, very wonderful, the bread chewy, the meat salty and delicious. Twenty feet away, a voice full of heart sang notes that could have been golden spheres, expanding out into the audience.

"Why is blues music so oddly comforting?" I asked Sam.

"Even though it's full of pain? Because it says you're not

alone in your troubles, and there's still life and hope."

"Mmmm." The beer was cold and just as delicious as the pastrami. "Mmmmm."

Sam said, "Saturday is my day off. Let me take you out to dinner."

Well—after all, I had broken off my relationship with Mike at last, or at any rate for the last time, and John was in Hong Kong researching a company to underwrite. This was Monday. I had until Saturday to find out more about him. Sam had liquid dark eyes, with bushy, intense eyebrows. I liked that. He was medium height, solid in the shoulders, but bony-solid rather than flabby. I liked that. Plus—I thought he had an independent quality that appealed to me. He might be able to be close without leaning on me, like Mike did. Of course, quite often, they look better before you get to know them.

I said, "Love to."

"Great."

He put his arm around my shoulder while the singer finished his set and I finished my beer. "Now," I said, "I've got to get home."

"So soon?"

"Absolutely. You've been a good doctor. This was just what I needed, but I'm fading."

Which was putting it mildly. I felt like Silly Putty. My Lord! What a day!

"Well, all right. I'll walk you to your car."

We had driven to the Indigo separately because I had my Bronco and he had his Range Rover. I was a little surprised that he, like me, had a four-wheel drive. His was much more expensive, but it formed a bond between us. He said, "I have to get to work, even if it snows."

This was my reason, too. Soul mates.

So I arrived home at my apartment next to the El tracks on Franklin at one A.M. and found a parking place only a block and a half away. The old feet were dragging when I approached the door, but at least writing up my notes on the trauma center could wait until tomorrow. Right now deep sleep was all I wanted.

The outer door is slightly recessed, so I saw only half of the person who sat on the step. There was a sleeve, a shoulder, and two legs protruding.

In my pocket I carry two tubes of spray stuff. One is breath freshener; the other is Mace. Quite often I remind myself not to get them confused. I certainly don't want to Mace my throat by accident. Now I picked one and glanced at it to be sure what it was, because mint-freshening a mugger probably wouldn't be a big deterrent.

Tonight I didn't need this grief.

Anyhow, it was probably some homeless person, who would wander off harmlessly and let me get upstairs to sleep.

As I approached, he stirred, then lurched to his feet.

"Cat! I've been waiting for hours."

Mike. Oh, hell.

· 6 ·

He stood there half in the light from the street lamp, half in shadow from the doorway, and it flashed into my mind what a metaphor that was for Mike himself. There was so much about him that was good. He could be such fun, and his observations about the world often shed light on things I hadn't even noticed before. But I couldn't be chained to his dark side. There was too much self-destructiveness there.

"How long have you been here, really?" I asked. He wouldn't have waited hours. He would have found a bar.

"Well, half an hour anyway," he said, grinning.

He stood very straight. Then he walked toward me, carefully, very straight. He'd been drinking again. Until they are very far gone, you can tell when people like Mike have been drinking, not by their wobble, but by their unnatural straightness.

"Mike, I'm tired. I have to get to bed."

He wasn't listening. "You know, Cat, I've been thinking. We can work this out. We have too much good history behind us just to call it quits."

"I'm sorry."

"And what I think I'll do is get into an outpatient treatment program, so you can see I mean it."

"It doesn't matter, Mike. I mean, I hope you do, but I can't go on with this relationship. I made that clear on Friday."

"I think I'll start going to AA again, too."

"That's a fine idea. You have friends there who care."

Finally, the message was getting through to him. "Cat, come on. Don't turn me away."

"I'd like to stay friends."

"You know that's not what I mean!"

We were standing on the street, right in front of my building, so I was not happy that his voice was rising. "Look, go home for now. Call me when you get up tomorrow. I'll be working here up to about two."

"I don't *want* to go home!"

"Well, you need to."

"Cat, let me come upstairs with you."

"No."

"I'll sleep on the sofa." He lurched against the wall. He was losing it.

"No, Mike, go home."

"Don't do this to me. I'm not a"—he started to choke up—"not a criminal."

"That's true. You're a good person. But I can't *do* this anymore."

He tried to grab the keys out of my hand to open the front door. I snatched them back and he fell forward. One of the second-floor tenants opened a window and called, "What's the trouble?"

"No problem," I said. "Just a breaking-up kind of thing."

"Oh. Well, make it short, will you?"

"You bet."

Meanwhile, Mike had been saying please over and over. I said, "No. No no no."

"Ah, jeez!" He swung angrily away toward his car, which, I now noticed, was parked next to the alley, fortunately not at a fire hydrant and not blocking a driveway.

"Hold it!" I ran after him.

"Cat?" He turned around, looking hopeful. Oh, damn.

"You can't drive."

"Oh, forget it! Just leave me alone." He had his keys in his hand and he lurched against his car. He had been too far gone to grab my keys, but I got his in a quick lunge.

I don't live on the quietest street in the world, what with the El going by and all, and in addition it's on a route a lot of cabbies take to bars. Two or three cabs had passed while we were arguing. Now there were none, but any minute—

"Mike, I'm going to put you in a cab."

"Gimme my keys back." He grabbed for them and I stepped back. He fell forward on the ground. Good God, it hadn't been my intention to humiliate him.

"Please, Mike, please, come on, get up." There were three cars coming along the street. No cabs. "Get up, Mike." I pulled him to his knees and then he stood on his own.

Finally, a cab! I left him swaying, stepped halfway into the street, and hailed it. Sometimes they don't like to stop if they think they're going to be picking up a drunk. For one thing, they think he may barf in the car. Also, they may have to pull him out and carry him to his door. But there's a real public interest in getting intoxicated people into cabs instead of behind the wheel of a car, and the taxi authority keeps telling the drivers that they have to accept these customers. This cab had its light on. I made it so obvious that I was waving down a cab that he had to stop.

I opened the cab door and gave the driver Mike's address. He said, "Uh, lady, that's way out of my way."

"It's nine blocks. It's not out of your way."

"It's—"

"He's not gonna be sick. Just get him home."

Mike meanwhile had done absolutely nothing. He stood like a pillar of salt. This was good. I had expected to find him sneaking toward his car, keys or no keys.

"Come on, Mike. Into the cab."

"My car'll get a ticket."

"Not before noon tomorrow it won't."

Should I keep his keys? If I gave them to him, would he have the driver drop him right back here? I took out a five-dollar bill.

I pointed to the photo ID of the driver in the cab. "You know there are regs on this. I have your name and cab number. Get him to that address."

"Lady, you know I'm not gonna dump him," the cabbie whined.

"Don't let him dump you either."

I put Mike's keys in his hand, slammed the cab door, and stood with my hands on my hips until they took off. The taillights disappeared up Franklin Street as an El train rumbled by overhead in the opposite direction. Mike wouldn't be back for the car. Whether he'd go to bed when he got to his apartment or wander down his street looking for a bar was another question. But if he didn't drive he was less likely to kill himself and much less likely to kill somebody else.

I dragged myself upstairs to my place.

At six forty-five Tuesday morning a voice in my bedroom shrieked, "Methought I heard a voice cry 'Sleep no more! Macbeth does murder sleep!'"

Blast that parrot! He's asking for murder himself. People tell you that if you cover a bird's cage at night, they won't wake up until you uncover it in the morning. Nobody seems to have told Long John Silver this, however.

LJ is an African gray parrot. They are without doubt the ugliest parrot in the world—drab gray color with random blotches of a clotted-blood color on the tail. But they are the very best talkers of the bird world. Wonderful at duplicating human speech, although not quite so delightful when their owner has had six hours of sleep.

"Button your damn beak!" I said into the pillow, without opening my eyes.

LJ said, "Night's candles are burnt out, and jocund day stands tiptoe on the misty mountaintops."

I opened my eyes.

Nearest thing to a misty mountaintop in my sight was the John Hancock Building, and as for jocund day, I doubted there would be much merriment today at the trauma center. LJ is probably about forty-five years old and was brought up the river from New Orleans thirty years ago by an old captain of a shrimp trawler, who for some weird reason of his own thought Chicago was a good place to retire to. Then LJ was owned for twenty years by a professor of English whose area of expertise was Shakespeare. I suppose this is better than a parrot who shouts salty curses and can't be allowed near elderly relatives and small children.

I got up with a certain amount of salty cursing of my own and swept the cover off of LJ's cage. I said, "Cursed be he that moves my bones," but he pretended not to understand. Since he was getting his way, he didn't say anything. LJ is smartest when he is most angry, and he's always annoyed if I lie in bed and ignore him.

The refrigerator yielded several pieces of cold pizza. Way ta go! This is unusual. My refrigerator is a magic box that seems to make everything vanish except limp celery and refried beans with white mold on top.

Of course, I had plenty of bird food. LJ doesn't take to austerity.

We had a nice little breakfast together, during which he said, "Polly wants a cracker." He drops fifty points in IQ when he's happy.

Sometimes I think LJ is psychic, too. He was just a bundle of feathery joy while I finished eating. He played on the floor with his Nerf ball and then flew onto the curtain rod, where he sat cocking his head back and forth like a seer. He loves to have me at home during the day, and somehow he realized I wasn't going right out.

Then I sat down with my coffee at the word processor and he flew over and sat on my shoulder.

Some reporters use tape recorders constantly. I find for most purposes it's better to make notes on file cards and then transcribe them onto a file in the computer before I forget what they mean. For instance, today I was mainly getting down my impressions of what the trauma center looked like physically and felt like emotionally. If I had talked into a tape recorder as I went along through the day yesterday, I would have generated thousands and thousands of words about the place. It's too much easier to talk than write. You don't realize until later how much of what you say is repetitive or useless. Transcribing the whole thing would take hours. When you handwrite your notes, there's enough added difficulty that you edit yourself to a certain extent. You ask yourself whether this observation is really vivid, or whether it will be important to know this detail to give people the sense of the place.

The other problem with audiotape is that, if you want to use just certain parts, it's very hard to locate the exact sentence you need without playing through the whole thing. You find yourself thinking, "Well, it was just before lunch I noticed that machine they use for suction. Now where—gee, maybe it was just *after* lunch." And you fast-forward and reverse until you're really sick of hearing your voice sound like a terrified chipmunk's. My two nephews, who speak six computer languages and could program the VCR before they could walk, think I'm just an old fuddy-duddy who could use a tape recorder much more efficiently if I put my mind to it. They may be right.

But with file cards, I am able to flip through them in an instant. A little category code at the top right—A for atmosphere, P for people, T for technology, nothing subtle about me—and I'm home free.

The next step is to transfer the information on the cards to a file on the word processor. This means translating the squiggles, adding recollections that I didn't write down, and getting it into full sentences. This is preliminary. It does not involve actually writing the article. At this stage I don't know enough to write a finished piece. If I start writing too soon, I generate lumpy, ugly material. Then it gets built on, or fitted into the final piece, and I can't get rid of it later, even though it's bad.

The one thing I've found audiotaping irreplaceable for is interviews. Very often I want to quote the exact words of the interviewee, and with a tape I can be sure I'm getting them right. Except for eliminating "ums" and "you knows" and some repetition, I believe that you owe it to the interviewee to quote the precise words when you quote at all.

So here we were, LJ and me, sitting at the word processor for three hours, transcribing and organizing. To other people, people who don't do it, reporting looks easy and glamorous. Ho, ho, ho. Actually, I guess any job looks easy from the outside. One thing about mine—there's no heavy lifting.

• • •

I watched the eleven-thirty local news on Channel 7, where they reported the mysterious death of Dr. Grant, "respected director of the University Hospital trauma center." Sergeant Hightower was shown briefly, looking handsome and in charge and announcing that he was "pursuing several promising leads." Right. Promising to lead to dead ends. Channel 9 at noon was similar, but instead of Hightower, it showed tape of the hospital administrator, one Henry DeKooning, wearing a three-piece suit, regretting the loss of Dr. Grant.

In a weak moment the night before at the Indigo, I had agreed to meet Sam Davidian for lunch at Greek Islands at one. So at noon I hosed down the body, put water in LJ's water holder, food in his dish, left the cage door open, made sure the television was off—he hates game shows—and left in my aging Bronco.

◊ *7* ◊

Lunch with Sam was a good change of pace. We ate moussa-
ka and drank a little retsina. A very little for him, a sip, Sam
said, because he did not drink before going on duty.

Sam had asked me to his apartment after work tonight to
see a movie. I'd said maybe. Maybe we were moving too fast.
Lunch today, and a big date planned for Saturday. I'd had a
few romantic disasters, and I was cautious.

I arrived at the trauma center promptly at three o'clock
that Tuesday afternoon. The second day on a location, you
notice different things. You've got past the total confusion
stage. For instance, when I entered today, just inside the
double doors I saw a large gray cart on wheels, maybe three
feet by six feet long, by five feet high. I had walked right past
it the day before and never noticed. It had folding doors on
one side, closed by a hasp and staple lock and sturdy padlock.
Stenciled on the side in red were the words DISASTER SUPPLY
CART.

I felt that yesterday had supplied us with enough disaster
and we needn't open it.

There was also a cardboard box, maybe three feet square,
labeled PROPERTY OF THE RADIATION SAFETY OFFICE. USE
ONLY FOR A RADIATION EMERGENCY. I wished I could see what
was inside it.

Sergeant Hightower and two detectives, all in plainclothes and all nevertheless obviously cops, were in occupation of Dr. Grant's office. Their idea of plainclothes was navy blue creased pants, shiny black shoes, and a white shirt with a dark tie. I walked over and paused in the doorway until they noticed me.

Hightower said, "Yes, Miss Marsala?"

"Hi. I've been thinking about whatever evidence you find in the lounge."

"Yes?"

"It seems to me whatever you find there isn't going to tell you very much. Everybody on the staff is in and out all day—"

"Frankly, Miss Marsala, we're aware of that," he said. Then he chuckled and added, "A fingerprint on the Coke machine is not going to get anybody arrested."

Condescending ass. "I'm sure it wouldn't. Most of the stuff you find lying around would be there legitimately. But, you know, the wastebasket is another matter."

"Oh?"

"Whoever brought in the tongue depressor and sponge may have carried it in something, especially the tongue depressor. I suppose you might find fingerprints on the tongue depressor—"

"How did you know we could get fingerprints off surfaces like that now?"

This was no time to tell him I knew people in high places in the CPD, or that I did stories occasionally on crime investigation techniques. In a kind and gentle voice, I said, "I thought everyone knew."

"I'm sure you realize"—he smiled again—"the tongue depressor was probably carried in a pocket. Everybody around here seems to have big pockets."

"They'd have to take it out of the pocket sometime. I

might be able to help you, if I knew what was in the waste-basket."

"Thank you. We'll handle it."

"And then there's the question about which staff members could walk away from their patients—"

"We've taken statements about the movements of the staff at about the time of death. We're getting them collated, Miss Marsala, I assure you."

"Have they explained who was able to move around freely? I can tell you it's not equally easy for everybody. I could take you through a list of who can leave a patient and who can't. And I'll know even more about that after I've been here a couple of days."

"I'm very grateful," he said, smiling like an alligator. "I'll certainly let you know if I have a question."

I nodded, turned, and walked a few feet down the hall, from which distance I heard the three cops laugh. Very grateful, indeed! He'd be very sorry, if he wasn't careful. During the chat, I had made a point of looking around Grant's office and noticed that they had opened her file drawers, put her papers in piles, and were going through them. I wanted to see them myself, but they wouldn't have allowed it. Yet.

I wasn't looking to play Sherlock Holmes here. I really wanted to help. Actually, it would be fine with me if the police solved Dr. Grant's killing. It would be fine if *anybody* did. Dr. Grant deserved it. Hers was a particularly nasty, ugly death. I had had waking nightmares several times in the last twenty hours about her, imagining her with the gauze sponge rammed down her throat.

The use of the gauze sponge was really brilliant, because it would stick in place. I hadn't realized this at first, but this morning I had experimented. When you try to guess how an event happened, it's important to make sure your physical assumptions really work. So often people just think, Oh, somebody pushed a sponge down her throat, and leave it at that. You need to ask how. And why a sponge instead of something else. And would it work. And you need to picture every step, so you can find flaws in your picture. You can't gloss over anything.

It was obvious why a sponge had been used, and it re- minded me that the killer was very smart. Any dry, absorbent material will stick to moist membranes. This is easily demon- strated. If you try to take hold of your tongue, you can't hold it. It keeps slipping away. But take a dry towel or washcloth or a sheet of Kleenex, and you can get hold of it easily. The capillary action of the absorbent surface "grabs" the tongue surface. And sponges are even more absorbent than a wash- cloth. They are made of fibers especially selected to absorb blood and other fluids during surgery. Rammed down Dr. Grant's throat, the sponge would adhere to the walls of the throat and be very hard to dislodge.

I wondered whether she would have attacked the killer, and whether the killer would have scratch marks or bruises, but after picturing the murder, I thought not. Not after the instant the sponge went into her throat. When any object ob- structs a person's breathing, every instinct is to get it out, get the air flowing. I'd been choked once and I knew that need overwhelms every other thought. From that moment, she would scarcely have been aware of the killer's presence. Whether he stayed to watch—which I doubted—or left fast to get out of there before anybody chanced to come in, she wouldn't care.

She would have clawed at the thing in her throat, desper- ate, frantic, strangling—strangling slowly, getting the tongue depressor out easily but still unable to breathe because of the sponge. It takes a couple of minutes to die of suffocation. The light would fade before her eyes; she'd see black spots in her field of vision. The black areas would coalesce. The agony would seem to take hours while at the same moment, as a doctor, she would know she had no time, no time left at all.

My God!

So when I turned to the rotunda again, I looked at the staff differently. Assuming there was just one killer, then out of the whole crew, maybe fifteen people altogether, there were fourteen skilled, caring, hard-working individuals and one extremely loathsome killer. It wasn't fair to look at each person as despicable when only one was, but at the same time I couldn't be sure that any one of them was not the murderer.

Could it *possibly* be anybody from outside?

I didn't see how. The rotunda was a large room with only three entrances. The central one was the emergency door where the paramedics with gurneys entered. That door beeped when it opened, and anybody coming in would be noticed. Not necessarily responded to, if they were not an emergency, but they would be seen.

Standing in that door, if you looked to the left, you saw the office corridor. Off that corridor were several attending physicians' offices, Dr. Grant's office, the rest rooms, the lounge, and several supplies closets. But it was a dead-end corridor, and was intended to be, to give the staff some privacy. It didn't go anywhere else. As required by the fire code, there was a fire door near the rest rooms, but it was locked from outside, and if it was opened from inside, an alarm would ring. No one could have come into the rotunda by that corridor from "outside."

The only other outside entrance was the set of double

doors on the right that led into the hospital. But the staff always glanced up when they opened. And for good reason. Patients being returned from X-ray came in that way, as well as people from the radiology department carrying X-ray films and other personnel bringing supplies or records. There had been very few during the shift, so far as I remembered, who came in from there at any time, and always with papers or with a patient. They had no need to cross to the office corridor. If they had, somebody here would have noticed.

Another point: When I talked with Sergeant Hightower, I said that certain staff members had to stay with their patients and others could move around more freely. What I meant by that was that the attending physicians, and for that matter all the doctors, including residents and senior staff, including Fern as charge nurse and the nurses Sue Slaby and Natasha Horne, were more their own bosses than the trainees were. It would be more difficult for a student nurse like Marveline, say, to leave a case, unless she was dismissed or asked to go get something, than it would be for Dr. Coyne, for example. When the unit was busy, the students had specific responsibilities. This didn't exactly eliminate the students from possibly being Dr. Grant's killer. But it made it less likely.

So, high on my list of possible killers would be Dr. Coyne, Dr. Michelson, Fern Butler, and, to be fair, Sam Davidian, although I was certain he didn't have either the motive or—considering his passion to save life—the temperament of a killer.

Slightly lower on the list: Dr. Sonali Bachaan, the fellow, and Dr. Zoe Peters, the resident, because people kept track of them.

And still lower on the list: the two nursing students, Marveline Kruse and Belinda Fowler.

And this tied in with a talk I had had with Sam at the Greek Islands restaurant at lunch, trying to confirm or reject my suspicions.

"Would you say staff members walk around with tongue depressors and sponges in their pockets?"

He said, "No. No reason to. There are hundreds of them in every treatment bay."

"So somebody came prepared to kill Dr. Grant."

He looked pained, but answered, "To be honest, yes."

"So somebody didn't just wander down to the lounge, see her there, and kill her. This wasn't a crime of opportunity."

"I don't see it that way. No."

"Me, too. So either somebody went to the lounge for another reason, saw her there, and, realizing it was a chance to do murder, went back and got the sponge and tongue depressor—"

"I hate to think so, but yes."

"Or had already arranged to meet her there."

"Lord. I suppose so."

He was sad, as well he might be. These were his colleagues. I did not draw the conclusion for him. But what I was getting at was this: The crime took time. Not a lot, but more than half a minute. Whoever did it had to be able to get away from the treatment rotunda long enough either to meet her there by arrangement or go see her, go back to the rotunda for the tools of death, and return to the lounge. Not everyone on the staff had the luxury of taking a minute off to move around.

Dr. Jacob Coyne had been on the periphery of my attention yesterday. There was something reserved about him, which is no bad thing, and no guilty thing either, for that matter. He was entitled to be a private person if he wanted. But I wondered about him. And I was feeling irritable after my unsatisfactory talk with Sergeant Hightower. When Coyne passed by me without a word, on his way to put a chart in the vertical file, I said, "Mind if I follow you around for a while? I'd like to see what each level of staff does."

"No problem," he said. But he did not look pleased.

"So, you did your residency at Northwestern?" I asked. There was time to make conversation because we were again in one of those trauma center lulls.

"Yes."

"Is this is your first year at U-Hosp?"

"Yes." He seemed to feel a longer answer was called for, as in fact it was, if he wanted to be polite. "This is a good place to work. Later on, though, I'd like to move to the suburbs."

"But stay with emergency medicine?"

"Oh, absolutely. That's the speciality I'm trained in."

"So you've had how many years of training to get here?"

"Well, four years of college. Four years of medical school. Four years of residency and one year of fellowship in emergency medicine."

"If you include grade school and high school that's twenty-five years you've been in school!" I said it with awe and meant it. "That's dedication!"

There was a double bell, and the doors opened. At the same moment, Fern said, "Dr. Coyne, you're up."

I headed toward the gurney. Davidian was with a slashing victim. The two residents, Michelson and Qualley, were busy. Dr. Qualley had been on break yesterday when Dr. Grant was killed and even now I barely recognized him. Zoe Peters and Sonali Bachaan were watching Davidian operate and presumably learning from him. Fern and Marveline Kruse came with us.

Two EMTs came in fast with a man of maybe forty. It was hard to tell, because his face was covered with stubble and his hair was gray partly from dirt and dust. He wore several layers of clothes, covered by a worn overcoat. A street person. The layers almost always mean a street person. His pants leg was cut open and flapped beneath a large pad of gauze bandage. The pad was soaked with blood.

"Fell in front of a CTA bus," one of the EMTs explained.

The other said, "Compound fracture of the right femur, some other lacerations. He's lucky it wasn't worse."

"Come in here," Coyne directed them to treatment bay seven.

Fern, Marveline, and one of the EMTs transferred the man to the table. He groaned. The other paramedic said something to Dr. Coyne about having given the man some painkiller and added in a quiet voice, "There was a bottle in his pocket that got broken. Caused some of the arm lacerations. You're probably dealing with an alcoholic here."

Things began to happen fast. The record of the man's vital signs on the accident site and in the ambulance were on a chart on the stand, which Fern consulted. She took his blood pressure. It was falling. Coyne asked for a blood type and cross-match, an SMA screen, and a stat crit and globin. Sue Slaby, the nurse, appeared and took the samples.

The leg was a thing of horror. The man's thigh was bent almost at a right angle, the flesh ripped open and bone protruding both above and below the opening. Coyne sent Marveline Kruse to page the X-ray tech to do a portable. There was a tight bandage around the upper thigh, probably a type of tourniquet, but blood was still leaking from the wound. The leg below the bandage was bluish, and I knew that Coyne would have to restore circulation pretty fast.

And he did move fast. He yelled, "Kruse, where the hell is that X-ray tech?"

He sent Slaby to call for a vascular surgeon, an orthopedic surgeon, and the anesthesiologist. The X-ray tech appeared and slipped plates under the patient. Coyne said something about a clean break. It didn't look clean to me, but I suppose he meant that the bone had not splintered.

Meanwhile, Kruse stood near the patient, wiping his forehead and saying, "Don't be afraid. It's going to be all right."

He grabbed her hand.

Kruse said, "You're going to feel much better soon. They'll give you a spinal, I think, and the pain will all go away."

Coyne said, "Prep the patient for the OR." He said to me, "We'd use a general anesthetic, but not with an alcoholic street person. Not unless it was absolutely necessary."

I wondered whether the man heard Coyne, but he gave no indication. He just breathed loudly. His face was stubbly, his cheeks sunken, his mouth open. If he was offended by what Coyne had said, there was no sign. Now a nurse put a cap over the man's head and prepared him for the OR.

The big guns finally arrived, the orthopedic and vascular surgeons, talked with Coyne, and then they all went into the scrub room. The scrub room, with closed doors on both sides, was the only way into the OR, an air-lock arrangement that kept any germ-laden air from blowing in. Clean air goes into the OR from the vent system, and then the air circulates out to the rest of the unit.

I watched through the window. Slaby came over and gave me a running commentary. I saw them turn the man on his side. "They're giving him a spinal," Slaby said. "Usually they sit the patient up, but not in this case."

I winced at the thought of a needle sliding between my vertebrae. I winced even more a few minutes later when the orthopedic surgeon seemed to be sticking a knitting needle through the man's lower leg.

"That's a Steinmann pin. They'll put traction on it to straighten out the bone."

"Ummh."

I barely caught glimpses, fascinating glimpses, as the vascular surgeon rejoined the ends of the great leg vein that had been torn. At one point Slaby said, "Now he's flushing out the whole circulation of the lower leg to prevent clotting. Because, you know, the blood flow was disrupted. If clots form in the leg vein, they can get loose when the circulation is restored and move up and be pumped into the lungs by the heart."

It was absolutely amazing, but I *saw* that leg go from bluish to pink!

Before they closed up, there were more X-rays. Then the surgeons and Coyne shifted the man onto a special bed that had been wheeled in. They fiddled around with some weights that pulled on the pin in the lower leg. Finally, the big guns left. I could hear one saying cheerily, "Call us again sometime," to Coyne as they slapped their gloves into the waste can.

Coyne came out and saw me waiting faithfully at the window. I guess he took pity on me, because he stopped long enough to chat.

"Interesting, isn't it?" he said. "We could have pinned the broken place in the bone. Or put in a plate. But whenever you introduce a foreign object into the body, you run the risk of infection later. And this isn't a man who'll take care of his health."

"No, I suppose not."

"You debride—that means clean it up—and start the wound healing. Won't heal as well as it would in somebody who takes care of his health, anyway. Get him in traction. It was a clean, diagonal break, as far as the bone is concerned. Traction and medical management ought to work."

"Plus, he could probably benefit from some time in a clean bed with regular meals."

"I suppose," Coyne said, slightly surprised. "He's hypotensive, of course, but that's temporary. The crit suggested that he had lost a fair amount of blood—"

"Crit?"

"It's a perfectly simple measure. Say you come in and we think you've lost blood, but we don't know how much. Your blood pressure gives us a hint, but the EMTs have given you IV fluids to keep it up enough to combat shock. So—oversimplified, of course—what we do is we take a small test tube of your blood, spin it around in a centrifuge until all the cells clump at the bottom and the fluid rises to the top, and then measure how much is cells and how much is just fluid. If there are fewer blood cells than that amount of fluid should have, we know you've lost blood."

"That does sound simple. And you said he was hypotensive—"

"Low blood pressure. Opposite of hypertensive. I'm sure you know 'hypo' means low and 'hyper' means high."

"In that case, I'm hypocaffeinic."

"What? Oh, I see." He smiled, but not much. I felt like quite a success, having wrung from him the only smile I'd seen him produce.

He said, "Are we allowed to use the lounge yet?"

"Yes. The barrier tape is off the door. The techs have collected all the evidence they figure there is."

We walked down the corridor to the lounge. He and I both glanced into Dr. Grant's office, where Sergeant Hightower and his crew were still reading Grant's papers.

"I don't imagine they understand a quarter of what they're reading," Coyne said.

I'd been thinking the same thing, but Coyne's arrogance bothered me. He went on, "It's all patients' charts and reports to the hospital board and student recommendations and so on. They've had me in a couple of times to decode, but they don't have the background to understand even if I explain it."

"They probably can figure out the recommendations."

"Even that's pretty technical. And the charts are impossible. Think of the abbreviations."

"Such as what?" I suspected he was needling me, not just the police, but I do this kind of interview for a living, and it does *not* bother me not to know something. I ask questions. I'm here to find out.

"Well, like 's.o.b.' on a patient's chart."

"I take it that doesn't mean he's a son of a bitch."

"Nope. Means 'short of breath.'"

We poured coffee from the ever-brewing pot. A hand-lettered note next to it said, "If you've used the last cup, BREW MORE OR DIE!!!"

Coyne got a chocolate bar. We both sighed when we sat down. For a moment I felt a kinship with him. He'd put in a lot of hard, fast work on that patient and he was justifiably tired. At the same time, I was beginning to have ideas about Jacob Coyne's personality. If my article was partly about the kind of person who works in a trauma center, my answer in Coyne's case was this: He wanted to be a doctor, whether for prestige or the money or intrinsic interest I didn't yet know. But he didn't want long-term relationships with the patients.

Hell, from my observation, he didn't want *any* relationship with patients, not even as much as a surgeon would have. He scarcely spoke to them, seeing them as problems, not people. Which was probably all right in its way, since he did good work. If I had a choice between a competent doctor with a lousy bedside manner and an incompetent doctor with a wonderful bedside manner, I'd pick the competent one.

He was completely unlike Marveline Kruse, who had sympathized with the injured street person even if he wasn't a socially prominent citizen. In fact, Marveline seemed to subtly try to avoid doing medical procedures and to prefer talking with patients and encouraging them. Also good, but she would have to be able to do both if she was going to be an effective R.N.

Coyne was staring at the place on the lounge floor where Dr. Grant's body had lain.

"What a shame," I said. "Hannah Grant's death."

"It certainly was. And what a total mystery."

Maybe he hoped it would remain a mystery. Slyly, I said, "Yeah. All the so-called clues in here yesterday, and I can't imagine any of them will be of any use."

"Clues such as what?"

I hoped I'd surprise some look of recognition or guilt from him. If he was guilty. "Well, there was some spilled coffee. From the color, I knew it had cream in it, and Dr. Grant didn't take cream. There was a cup on the table that didn't have cream in it. That one was probably hers."

"Right. She drank hers black."

"There was a clipboard on the floor, with no paper in it and no name on it."

"Mmm."

"And there was a quarter."

"No kidding. Where?"

"Sort of behind the table leg."

"So *that's* where it went!"

"What?"

"I was trying to get a Snickers bar out of the machine and I dropped my last quarter. I looked everywhere for the damned thing, I thought. I finally decided it must have rolled under one of the machines."

He certainly wasn't hiding the fact. His frankness was extremely convincing. One clue bites the dust. "Well, that explains that."

"Plus, I tried the dollar-bill changer and it didn't work, so I never did get anything out of the machine."

Poor baby. No chocolate. What bad luck. Dr. Grant had worse luck, though, didn't she?

Maybe something in my body language telegraphed to Dr. Coyne that I didn't like him much. Glancing sideways at me he said, "Well, I guess Sam Davidian will have to take over again for a while."

I knew he'd seen me chatting with Sam. I think he'd heard Sam ask me to go see a movie. I said, "Take over again?"

"Oh, yeah. He was the department director before they brought Dr. Grant in. Didn't you know that?"

"No. No reason I should, especially."

"Mmm. Yeah. They asked Davidian to step down. The hospital board did."

"Why?"

"They said the department wasn't being run well. There was some theft and a missing drug thing."

"What kind of missing drug thing?"

"Well, missing narcotics. That's always a problem in hospitals, of course. This was about a year ago. To be fair, Dr. Davidian actually found out who was taking them quite a

while before he was replaced, but the board said they needed somebody who was more on top of things."

"Who was it?"

"The person taking the drugs? Oh, a med student.
Overworked. Kind of frantic. Medicating himself. All you
could do is fire him, of course. Not an unusual story."

"Pity, though."

"I guess. I've often wondered whether old Sam resented
getting replaced. Must have, I suppose." He glanced at me.
"Must have, since he doesn't talk about it. And I've often
wondered whether he resented Dr. Grant."

◦ 8 ◦

I felt so alone.

Why hadn't Sam told me? Why was he hiding the fact from me that Dr. Grant had replaced him as director? And he *was* hiding it; he'd had plenty of opportunity to tell me.

Meanwhile, I was careful to keep my face calm. Dr. Jacob Coyne was not going to get a reaction from me.

Maybe my lack of reaction disappointed him. He looked at his watch and said, "Enough break time."

We both got up and threw our cups in the wastebasket.

As I walked down the corridor toward the rotunda, I passed Dr. Grant's office again. The voices of the cops inside were lower. One of them growled, "Well, what then?"

Hightower's voice, also gruff said, "Keep reading."

The growler said, "Oh, right. Keep reading. Keep reading."

They sounded like men who were getting nowhere, getting frustrated, and getting angry.

Dr. Sonali Bachaan and a nurse I hardly knew, Natasha Horne, were meeting an incoming patient as Coyne and I reentered the rotunda. I said, "Thanks for the information" to Coyne, not specifying whether I meant the info on emergency medicine or the info on Sam, and followed Dr.

Bachaan, Horne, the patient on the gurney, and two EMTs into a treatment bay.

Horne had been on break when Dr. Grant was killed, but Sonali Bachaan had been on duty. And Bachaan, as a visitor and trauma surgery fellow, was still on approval, so to speak, vulnerable to any negative evaluation by Hannah Grant.

The patient was half conscious at best and had a collar around his neck. He was dressed in blue denim overalls and a plaid shirt. The shirt had been peeled back and he was hooked up to a cardiac monitor. His head was swollen over the left ear and eye. His eyes, half open, were bright red. There was a large laceration on his shoulder and the front of his chest.

Dr. Bachaan checked his eyes, palpated his skull very gently, and asked him questions in a soft voice while Natasha Horne took his blood pressure and checked his IV.

It was a construction accident, one of the EMTs said. A girder had collapsed when it was being placed and the man fell. As he fell, the loose horizontal girder had knocked into another vertical girder, which then toppled also, striking the man in the head.

Dr. Bachaan ordered a portable X-ray, but while the patient was being X-rayed, she said to Horne, "We need the neurosurgeon here, stat."

"Right."

She and Horne exchanged words about "closed-head injury," which this was, and that the patient was a "ten on the Glasgow Coma Chart."

Then Dr. Bachaan said, "Dr. Davidian?"

Sam came over.

"Would you look at this, please?"

Quickly she told him the nature of the accident. "It looks like a head injury, but I suspect a gut bleed, too."

"Crit?"

"Twenty-two."

"Pulse?"

"One hundred and thirty."

"Systolic BP?"

"Eighty-eight."

"Yes. He's shocky. Let's hang some blood and then see what we can figure out."

From here on, things went fast. Sam suspected a lacerated liver and talked about the man possibly having fallen abdomen-down on another girder. Horne put several units of blood in the warmer. Fern had the OR set up stat. Within fifteen minutes, the patient's blood pressure was plunging faster, and they were in a life-or-death situation. He was moved to the OR. Fern beeped the anesthesiologist, who came and got instantly to work. The neurosurgeon came in and gave his okay. Within twenty minutes, Sam was up to his elbows in blood.

Sam gave me permission to go into the OR, so Fern showed me where to get green scrubs. I changed fast. She handed me a plastic cap to put over my hair, and a mask, tucked some hair I had missed under the cap, and said, "Don't get in the way. Don't get near the table. Don't touch anything or anybody. Don't say anything. Stand back. If you feel sick, get out."

I was in the operating room in three minutes.

The look of abdominal surgery in action generates enormous ambivalence. It is oddly both primitive and high tech. There's a feeling very much like that caused by watching films of lions tearing open a gazelle and feeding on the entrails. At the same time the players are surrounded by electronic gear that ticks and beeps and whirs. The electricity of the heart traces itself as a rising and falling line on a screen.

The activities of the doctors and nurses, too, are difficult to get in a mental grasp. They are brutal—slicing the skin and muscles open, pulling tissue back with cruel-looking, shiny metal scoops and rakes. And yet there's a reverence for the tissue, for the substance of a human being, that is almost religious.

The body lies open and brightly lit, multicolored, with red and yellowish pink predominating. The group around it, dressed mostly in green, masked and abstract, pick and cut and mop at the gaping opening.

The assistant, Bachaan, reacted instantly to Sam's every request. Sam asked for a bleeder to be cauterized, a vessel to be tied, as he made his way to the tear in a blood vessel that was causing the hemorrhage somewhere deep in the liver. I could see from their responses how much the staff respected him. Once in a while, Bachaan or Michelson would ask why he was doing a specific thing, and would listen to his answer. I could feel them filing this away, knowing that someday it might be them alone against death in a situation like this. Time passed, and the tension mounted. "Liver's a bitch," Sam said. "It's too soft to sew up. It gets away from you when you want to—damn!"

Several more minutes passed. The anesthesiologist announced the blood pressures in a tense voice.

Suddenly, Sam said, "Got it!"

Somebody sighed. After that, they finished rather quickly. Sam reconnected some of the musculature they had cut through. Then Sam let Bachaan close the skin.

Finally, Dr. Bachaan swabbed the head laceration with brown Betadine, injected a local anesthetic, and began to stitch it up.

I watched her work. Dr. Sonali Bachaan was either Indian or Pakistani. About thirty. She was the type of woman people would call birdlike, with little thin bones, large eyes, a thin nose. She made quick moves, but she paused in between them, as if to judge exactly where to place the next stitch. Compared with the work of the other doctors, her stitches were smaller and closer together. It was more like embroidery than surgery. The tip of her tongue occasionally appeared between her lips as she concentrated.

"What is a Glasgow Coma Chart?" I whispered to Natasha Horne.

"Basically, how deep in a coma they are. Fifteen is good, eight is bad."

Horne, who was a black woman of maybe forty, obviously had a lot more experience than Dr. Bachaan. She kept the supplies flowing for the doctors, even before being asked for them, made notes on the charts, sent the student nurse Kruse to call the neurosurgeon after Sonali asked for him, sent Kruse for the suture cart before Sonali Bachaan even asked for it. As Sonali stitched, Horne had the fresh sutures ready for her hand as soon as the earlier stitch was placed.

Strange, the hierarchy here. There was no doubt that Horne could have done everything Dr. Bachaan was doing, and probably much better, but she was not allowed to. She was a nurse. Sonali was a doctor, a junior doctor and relatively inexperienced, but a doctor nevertheless.

I wondered about how much resentment nurses must have.

I watched and listened as Sam and the neurosurgeon looked at the X-ray films, but I could hardly understand anything they said, except that he was going to recovery and when he was stable would go to radiology.

The patient was wheeled out to radiology and the neurosurgeon followed.

• • •

I hadn't exactly been avoiding Sam since Coyne's revelations. I just hadn't gone anywhere near him. Well, maybe that's the same thing. He approached me now, as I stood staring at the board. Sonali Bachaan had just made an entry on the board with the red marker, showing that the construction worker, whose name was Konstantis, had left OR to go to recovery. She represented this by just writing in "recovery" and an arrow pointing up.

When Sam came up I was caught off guard, because I hadn't decided what to say to him yet. I blurted out the first thing in my mind: "I wish we'd saved what was on this board when Dr. Grant was killed yesterday. It might have helped tell us where everybody was."

"We couldn't. There were other patients coming in."

"Well, we should have photographed it."

"I suppose." He pointed at the clock. "It's five of seven. I'm going on break. Want to do lunch in the cafeteria?" He smiled. "It's the best I can offer. I can't go out of five-minute range."

I didn't smile. "Sure. Let's go."

"I want to get an idea of where everybody was during the murder," I said as we settled at a table. His plate held a Salisbury steak dinner with mashed potatoes and carrots. I was having iced tea and an apple. I wasn't feeling very hungry.

"Why?"

"We need to know who had the opportunity to kill her."

"Don't you think the police can handle it?"

"No, I don't. They don't understand the system here." Was he objecting because he hoped it wouldn't be solved? I reminded myself of my conclusion—Sam Davidian couldn't possibly be a murderer.

"Did they ask you what the staff was doing yesterday?"

"Roughly."

"How roughly?"

"Well, very, if you put it that way. They wanted to know whether people had to stay at certain posts all the time, and I had to say no, it wasn't quite that rigid. They asked whether I had seen anybody at one specific place constantly from three-thirty to four-thirty. And naturally I hadn't."

"Well, did they at least ask where you were?"

"Yes. And I told them." He studied my face, trying to read my mood.

"I'm asking because if they took everybody's statements they could put them together and get a good picture."

"Mmm. No."

"Why not?"

"It's too approximate. Take me, for instance. I was working on the teenager with the bullet wound. He came in at three-twenty, precisely. That kind of data we keep. We had the boy in the OR by three-thirty and the bullet out in fifteen minutes or so. Fortunately the bullet hadn't penetrated far and hadn't damaged any major blood vessels. A pneumothorax looks and sounds bad because it sucks air, but it isn't especially difficult from a surgeon's point of view if it's a clean entry and the bullet hasn't fragmented or tumbled. After we finished, I got coffee but put it down and forgot where I'd put it, probably in the lounge. That was when we tried to resuscitate Mrs. Holyrood. I started to the lounge to get more coffee, but on the way I got beeped by Fern to look at that little boy from the automobile accident. But if you asked me exactly what time I went over to see the little boy, I'd have to say sometime around four-fifteen or four-twenty. I just wasn't keeping minute-by-minute track of time. And I'll tell you something else. I don't believe anybody else would have noticed exactly when I left the OR or exactly when I approached the child."

Now I had to wonder whether he was telling me this to convince me he hadn't killed Dr. Grant. Unfortunately, he was probably right about the time problem. "People went out to the lounge and rest room all along, too," I said.

"Right." He ate for a little while. I worried and sipped tea. His tone of voice and his body language, a little subdued, told me that he realized the relationship between us had changed. He didn't ask why.

"Okay. Now tell me if some of my ideas about how the unit works are right. When you ask a nurse or a med student to stay with a patient, they stay, right?"

"Right." His tone was cautious.

"Help me make up a chart, then. You know these people. I was still confused about who was who yesterday."

He studied my face for a couple of seconds, then said, "Go ahead."

I had brought along a couple of the forms that are used for charting and turned them over to the white backs. "Okay. I arrived at three. There was a patient just leaving for—somewhere?"

"Radiology."

"Right. Then there was one of those mysterious lulls."

He smiled at that. I didn't smile back.

"Then DeeDee arrived, the burned child."

"At three-fifteen."

I wrote that down. "The people who started to treat DeeDee were Dr. Michelson, the resident, as the primary physician, I guess, Fern Butler as the nurse, Dr. Grant briefly, and a person I don't know."

"Brunniger. He's a med student. When they sent DeeDee to the burn unit, Brunniger went along."

"Good. Grant left to do something else, but Michelson, Fern, and Brunniger stayed with DeeDee. Then the teenager came in."

"Colczyk. Jim Colczyk. The pneumothorax. Did you know we didn't track down his mother until noon today, and she hadn't even noticed he was missing?"

"No. I'm sorry to hear that." But I wasn't going to be distracted. "He came in at almost exactly three-twenty."

"Right. And was treated by me, assisted by the nurse, Sue Slaby, and by the student nurse Marveline Kruse."

"Good." I wrote that down. The tension between us was growing, but we were both pretending there was no problem.

Once he went into the OR, the thoracic surgeon arrived, scrubbed and operated. When he was finished, he left without going *anywhere* else in the unit.

I said, "Okay. Then at four o'clock, suddenly we were swamped. Five people from the truck-car accident."

"Right. The Holyrood family."

I was beginning to notice that he remembered the cases as people with names first, and diagnoses second. Coyne was the opposite. To him, Colczyk would have been "the pneumothorax" and no name.

I said, "Fern Butler and Dr. Zoe Peters went to the elderly woman."

"Georgia Holyrood. She had a lot of bruises, a few lacerations, and a huge hematoma. A hematoma is nothing but a large bruise. It's a place where an injury to the blood vessels causes a lot of blood to seep out into the tissues. Hers was so large it contained enough blood to drop her blood pressure. Except for several cuts, there wasn't much to do for

her except keep her under close observation and on an
IV. She had been taking hydrochlorothiazide to lower her
blood pressure, and the flood of blood to the hematoma had
lowered her pressure more, and with the shock and emotion-
al horror, when Peters sat her up to check the cuts on her
back, her blood pressure went into the basement and she
died."

"Was Peters at fault?"

"No. It was sudden and she didn't show signs of being in
real trouble. You have to realize, accident victims are fragile.
They can be unpredictable for hours afterward. You can't
anticipate everything."

"Was anybody else in the rotunda then?"

"Sue Slaby, but she went on break about five after four.
I saw her leave. Perkins was there, I think. He's a med
student."

"Now, Fern and Zoe Peters were tied up with Georgia
Holyrood from when to when?"

"One or the other to four-thirty at least."

"The middle-aged man—"

"John Holyrood. He was a hopeless case from the start.
The EMTs had a heartbeat when they got him in the ambulance, but they lost it twice on the way, and by the time they
got here, there was nothing."

"Dr. Coyne was handling him."

"Right. He tried the usual, but it was just a massive chest
blow of some kind. He may have been crushed between the
car door that came in sideways and the steering wheel. Or
maybe a simple steering wheel thing. Basically, the entire
front of his chest was pushed in three inches. The ribs were
broken in several places, so when the victim tries to breathe,
the chest collapses in."

"So Coyne was tied up with him—"

"From four to maybe four-twenty."

"Then what did he do? Not just walk away from the body?"

"He left the student nurse, Fowler, with the body and went to get chocolate. He was stressed out and disgusted."

"He doesn't seem terribly compassionate to me."

"He's not. But he likes what he does to have a positive effect."

"Can't blame him for that. Then, Billy Michelson was treating the woman with the back injury."

"Shirley Holyrood. She was stable and not in any immediate danger, but he ran some X-rays and could see she needed more careful study. A myelogram, which just means you shoot radiopaque dye around the spinal cord to see whether there's evidence of damage. We don't do that here. We send them to radiology."

"So Michelson was free—"

"They called the med student, Perkins, from Georgia Holyrood, and he and the orderly went right out to radiology with her. Michelson was free by four-twenty. He went to the rest room."

"So Perkins was out of the trauma unit by four-thirty."

"Yes."

I noted to myself—talk with Michelson.

"And what about the little boy? Wasn't Marveline Kruse with him?"

"Yes. John, Jr. Although he claimed his name was Michael Jordan Holyrood. She took his vital signs and found he had a tremendous amount of vitality." He smiled, but I didn't. "He wanted to take the stuff off the suture cart and ride it around the rotunda. She got him a fuzzy bunny we keep around, and then I came in and sutured one small cut he had. Then the relatives showed up and took care of him."

"Marveline is kind to patients."

"She is. You're right."

"The last one was the young man with the injured eyes. Actually, I guess he was one of the first to be brought in, but I think he left the rotunda last."

"Antoine Holyrood. I think so, too. Sonali Bachaan treated him."

"Dr. Grant supervised, didn't she?"

"She watched. I would guess that when she saw that Sonali was doing the right things, she left. I know she wasn't there after four-ten at the very latest."

"The latest?"

"Well, my guess would be she left by four-oh-five."

"And nobody else says they saw Dr. Grant after four-ten?"

"Not that I know of. Not until you found her."

"All right. That means Brunniger and Perkins, the two medical students, couldn't possibly have killed Dr. Grant. They were with the patients, Brunniger with DeeDee and Perkins with Georgia Holyrood's body, until they went with them to other parts of the hospital."

"Yes."

"Why do the medical students get sent out with the patients?"

"They don't always, not if we need them here. But it helps them learn when they see the patient through several steps of treatment. See, the *first* purpose of the trauma unit is the treatment of patients. But the second is training. This is a major teaching hospital. It's one of the largest in the world."

"And you want to expose the students to as many types of cases as possible."

"Sure. Emergency medicine is actually an *optional* rotation. It ought to be required. Every doctor is going to run into a lot of emergencies in his career, no matter what specialty he picks. Even psychiatry. They ought to be prepared."

I pushed him back to the point. "So the medical students and student nurses go where you tell them to go and stay where you tell them to stay?"

"Yes. They're allowed off during their break, of course, and when the unit isn't busy, they wander around, but when they're told to stay with a case, they stay."

"So my point is, Marveline Kruse and the other student nurse would have stayed with that child until somebody said it was okay to leave, and Belinda Fowler would have stayed with the body of John Holyrood until she was told."

"Right."

"So the chance of their killing Dr. Grant was virtually nil."

"I—yes, well, they could have just abandoned the patient."

"But they would know the chance of their being discovered missing was high."

"Right."

"So Brunniger and Perkins are out, and Kruse and Fowler are unlikely."

"And Sue Slaby. She went on break to the cafeteria at the same time Colczyk went to recovery."

"Why lunch break? It was only four-twenty or so."

"She's on a different shift. She works twelve hours four days a week. She'd come on at eleven."

"Oh."

I spent a couple of minutes entering everything on the sheet of paper. Sam continued to eat, but he didn't look happy. Finally, I turned the page around to him and said, "Does this look right?"

TIME

3:15	3:30	4:00
DeeDee Williams treated by: Fern Butler, R.N. Dr. Wm. Michelson Dr. Hannah Grant Brunniger	Colczyk treated by: Dr. Sam Davidian Marveline Kruse (to child at 4:10?)	Georgia Holyrood treated by: Dr. Zoe Peters Fern Butler, R.N. Perkins Sue Slaby, R.N. (who went on break after 5 minutes or less)

4:00 (continued)

John Holyrood
treated by:
Dr. Jacob Coyne
Fowler

Antoine Holyrood
treated by:
Dr. Hannah Grant
(briefly)
Natasha Horne, R.N.
(who got back from
break at 4:30 or so)

Shirley Holyrood
treated by:
Dr. Wm. Michelson
Qualley

John Holyrood, Jr.
treated by:
Dr. Sam Davidian
(not until 4:20)
Marveline Kruse
(starting at 4:00)

Sam studied it for a minute or two, giving it serious attention. "Maybe I let Kruse go a little earlier. She had to get right over to that child, though."

"You saw her go to the child?"

"Uh—I saw her go in that direction."

"What you're saying is you saw her leave your treatment bay, but you didn't see her go directly to the one with the little boy and stay there. She could have taken a detour."

"She could have, but she *wouldn't* have. She'd know that at any moment I could leave my patient and go to get something or make a call and notice that Marveline was not taking care of the child."

"Listen, don't get so emphatic. I agree with you."

"Cat, why do you have to go into all this?"

"Don't you realize it's exactly what the cops are doing right now?"

Sam said, "So what? That's good. Let them. This isn't your job, Cat. Let the police do it."

"It *is* my job if I can contribute anything." I added sententiously, "And it's your job if you know anything, and Fern's job, and Billy's job, and Marveline's job, and Jacob's job. It's everybody's job to see that the police have as much accurate information as possible. There's a lot they don't understand about this place. They don't know how things work around here. You do."

He sighed. "Well, if you put it that way, I suppose you're right."

What I had not said was that it had become more my job since I discovered he had a motive for killing Hannah Grant. I realized that I liked him a lot. It would be impossible to have a relationship with him if no one ever found out who had killed her and I had to go on suspecting him.

◊ 9 ◊

Dr. Billy Michelson, the fourth-year resident, was working on a head injury. The patient was a girl of eleven who had fallen off a slide at school. I caught up with Michelson as he was putting the X-rays of her skull up on the light box.

He turned as I came up behind him. "Are you finding out what you need for your article?" he said.

"Doing fine, thanks. Just pretend I don't exist."

"Well, we wouldn't want to go that far." He gave me a friendly smile, and I could see the person under the layer of determination. "What is this?" I gestured to the X-rays.

"Well, that is a little girl named Halley who *doesn't* have a skull fracture."

"That's good."

"That's very good. The EMTs brought her here instead of the emergency room because they thought it looked serious. Well, better safe than sorry. So—we'll just get her fixed up."

"Pretend I'm a fly on the wall."

"No flies allowed here. We're too sterile for that. Come on, we'll pretend you're my shadow."

Halley was frightened but too brave to say so. Her eyes were big. Her reddish hair was matted with blood.

"Now, Halley," Michelson said, "I'm going to give it to you straight. The good news is you don't have a skull fracture."

"I didn't break my head? My best friend said I'd broken my head."

"Maybe you need another best friend."

This caused Halley to dissolve into a fit of giggles, partly nerves, partly relief, partly real amusement.

"What's the bad news?" she asked.

"Well, the bad news is that in order to fix that cut, I'm gonna have to shave off some of that beautiful red hair."

"Oh." Halley was solemn.

"What I suggest—course it's up to you—is you go back to school tomorrow and make quite a big drama out of it. Add some blood and all. You should be able to keep them interested in your exciting hospital stories, oh, at least until the hair grows back in."

"Yeah. I think I can do that."

"Let's start. There's gonna be a tiny prick when I put in some anesthetic, but not too bad. The scalp actually doesn't have a whole lot of sensitive nerve endings compared to other parts of your head."

"Really?"

"That's right. And it's a good thing, too, or else you'd never be able to comb your hair. I mean, think of combing your eyeballs, or your tongue."

This elicited another fit of giggles, and I saw Michelson sneak in four injections of anesthetic while she laughed.

"Why, if your scalp was as sensitive as your lips, you'd never even be able to wear curlers."

She laughed. "Or use a hot comb!"

By now, he had the hair shaved off. The cut had been cleaned by Slaby, but he cleaned it again. His hands made firm, rapid sweeps with the antiseptic. Slaby was handing him the materials. She had the threaded needles in a clamp-like tool, and when he held out his hand and said, "Suture," she slapped the handle in his palm. Halley was lying on her back, and Michelson sat to the left side of her head. He had gestured Slaby to his right, which put Slaby at about the crown of Halley's head and therefore out of sight to her. This meant that Halley didn't see the rather nasty needles and hypodermic equipment. Good for Michelson.

"Little tug here," he said to the child, "but it shouldn't hurt."

"It doesn't, Doctor," she said.

He said, "Call me Billy."

Michelson had a decisive, quick hand with the sutures. He'd grab one side of the cut with the curved needle, pick up the other side, and be through and tied off in fifteen seconds. Nice work.

"Now, Halley, I'll want you to go to your own doctor in a week to ten days so the stitches can come out. That won't really hurt much at all."

"Will you take them out for me?"

"Well, I don't work every day. And besides, this is really a place for major emergencies."

"Can I find out when you're going to be here and sneak in anyhow?"

He caught my eye and shook his head self-deprecatingly. But he was pleased. "Well, maybe we can fudge it somehow. Let's take a look at my schedule before you leave. Now let's sit you up real slowly here. Just swing your legs over the side but don't try to stand up yet. And Halley, next time you go down the slide, try to do it feet first."

"Was that local anesthetic you used Tegucaine?" I asked him as Halley walked out with her mother.

"No. I don't use Tegucaine."

"Why not?"

"It's new. I don't use new stuff. I guess I'm a conservative."

"Well, but it's been tested, hasn't it?"

"And approved for patient use. I realize somebody has to start trying it. I'm sure it's fine stuff. But when I have a patient on the table, I like to know *exactly* how the materials I'm using are going to work."

I certainly couldn't fault him for that.

I had never thought before I came here that you could deduce something about a person's character by how he or she sutures a cut. Now I knew you could. There was Dr. Jacob Coyne, who worked with what I could only call cold precision. Dr. Billy Michelson, who worked with intensity and quick competence. Dr. Sonali Bachaan, timid but very precise. She'd keep at it all day if she had to, in order to get it right. Dr. Zoe Peters—I was sorry to think it, but if I were injured, I would rather not have her on the case. Angry on the surface, she was probably fearful underneath, but if so, she fought back her fear of inexperience with bravado and sometimes skipped a step or did something too fast.

Of all of them, I'd want Sam Davidian. He had the combination of easy skill—well, after all, he'd been doing this for ten years—and a kind of enjoyment. You were injured, but he and you together were going to get you fixed up, and together you were going to beat death and beat disfigurement and by golly! it was satisfying!

After work, at eleven P.M., I ducked out on Sam's offer to watch a movie at his house. Instead, I drove Marveline Kruse home to her apartment. She lived a few miles north of the Loop in a deteriorated part of Rogers Park. Rooms would be comparatively cheap, but the streets could be dangerous.

Apricot-colored lights lit the area, making the few pedestrians look like victims of liver disease.

We'd been walking out of the trauma center at the same moment. She said good night and headed toward the bus stop. But a bus was just pulling away. It was as warm as it had been earlier in the day, and the heat was a surprise after eight hours in the air-conditioned hospital. But the dark skies were leaking a blood-temperature rain. I asked her if she'd like a ride home. I assumed I would drop her off in front of her place.

"Come up and see my apartment, Cat, please?"

"Um. Well, it's almost midnight."

"My place is small, but it's real, real nice."

She meant it; she wanted me to see it, so I parked in the only place on the block, just slightly overlapping the bus stop. Cars longer than my Bronco had not made any attempt to fit into the space. I could always use the possibility of getting a parking ticket as an excuse to leave if she seemed to want to talk all night.

"I'm right on the bus line, so I get on and get off right in front of U-Hosp. Isn't that lucky?"

It was a tiny apartment, really a bed/sitting room. My own apartment was small, but this was miniature. The "bedroom" was separate only in the sense that the bed was in a dead-end alcove under a sloping ceiling that must have been the underside of a stairway that went down to the back hall. On the bed was an inexpensive but cheerful pink and green quilt that served both as bedspread and blanket. The landlord had fitted a former closet with an under-the-counter refrigerator, a two-burner stove, and some chipped pressed-wood cabinets. The bathroom had no tub, just a prefab shower, toilet, and small sink. You could find bigger bathrooms on submarines.

There was an overstuffed green chair in the central part of the room and a brown sofa of unmatching, abstract design with telltale bulges where some springs were letting loose.

"Can I get you some tea?" Marveline asked.

"No, really. I can't stay."

"Well, let's split a Coke."

"All right."

While she poured it, she said, "Isn't this great? I found the chair at a used-furniture store. It's real comfortable. Try it!"

I sat. "It is nice." And in fact it was very comfortable, even though the arms were worn.

"I got the table"—she gestured at a scarred coffee table between the sofa and chair—"when some people were getting rid of furniture. Right on the sidewalk! They were just throwing it out. Then, some people who were moving couldn't get this sofa into the U-Haul and said did I want it. For free. Can you imagine!"

"It's great what you can get, if you keep your eyes open."

"I worked all the time I was in high school and saved all of the money." She smiled. "Well, like, I saved a lot of it. And then, my uncle said if I stayed in nursing school, he'd give me an allowance. And plus, they pay me for working three to eleven as an extern. So I don't have to live in the student housing. You know, the student housing is about the same cost as this, really, unless you have a scholarship. But I like it here." Her face was glowing with pride.

So the uncle gave her an allowance. Where were her parents?

"You want to be a trauma nurse?"

"Oh, no! I want to be a pediatric nurse."

"Really? I thought—"

"I want to nurse children. I love working with children. You thought I wanted trauma because I'm there now? That's just a rotation. I do it six weeks and then I'll go to, um, I think it's psychiatric next."

"You don't like the trauma work?"

She shook her head, then looked down at her lap. She didn't want to admit it; somehow she thought she was supposed to like all of it. "Not so much. Not really. There's too much stress. And everything happens too fast. You don't get to deal with one patient before the next one comes in. You don't get to know them at all."

"I bet some of the staff likes that."

"I guess." She wouldn't be drawn into giving names.

"What do you think of the staff?"

"They're great. Sonali Bachaan and Zoe Peters are trying so hard. It's sort of the same for them as for me. You know, being watched every second to see how we're doing."

"Does that bother you?"

"Well, it has to be that way, doesn't it?"

"What do you think of Dr. Michelson?"

"He's very strict about things, but nice."

"What about Dr. Coyne?"

"Oh, he's just great! And he's really such a hunk! Well, I mean, you know—" Flustered, she stopped.

I couldn't resist asking, "What do you think of Dr. Davidian?"

"Oh, he's wonderful! If I were in an accident, that's who I'd want to have take care of me."

"He was director before Dr. Grant, wasn't he?"

"Mmm-mm. Yes."

"Do you think he resented being replaced?"

"I don't see why. He loves what he's doing. He likes trauma surgery. I don't think he minded at all."

We finished our Cokes, and I got up to leave.

"Thanks for the Coke. I'm glad you invited me in. It *is* a

nice place." The coffee table was so covered with nursing textbooks and nursing magazines there was no place to put my glass down. I took it into the closet/kitchenette. "See you tomorrow."

I left her as she turned back with a smile into a room that to her looked lovely. Because it was all hers.

By the time I got home, it was past one A.M. My message machine was blinking. It could be an assignment, couldn't it? A glossy magazine begging me to eat at twelve famous restaurants at their expense and report my impressions? For a six-figure payment? Probably not.

I punched the message tab.

"Cat, this is Mike. Let's not be hasty."

He thinks I'm being hasty? After three years of hassling over this?

The voice went on. "Why don't we get together and talk? You and I have a lot of history. Let's not waste it."

• 10 •

The trauma center was more cheerful Wednesday, more normal, probably, even though I had only seen it "normal" for about an hour and a half on Monday before Dr. Grant was murdered. Now that I'd talked with Marveline, I began to notice that when she had a moment free, she would drop by wherever Jacob Coyne was working and watch his cases. Actually, of course, she was watching him.

At one point he said to her, "Take a look at this," and showed her an especially tricky running suture.

Love blooms in the trauma center?

Even Lester Smalley mopped more cheerfully.

There were always specimens being collected in the unit—blood in tubes, urine in plastic bottles, tissue slides in plastic covers, more rarely actual tissue pieces floating in preservative in small plastic jars. There was a table where specimens were left for pickup by the hospital lab. Those that had to be refrigerated were stored in a refrigerator near the door that led to the rest of the hospital. The staff was constantly calling the lab for quick pickup of specimens they needed fast results on. There was also a mini-lab in the rotunda where the staff ran simpler tests that they needed in a hurry—crits on blood to tell about blood loss, paper tests of urine for diabetes, some quick tests for pregnancy, in which

case they wouldn't X-ray the lower abdomen if they didn't
absolutely have to, and so on.

Michelson was looking for something. He checked the
table, asked around, and finally, since we didn't have any
patients, his being currently in X-ray, stood in the center of
the rotunda and shouted, "Where's my urine?"

Fern yelled back, "If you don't know, you're in deep trouble."

Sam and Sue Slaby laughed. Marveline Kruse and Sonali
Bachaan giggled. Zoe Peters, who didn't have much sense of
humor, said, "I'd better take my coffee break now. You know
what happens when it gets empty like this."

Fern said, "Yeah. Multiple car pileup on the Edens."

This was probably the way they carried on in normal
times.

The door beeped. The EMTs had another case for us.

Nhu Duc Tran had been struck by lightning. He was fishing off the end of Navy Pier. The sky was overcast, the late afternoon was hot, but there was no rain, no thunder, nothing
to suggest lightning. Suddenly the people fishing near him
saw a blue-white flash, and Nhu Duc Tran was lying on his
back on the concrete.

Sam met the gurney. The man was conscious, unbelievably. Lightning had traveled down the fishing rod, through
Tran, into the ground. His right arm was burned in a jagged
line. His Levi's were singed. His right foot was burned all
around the toes, and the rivets in his right boot were all
popped out. His right thumb had exploded.

He chatted with the nurses. He felt lucky to be alive, and
most certainly, he was right.

Sam said, "Hook up a cardiac monitor. Fern, get blood for
a CBC and cardiac enzymes. A urinalysis. Tetanus booster.
And cut the flow in that IV."

"Why slow the IV?" Brunniger asked.

"Brain edema is always a possibility in lightning strikes. Although in this case, I doubt it. I think the bolt was across the outside of the body."

While running through the usual exam—heart, eyes, questions about what day it was—Sam asked Tran how he felt.

"Good. Good."

"You're going to need plastic surgery on that thumb."

"That's not the only thing."

"What else?"

"New fishing pole."

"Did you catch any fish?"

"Should have. Be first time anybody catch already-fried perch."

Besides Tran, two patients were due back from radiology. That was all we had in the unit. As always when there was a short break, the unit went into its cleaning, replenishing-supplies, straightening-up-the-paperwork mode. The staff was busy and chatty.

Then the door beeped again.

It was Sergeant Hightower and another cop. They didn't turn right to go into the corridor door. They came straight on through into the rotunda. This was odd. Sam Davidian stepped forward, about to speak.

Hightower said, "Marveline Kruse, will you please come with us?"

The rotunda went dead silent.

Marveline stood still, her mouth slightly open. After a few seconds she said, "Why?"

"Routine questioning." He stepped closer.

Jacob Coyne said, "What is this? Why are you after her, especially?"

"We're not 'after' her, sir. We just need to go over some questions."

Marveline got control of herself. You could see her stand taller. She said firmly, "Are you suggesting I'm a suspect?"

"We'll decide that on the basis of your answers."

I said, "Wait a minute. If you question a witness, you don't have to caution them. But if you question a suspect, you do. If you decide later that she's a *suspect*, and you haven't cautioned her, you could be in trouble."

If looks could kill, Hightower would have zapped me. He said, "Miss Marsala, this isn't your problem. Miss Kruse, please come with me."

Coyne said, "You don't have to go—"

But Marveline said, "I don't have anything to hide," and walked toward Hightower.

I said, "Wait a minute. Marveline had *less* opportunity than any of the rest of us—"

"*Miss Marsala! Be quiet!*" Hightower boomed. "*If Miss Kruse has an alibi, she can tell us herself!*"

This was no time for a fight. Instead, I caught Marveline's eye. "Don't answer any questions without your attorney present, no matter how harmless the questions may seem. Just say you're waiting for your lawyer."

Hightower was furious, but he didn't dare say anything negative about her getting a lawyer. Especially not with all these credible witnesses watching. Marveline, though, said, "I don't know any lawyers!"

"I'll *send* you one," I said. "Just don't talk until he gets there."

My first call was to my first choice, Alyssa Bergman. If I were in trouble, she'd be the attorney I'd turn to, and I'd also take her advice. Taking anybody's advice is difficult for me, so this shows huge confidence in Alyssa.

I explained the situation to her.

"Cat, I really wish I could! But I'm due in court in twenty minutes and I'm on trial in a major case, probably for the rest of the week." Lawyers, for some reason, say "on trial" when we laypersons would say "in a trial"—leading you to think for a second that they're the defendant and bound for the maximum security prison at Joliet in a few days.

"You were my first choice, Alyssa."

"Thanks. Have you thought of Jim Cermaier?"

"I was about to call him next."

Which I did. Cermaier, according to his secretary with the honeyed voice, was in China. "A lifelong dream of his," as she put it, in golden tones.

My last best choice, Tony Marino, was in Springfield, arguing a case before the Illinois Supreme Court.

Strike three, I was out.

Fern, Sam, Jacob Coyne, Billy Michelson, Zoe, Sue Slaby, all of them kept crowding around me asking what I was going to do. "That's my top three choices," I said. "Don't any of you know any lawyers?"

Slaby said, "I heard of a great divorce lawyer."

"I know a good tax lawyer," Sam said.

Fern said, "My cousin has a guy who looked at the contract when she bought a house."

"Hell." The only other person I could think of was a man Mike had profiled in a big article last year, a defense attorney who took a lot of pro bono cases, but I couldn't think of the guy's name. The only way I could get it was to call Mike. And that was something I didn't want to do. He didn't owe me any help; I'd just made him pretty unhappy. Even more, I didn't want to get him thinking that I came running to him for help.

But it was life or death for Marveline. The justice system does make mistakes. And Marveline was exactly the kind of defendant who gets into trouble. The kind who's innocent, so she just rambles on, telling the police everything that occurs to her. And then they come back later and say, "She claimed this happened at three forty-five and it was really three-fifty. She must have lied intentionally." As if everybody remembered to the minute exactly what they were doing all day.

I'd talked myself into it. I had to call Mike.

He said, "Cat! Thanks for calling me—"

"Mike, listen, I'm not returning your call, exactly." I had to stop him before he got too carried away. "I did get your message, but I meant what I said before."

"Ohhh. Yeah. Well."

"We've had a crisis here at the trauma center. About Dr. Grant's murder. The police have taken an innocent person in for questioning. I need the name of that defense lawyer you told me about. The one you profiled."

"Oh." Now he got a businesslike tone in his voice, making it obvious that he was really hurt. "It's Stanley Kupferman. The office is on LaSalle someplace. I can get the phone number for you."

"I'd appreciate it."

I called Kupferman. He'd leave for Area Two police headquarters immediately. When I hung up, Dr. Coyne, who had been listening closely, said, "Thanks, Cat." Then he blinked, as if surprised at this big show of emotion.

The rest moved away. There was work to do. Only Sam hung around.

"Cat, why didn't you want to call that guy, Mike?"

"Was it that obvious?"

"Of course it was."

"Old boyfriend. I didn't want to be obligated."

A couple of seconds of silence went by. I didn't break it, because I hadn't decided yet how to handle my suspicions of Davidian. He said, "Is Saturday night still on?"

"I don't know. Can I tell you later?"

He studied me. "Sure. You let me know."

The three hours that followed were extremely awkward. Several patients were brought into the unit. One was basically DOA. The others lived, but Michelson predicted that his, a cab driver who had picked up a fare who bashed him on the head with a hammer, would have some permanent brain damage.

There was no gossip, no joking around, no talk about what was happening with Marveline. The patients wouldn't have noticed anything wrong, because they are so involved in their own precarious physical conditions. And even if they had noticed, they'd probably think the trauma center was always silent and businesslike.

Fern and Zoe and I took a coffee break together, during which we talked only about which major clothing stores were having sales. We also didn't exactly look each other in the eye. Billy Michelson came in while we were there, sat down, took out a cigarette, and lit it. Then he said, "Damn! I'm supposed to be quitting," and put it out and left.

The problem wasn't that anybody was being careful about what they said because I was there. They were accepting me now as part of the furniture. It was fear for Marveline and fear for themselves, too.

In sociology there is a study method called participant observation. What this means is simply that when a sociologist

wants to study a certain group of people and analyze their
habits and values and lingo, he just goes and hangs out with
them long enough so they feel he's part of the group and they
act natural around him. That's what I do when I'm researching a group for this kind of article.

The trauma center staff was used to me. This was a boon to
my future article. It also put me on the inside as far as finding
out who had murdered Hannah Grant. But if I asked questions that were too pointed, I'd put myself back outside the
group again. I couldn't afford that, because I had to have a
version of the article done by Saturday.

Specifically, what I would have liked to do was refine my
list of the sequence in which people went to the lounge or
the rest rooms near it. But I couldn't very well go around
with a notebook asking everybody, "Did you go to the lounge
and what for and at what time and was Dr. Grant there, dead
or alive?"

As far as they knew, all but Sam, my only interest was in
writing an article about them. And the only questions I asked
related to that.

At seven P.M., Marveline came back.

Everybody who wasn't tied up with a patient crowded forward to see her. Sam, Billy, Sonali, Fern, and me.

Fern said, "Thank goodness! Are you okay?"

"Uh, sort of."

Her eyes were big with fright. The wispy red-blond hair
hung stringily, as if she had been pulling at it nervously for
hours. Her pale skin was whiter, and her eyes were red.

She said, "They found this note. Dr. Grant wrote a memo
to herself."

Fern said, "What did it say?"

"It said 'Warn Kruse. Again!' They asked me what it meant, and I said she probably was going to tell me to try to do better. That was her job, I said."

"Marveline, did your lawyer let you answer that?" I asked.

"He wasn't there yet."

I groaned. "But I told you—" I stopped. What would be the use, now, of making her feel she'd screwed up?

Fern said, "What happened then?"

"They said maybe the note meant she was going to fire me. I said it didn't. That it was her job to keep people up to— up to their best."

Sam said, "Marveline, would you like to go home? You don't look well."

"No! I want to be doing something! I want to work and get it off my mind. You know what they think? They think I killed Dr. Grant. Me! I admired her so much. How could they possibly think that? Do I look like a murderer?"

"Absolutely not!" Jacob Coyne said. He put his arm around her shoulders.

Her voice started to break as she said, "They told me I'm the only one who had a motive."

I was careful not to look at Sam when Marveline said she was the only one with a motive. He had a motive that was at least as strong. And Marveline would have had much less opportunity than he had.

Marveline settled gratefully to work, stripping the soiled sheets off an examination table, wiping down the rails with disinfectant, then restocking used equipment. It was seven-thirty. Just about "lunch" time. I approached Sam, who was washing up from a minor surgery.

"We've got to talk."

His face lit up.

I said, "We can't let this happen to Marveline."

He looked less happy now that he realized I didn't want to get personal, but he said, "I agree. Okay, let's talk."

We went to the cafeteria. He had the tuna salad sandwich, and I wanted that, too, but I had reservations about looking like I was soul mates with him. Then I decided that was stupid, I'd eat what I damn well wanted. We both took coffee with a small amount of cream.

"Sam, when you agreed with me that Marveline and the other students didn't have time to slip out and kill Dr. Grant, you meant it, right?"

"Of course. I wouldn't have said so if I didn't."

"So you think Marveline isn't guilty?"

"Sure, that's what I think. It's a question of probability. The students are the people least likely to be able to get away unnoticed."

"They didn't have the time."

"Right."

I said, "You realize that just because the cops didn't hold her doesn't mean they won't go ahead and arrest her tomorrow or the next day."

"They can't have any evidence against her."

"Unfortunately, they've arrested people before without a lot of evidence. Especially in high-profile cases like this. Even if they eventually let her go, it would be a ghastly experience for her. And sometimes people are tried even without much evidence and sometimes they're convicted."

"I know."

"As far as I can see, the only way to make sure the cops don't actually go ahead and charge her is to find out who did it." I said this pointedly. If Sam were the killer, he wouldn't want more investigation.

"I wish—well, wishing doesn't help. I have to admit it looks like they're blundering."

"You'll help me figure it out?"

"Sure."

So far I hadn't eaten a bite of lunch. Quickly, I ate half my tuna sandwich. "What I need to know about is Dr. Grant. See, the question is this: Was she in the lounge expressly to meet somebody?"

"We can't possibly know that. Unless somebody admits to it."

"Which isn't likely. He's likely to be the killer. I think she must have gone there to meet somebody."

"Why?"

I told him my reasons why I thought the killing was premeditated. Why I thought nobody would carry a sponge and tongue depressor around.

"So either Dr. Grant told somebody to meet her in the lounge and the person already knew Grant was a threat and brought the murder weapons along, or the person had a talk with Dr. Grant in the lounge, found out that Grant was a threat, went back to the rotunda and got the tongue depressor and sponge, and *went back and killed Dr. Grant*. Going back to the question of time, that would take even longer. Plus the time it took Grant to tell him or her about what her problem was."

"You've really thought about this, haven't you?"

"Naturally I've thought about it." I wasn't sure whether his tone of voice was admiration or regret. I was going to say, "Haven't you?" but thought better of it. "So it's important how Dr. Grant did things. So—whoever Grant met in the lounge, they may have met there at her request. Why? Why not her office? For what kinds of reasons would Dr. Grant call people into her office?"

"Serious things. She'd consider that a pretty heavy move, like being called on the carpet."

"That's important to know. What would she consider serious?"

"Firing somebody. Actually, she couldn't fire them herself, but she would recommend to the director of nursing to fire a nurse or an extern or recommend that medical education fire a resident or fellow."

"What else would be serious?"

"Accusing somebody of stealing. That happened a few weeks back, just after she came on."

"What were the circumstances?"

"One of the orderlies was stealing from patients' clothes."

"No kidding?" I realized that would be quite easy. Clothes and belongings of the patients, like purses and wallets and briefcases, were placed on a rack near the examining table. If the patient died or was transferred someplace else in the hospital, the belongings went into a bag to be moved with him. But up until then, they were quite accessible. "What else?"

"Theft of drugs, probably."

"Is there much of that?"

"It's a constant problem in hospitals. Nurses take drugs. Residents take drugs, mainly to keep awake because they're overworked. Older doctors take drugs to cover burnout."

"How do they steal them?"

"Well, the simplest way with narcotics is to shoot half a dose into yourself and half into the patient. Or if it's pills, you can do a switch and give the patient some other, more or less harmless drug and keep the narcotic for yourself."

"How do you catch these people?"

"Oh, lots of ways. Say a particular nurse has an unusual number of patients that claim that their painkiller didn't help. We keep track of that. And any evidence of being impaired on the job, of course."

"Yes, okay. Are all your drugs locked up?"

"Only the narcotics. They're in a locked cabinet and only certain authorized people have keys. Regular meds aren't locked up. We keep track of regular medication, but not as tightly. Most of the stuff—insulin, thyroxine, nitroglycerin, Tagamet, hydrochlorothiazide, all the ordinary things—aren't abusable."

"Let me get to the bottom line. Do you have any reason to believe anybody's stealing drugs right now?"

"Absolutely none."

"Or stealing from patient's belongings?"

"No. We'd hear about that. It's a lot easier to get away with stealing drugs than wallets."

"So you don't think Dr. Grant called anybody into the lounge for that reason?"

"I doubt it. She was very sensitive to the implications of her actions. If she called the person into her office, she would have two choices. Leave the door open, in which case everybody would see that the person had been called on the carpet. Or close the door, which would look even more serious if a person passing down the hall saw them going in or coming out."

"That's why she tended to see people in the lounge?"

"Sure. She could just say, 'Let's get coffee and talk,' and they would be private there until another staff member came to get coffee or whatever. When anybody else arrived, it would look like Hannah and whoever just happened to be taking their break at the same time."

"Yes. That makes sense," I said.

"Which suggests to me it was one of two things. One, Hannah just wanted to tell somebody to shape up their work. Or two, it was something that might be serious, but Hannah only suspected it was going on and either wasn't certain that the crime was taking place or that this particular person was guilty."

"Would somebody kill just for being told to shape up?"

"Well, for students her recommendation was crucial. And Marveline didn't come right out and say it, but the crucial word in the note was 'again.' 'Warn Kruse. Again!' Somebody on the staff may have told them that Hannah would warn a person just so often and then—out. So, if they asked or if somebody volunteered it, the note can be called extremely urgent for Marveline."

"But her recommendation was crucial even for residents?"

"Sure."

"Still—"

"It all depends on how threatened the person feels, doesn't it?"

His assessment was plausible. His concern seemed genuine. And he certainly hadn't tried to offer me a whole bunch of suspects, like a guilty man might do.

"Sam, what about opportunity? Do you know for *sure* of anybody who went to the lounge or rest rooms around four? Not what they say, but what you know."

"Me. I went and got coffee."

"When?"

"Maybe ten after."

"Did you pass anybody in the hall?"

"No, but I saw Jacob Coyne heading that way a few minutes before I did. He's a chocolate addict. Singlehandedly keeps the candy machines profitable."

"Did you notice anybody else going into the corridor after that?"

"No. But I was concentrating on what I was doing. See, I would notice unusual things, which is why I've said I'd probably notice if one of the students left a patient. You've seen how careful we are to keep enough staff on the floor. We stagger our coffee breaks—we schedule lunch so that there's always at least one attending physician in the rotunda. When the place is deserted, it's different. People can wander down to the lounge and hang out, even the med students and nursing students. But even then, they can't leave the unit without getting permission and they always carry beepers."

I thought I'd try one more approach on him. "Well, maybe you can tell me about this. When I found Hannah Grant, there were some items on the table and floor near her. A quarter, a clipboard with nothing clipped onto it, a cup of coffee that was spilled. Coffee with cream. Hannah took hers black—"

"So *that's* where I left it!"

"Left what?"

"When I finished with Colczyk, the pneumothorax, I went to the lounge to get a cup of coffee. Then I went back to the rotunda. And I thought I'd put the coffee on the central desk, but it wasn't there. I must have left it in the lounge. I take cream, by the way."

"Oh."

I knew that. I'd been watching him drink coffee with cream for the last five minutes. His easy acknowledgment made the coffee "clue" dwindle in importance. In the detective shows on television, clues at the scene actually mean something. But not for me; not this time. Jacob Coyne had claimed the quarter without any evidence of guilt. Were all of my clues going to vanish like this? I said, "Whose clipboard do you suppose it was?"

"I don't know. We all carry them. We all leave them around, too."

I thought it over for a while. "What do you think of this theory? The murder must have happened because of something that came up that day. Dr. Grant must have confronted her murderer about her suspicions on Monday for the first time. Otherwise, it would have been so much safer just to mug Dr. Grant in the parking lot at midnight. Out there, the killer could be anybody in the whole city of Chicago. In here, it was one of a small number."

"I think that makes sense. I wish it didn't."

"And whatever it was, it was so dangerous that the killer had to finish Hannah Grant off before she talked with anybody else."

"Yes. And if that's the way it happened, the killer probably listened to whatever Dr. Grant said, claimed to be able to explain, left the lounge but went to the rotunda and got the tongue depressor and sponge, and went back."

"Saying something like 'I've been thinking it over. Let's talk.'"

"Right."

What I didn't say was, all of this was true except for one quite different motive. Hatred. Somebody who simply hated Dr. Grant. Hated her because she replaced him as director.

But even so, even in that case, why wouldn't he mug her in the parking lot? My head was filled with too many possibilities and too few certainties. Surely, Sam Davidian was not a *likely* killer.

Boiled down, the people who could have killed Hannah Grant were the people who had opportunity: Sam Davidian,

Jacob Coyne, Billy Michelson, Zoe Peters, Sonali Bachaan, and Fern Butler. That is, they were enough their own bosses to get away.

And when it came to motive, we had Sam Davidian, Marveline Kruse, and—

Well, Davidian and Kruse. Unless there were other motives I didn't know about. Certainly there had to be some. But no matter how I looked at it, so far only one name appeared on both lists. Dr. Sam Davidian.

I said, "So think hard. Is there anybody else with a motive to kill Dr. Grant, so far as you know?"

"No. Marveline is the only one. But I don't think much of her so-called motive either."

"The police think she's guilty."

He said, "And they've gotta be wrong."

"In that case, first thing tomorrow morning I'll have to go see my cop friend, Harold McCoo."

· 11 ·

Chief of Detectives Harold McCoo is a longtime buddy. I first met him when he was a detective sergeant, and I've seen him rise to lieutenant, then Area Commander in Six, which is central and west Chicago, then Chief of Detectives Group A, which basically means the north half of Chicago. There are cops who rise because of politics, and cops who rise basically on luck, being in the right place at the right time. McCoo rose on ability.

I went to his office early Thursday morning. His secretary, a woman cop named Bramble, waved me in. Bramble doesn't exactly like me, but she's decided I'm harmless.

McCoo was zooming across his office backward in his desk chair. He didn't see me come in, and I barely stepped back in time to avoid being run down. As it was, he clipped my foot.

"Yipe! Yipe-yipe!"

"Holy shit! Cat!" He jumped out of his chair and took hold of my arm. "Are you okay?"

"Yeah. I'm wounded. But not badly."

"Don't you know better than to come waltzing in without warning?"

"Well, jeez! I didn't expect the office to be a raceway. You've violated the speed limit, McCoo."

"Hey. It's *my* office."

"Where were you going in such a hurry?"

"The file cabinets." His office had no rug, partly because the CPD hadn't given him one, but partly because he didn't want one. It would impede the movement of his chair. He likes to keep copies of all his case files near at hand and zoom from file to file, as the whim takes him.

"What's so important in the file cabinet?"

"Nothing." His square brown face folded into smile lines. "I guess once I get started I just like to go fast."

While his office looks austere because there's no rug, it always smells of the finest coffee. He has a Krups grinder and a new French pot and keeps real cream on hand at all times, brought fresh every morning from home. Today, with the morning sun making the room honey colored and the rich odor of brewing coffee filling the air, it was a welcoming place. It's odd to say about an office in the big cop shop, but really a welcoming place.

"What's your coffee this morning?"

"Yemen Mocha with spicy Java Island. The Yemen Mocha imparts a robust, hearty body and the Java supplies the lively, impetuous overtaste and bouquet."

"Oh, Mocha Java! John's father used to talk about that!"

"Well I admit to being on a traditional kick today. But I've got a line on an audacious little Panamanian bean that's said to be a promising upstart."

He poured me a mug of the Mocha Java and refilled his own cup. "Panamanian is considered effervescent and a bit tart on the palate. Now, Cat," he said, "what favor have you come to ask me?"

"I've come to *do* you a favor."

"Oh, right."

"You know about the murder of Dr. Hannah Grant, of course."

"Please!" he said.

"Well, of course you would. High-profile case like that. I was on the scene."

I explained why I'd been there and also that I was still on the scene. And why Marveline Kruse wasn't a likely killer. "See, what I'd like to do is help Sergeant Hightower. He doesn't know the milieu from the inside, the way I do."

"I see. You don't want anything *from* him. You want to give information *to* him."

"Well, uh, there you put your finger on a kind of sensitive point. I do need a little information from him in order to—to put some others things together, if you see what I mean."

"I see what you mean. You've come to me for a favor."

"Well, shoot, McCoo. Put it however you want."

"What do you need to know?"

"I'd like to know what everybody told Hightower about when they went to the lounge. Or bathrooms. And whether there was anything interesting in the wastebasket."

"Well, Cat, you may have just lucked out."

"It's about time. In what way?"

"Hightower is due here in twenty-five minutes. I asked his commander to send him here at ten-thirty."

"And?"

"Why, we'll present your case. I've heard his reasons for liking Marveline Kruse for the killing. They're adequate, but I think the word 'warn' in Grant's memo is a little weak for murder."

"Good. I have to admit, McCoo, that some of the staff tell me Grant would warn somebody a limited number of times, though. My reason for thinking Marveline couldn't have done it is that she's just not her own boss."

"Okay. Your judgment means something to me. Now you

let me do the rest of this paperwork. You just settle back and luxuriate with fine coffee."

This was not a hard order to follow. Twenty-five minutes went by like five.

Bramble came to the door. "Your ten-thirty is here. Sergeant Hightower."

"Fine."

Hightower strode in, the picture of assertive, on-the-ball public official. He said, "Good morning, boss," to McCoo as McCoo greeted him. He half ignored me at first, not recognizing me out of context. Then memory kicked in and he missed a step as he realized who I was.

"Miss Marsala."

I said, "Good morning, Sergeant Hightower."

McCoo said, "Sit down, Hightower. Ms. Marsala, as you probably know, is working on a story about the trauma center for *Chicago Today*."

"Yes, I know that, sir."

"She feels she might be helpful in giving you some insights about the staff."

"Oh. Well, yes, sir. Of course, I appreciate that, Miss Marsala."

I could see Hightower looking back and forth between me and McCoo, on the pretext of talking to both of us, trying to gauge whether I knew McCoo well, and trying to figure out how pleasant he had to be to me. Did I have clout? Or was I just a reporter annoying McCoo? Hightower was asking himself, I think, whether he would gain points with the Chief of Detectives if he was firm with the media. Me being the media in question.

After this opening, nobody said anything for a few seconds, so I broke the silence and said, "Maybe we could narrow

down who was where when. Who really had opportunity."
McCoo wore the Poker Face of the Decade. Wily rascal.

Hightower's personality tipped him into making the
wrong choice.

"Well, you have to understand, Miss Marsala," Hightower
drawled, "that there's a problem with real life. Now these TV
cop shows you see, you always know exactly who was where
at what time. But that's not the way it works in the real world.
Ninety-nine percent of the cases any real detective works,
there's nothing you can pin down to the minute. It's all a little fuzzy around the edges. And don't let anybody tell you
you can just add up all the evidence like three and three and
three makes nine. Evidence is a mess. It's all over the place,
by which I mean it's pro and con and most of it you could
take either way. You get a technical fact and you'll find at trial that the prosecution and the defense both use it. Put a different spin on it. We go by motive. If you got a motive, it's
probable you did it."

"And in this case, the motive—"

"The nurse, Marveline Kruse. Dr. Grant was getting ready
to terminate her."

"Well, Sergeant, I don't think that's quite true. The staff
tells me Grant always cautioned people about their work if
they weren't doing it as well as she thought they should. And
she cautioned long before she even *thought* of recommend-
ing termination."

Still McCoo didn't enter the conversation.

I went on. "One of the staff told me that Grant saw people
in the lounge if she wanted to warn them. She would see
them in her office for serious matters, like termination. As
you know, she was killed in the lounge."

"Okay. Well, then, you tell me. Whatever it was, it was serious enough to get her killed, wasn't it?"

Touché. Hightower had a point.

"That's true. But that's equally true for whoever did it. It doesn't mean it was Marveline. Look. Let me explain about the pecking order in the unit. Marveline isn't a nurse, you know. She's a nursing student."

"I know that. Doesn't matter. Well, it does—it matters because she was on probation. She was in more danger of being canned than a real nurse."

"That's true. She was still qualifying. But because of that, they watched her almost all the time."

I explained the way the senior staff kept track of the students, so they didn't screw up and damage a patient. I explained how students were left to watch over patients while attending physicians and senior nurses went off to get test results or look at X-rays or whatever. Throughout, Hightower maintained his supercilious expression.

"Let's take a closer look at what you're saying, Miss Marsala. You think the doctors, like Coyne, Michelson, and Davidian, would have noticed if she wasn't there."

"They would and Fern Butler would. She's the charge nurse and she's on top of what's happening."

"Fine. But in fact, I've asked all these people if any one of them can tell me that they had any person under observation *all* the time, and they say no. Except for some medical student named Brunniger and two nurses, Slaby and Horne, who went out of the unit. Nobody can claim to have had Marveline Kruse under direct observation the whole time from, say ten of four until four twenty-nine, when you discovered the body."

"They wouldn't. That's not the point. The point is she'd know somebody probably would notice if she was gone."

"Probably? I'll even buy that. Miss Marsala, I guess she took a risk."

"It would be a crazy risk. There are probably lots of other times you could attack somebody more safely."

"Probably?"

I sighed. "Very likely."

"We don't know that."

"Well, did anybody see her go down the corridor?"

Hightower caught McCoo's eye. McCoo waved his hand graciously, meaning "go ahead."

"No. Nobody says they saw her."

"Who *did* they see?"

"I don't think that's your business. If you have anything to tell me, tell me. Although if it's as indeterminate as what you've told me so far, I frankly don't think you're gonna be much help."

At last McCoo stirred. Rumbling, stretching, sitting up more vertically in his chair, he moved into his avuncular mode. He tries this with me sometimes, but I've known him long enough to kid him about it.

"Now, Sergeant," he said. "You don't want to take this attitude. These aren't state secrets. And you don't have what I would call exactly an open and shut case."

Hightower blinked and sat *much* straighter.

"Yes, sir. Well, Dr. Coyne says he went to the lounge about four and met Dr. Davidian coming down the hall from the lounge. Dr. Davidian remembers running into Coyne, but thinks Coyne was leaving the lounge when Davidian was entering. They think it was around four o'clock. Neither one of them saw Dr. Grant's dead body, of course."

"Go on."

"Dr. Bachaan went to the lounge for some candy about then, five of four she thinks, and didn't see anybody going either way. Fern Butler thinks she went in about ten after four. She got tea and didn't see anybody. She didn't stay long."

I said, "They wouldn't. There were a lot of patients in the unit."

"Dr. Michelson went to the men's room and passed the lounge but didn't look in. Dr. Peters went to both the lounge and the rest room, but she thinks it was ten of four. She got an orange. No one else admits being down that end of the corridor at all."

McCoo said, "Now that wasn't so hard, was it?" Hightower blinked at him. There were about ten seconds of silence.

I said, "What was in the wastebasket?"

Hightower groaned loudly, but McCoo said, "Sergeant!" in a cautionary tone.

"The hell of it is, it was just stuff like all that other stuff we found. All ordinary items that were there naturally."

"Like the coffee and the quarter and so on?"

"Well, sure. And the hair and fibers we vacuumed off the floor. Those people are in and out of the canteen all day long. The fact that they leave hair or clothing fibers or coffee cups means absolutely zilch in terms of proving that they killed Grant."

"Okay. But anyway, what was in the wastebasket?"

"Yeah. Well." He rummaged in his briefcase, shoved a few sheets of paper aside, studied the headings on some form-sets, and finally found the one he was looking for. Personally, I thought he knew exactly where it was all along, and just wanted McCoo to think he had a lot of important papers.

"Uh-huh. Here," he said. "Nineteen pieces of skin from an orange." He looked at me as if to emphasize how ordinary this was. And how useless it was to bother to tell me. "Four used Styrofoam cups, two previously having held coffee, one cocoa, one tea. Seven wrappers, five from candy bars, one from potato chips, one corn chips. A discarded lipstick. The color is called Tropic Sun. We'll ask whose it was."

"Sonali Bachaan probably," I said.

He looked sourly at me. "A Kleenex with a touch of eye makeup on it. Eye shadow, to be precise. Light bluish green. We'll try to find out whose it is."

"Fern maybe," I said.

"A broken cigarette. I suspect somebody is trying to quit."

"Michelson," I said.

"Uh-huh. Great," he said sourly. "Thanks. That's useful. Some hair, probably from a comb. Somebody combed his or her hair and didn't want to put it back in a pocket with the hair on it. Brown. Four inches long."

"Zoe Peters," I said.

He sighed. "Swell. Well, that's it. Help you any? 'Cause frankly, it doesn't help *me*."

McCoo said, "Sergeant Hightower, I think you're going to have to work on your pessimism problem."

I left the CPD and started walking north on State, and by the time I had gone five blocks I was feeling like hell. When Hightower had said Marveline was the only one with a motive, I had not told him about Sam. Obviously, nobody else had either. The more I thought about withholding this information, the guiltier I felt. Not so much about Hightower. But McCoo was a friend and I owed him honesty. I also owed it to Marveline. Lord only knew what I had let Marveline in for. With two people with motives, Hightower would at least be confused and might not arrest either one.

That would be better, wouldn't it? Wouldn't it?

It was quarter of twelve, and the combination of guilt and indecision made me think of ways to console myself. Lunch, a really good, big lunch, would help a lot. Complex carbos and an adequate amount of chocolate was just the thing for gloom. It might not solve the moral dilemma, but it would keep me alive long enough to decide what to do.

My friend Hermione runs a restaurant accurately called Hermione's Heaven. I walked briskly the six blocks farther to the restaurant and arrived, unfortunately, at the very busiest time of day. Every table was full. There was no place to sit.

I can't stand this! I need food! I thought, standing in the doorway, smelling the thick pea soup that Hermione called Superpea. On her blackboard of daily specials was Pasta-Blasta!, which was some new invention of hers, and Choc-Full, which I recognized. That was chocolate cake, dense not fluffy, with creamy chocolate mousse filling and hard chocolate candy topping, and I immediately became aware of the rich, spicy odor of chocolate that scented the air. The restaurant was a symphony of fragrances, a nosegay. I was going to burst into tears if I didn't get in.

Fortunately, Hermione saw me.

"Cat! You know better than to get here at this time of day."

"I was hungry at this time of day."

"You do look hollow-cheeked."

Hermione herself was round-cheeked. She's about a hundred pounds over the weight people think she should be, but solid, and she doesn't take any lip about it. She said, "Well, I certainly can't turn you away in a starving condition. Come here."

We trekked through the restaurant, me studying the plates on tables. Obviously one of the specials was her famous chili, the one she called Chili-Max.

Hermione led me into the kitchen. Chefs were flipping pans, flinging stir-fry; clouds of fragrant steam rose from simmering soups; red and green and yellow peppers sizzled in olive oil, a confetti of delight. Deep garlic and onion odors, like bass notes, underlay the crisp scent of chopped parsley and endive. Roast pork and frying chickens marinated in lemon and cracked pepper painted pictures of Italy in my mind.

"Here," she said. "Sit."

We were at her desk, which was really a white-enameled metal table in a corner next to the door to the cooler in the back of the restaurant. The desk was stacked with file cards and bills, as well as pens, herb samples, and flyers from meat suppliers. She shoved them to one side. "Wait there."

In about a minute and a half she was back with pasta. "Today's special," she said. "I'll be busy for half an hour, and then I'll be back."

"I'll be busy for half an hour, too," I said, seeing the size of the plate. But she'd left and didn't hear me.

When I tasted it I knew the name Pasta-Blasta! referred to the effect of a number of tiny finger peppers, tossed with the rigatoni pasta, sun-dried tomatoes, oil-cured olives, garlic, fresh basil, and oregano. It was spicy. It was great. My eyes closed for a couple of seconds in sheer delight.

After a while, the tempo in the kitchen became a little less allegro. The chefs were still working fast, but not frantically. Hermione's would be busy until about two, and then slow down until five, when the early dinner customers would start to arrive.

She showed up with two slices of the chocolate cake and two cups of coffee, and she placed one of each in front of me. This is a friend! Hermione is a former waitress and can still hold six full plates on her left arm while pouring coffee with her right hand. She put the other cup of coffee and slice of cake on the table for herself.

"All right, Cat. What's the matter?"

"Nothing. I was hungry. This was your best pasta special yet."

"You always say that. Don't get evasive with me. This is Hermione here, and you won't get away with it."

"What?"

"I've noticed something about you lately."

"What?"

"You're lonely."

"Lonely? How could I be? I have friends. You, for one."

"That's one."

"Like Hal Briskman—"

"An editor. A business associate."

"He's a friend, too. And a couple of the people in my building. Plus, Mike's getting more persistent than ever, now that I've broken up with him. He left some really wild messages on my machine last night. Mostly 'Please, please, please!' And then there's John."

"Well, your gentleman callers are half the problem, aren't they? You haven't settled down with either one of them. Why? Because they're not quite right for you. That's why."

"John is sensitive, helpful, and considerate, let alone rich—"

"And not quite right for you, is he? He's not exciting, am I right?"

"Well, no. But if a person is thinking of being married for decades, friendship is more important, isn't it?"

"Maybe. But shouldn't there be excitement at the beginning?"

"Oh, hell. Yes, I suppose that's what's making me hesitate. I kind of broke up with him, by the way. And he's out of the country, too."

"Tell me what happened."

Okay, maybe I was vulnerable. "Just before John left for

Hong Kong, we had a falling out." John Banks is a stockbroker, and as if he isn't making enough money that way, his family has money. Old money. You've heard of New Yorkers who think the world ends at the edge of New Jersey? Mrs. Banks is the kind of person who thinks a map of Chicago consists entirely of Michigan Avenue and two cross streets that contain Ultimo and Donna Karan. His father is the sort who would wear a three-piece suit and tie to scuba dive, if he could.

Not that John is like his parents. He's sensitive, not hidebound, not snobbish. He's considerate. One time, when my landlord, Snively Grinch, was refusing even to make minimal improvements, John bought me a new toilet. You gotta love a guy who can see what you really need.

"But you're right," I said. "I don't seem to love him quite enough. He asked just before he left whether I'd marry him. And suddenly we were right back to the old question. How much time did I have to spend on my work? Why couldn't I stay at home a lot, like most wives?"

Hermione asked, "What did you tell him?"

"I said, 'If we were married, you'd want me to cut down on my hours, wouldn't you?'"

"He said, 'Cat, you normally run a seventy-hour work week. Cutting down a little wouldn't hurt you.'

"I said, 'It would hurt my career.'

"He said, 'You're freelance. You can work whatever hours you want.'

"I said, 'It's not like that. It takes a lot of hours to do any story well. It takes a lot of good articles to build a reputation. And if I'm going to make a living income from it, I have to put in the time.'

"And then, Hermione, he said, 'If we were married, you wouldn't *need* to make a living at it. You could do it more as a hobby.'"

Hermione said, "Oh-oh!"

"Yeah. I didn't answer him. He could see he'd stepped in it. After a minute or so I said, 'A hobby?'"

"He said, 'All right. I'm sorry. I didn't mean that the way it sounded. But Cat, with my job, I get to go wonderful places. We could travel. You could go to Hong Kong with me right now, if you didn't have to work on this trauma center thing.'

"I said, 'I can plan an occasional vacation.'

"'What if we had a baby?'

"'If I had a baby, I'd take time off. That's important.'

"'You'd take time off for a baby but not for me?'

"'Well, a baby needs time.'

"He said, 'I see.' He was hurt, you know, Hermione. We were doing just great, weren't we, each of us damaging a person we were really fond of?

"I said, 'Please, you know a baby needs a mother differently. They need what they need *right then*. It's not forever. Eventually they grow up.'

"So he went back to his earlier point, 'If we were married you wouldn't need to work.'

"I said, 'Yes, I would.'

"'I can support us both.'

"I said, 'I'm aware of that. I meant that I need to work. John, when you stop to think of it, financially speaking, *you* don't need to work. Your family has money. Why don't you give up your job?'

"And Hermione, he said, 'What would I do all day?'"

Hermione said, "Oh-oh."

"Right. Well, that was when I was pretty sure we weren't looking at life the same way. He left for Hong Kong and I left for the level one trauma center at University Hospital. And whether it was a good choice, I don't know."

Hermione got a pot of coffee and poured more for both of

us. "You live alone, Cat, and now you're spending the whole day isolated in the trauma unit with a whole bunch of strangers."

"That's my job."

"And then you go home and talk to a parrot."

"Hey, watch it! Whoever disparages Long John Silver disparages me."

"Just because he speaks doesn't mean he's the basis of a mature adult relationship."

"Mature! That bird is five or ten years older than I am, at the very least! He's probably forty-five years old."

"He's not human."

"He's more rational than most humans."

"I can buy that. He's still not human." She poured coffee, thinking at the same time and finally said, "Now, what's *really* bothering you?"

So I told her about Sam Davidian. I told her he was attractive, and might be a murderer. I explained very carefully about his being replaced as director of the unit, and how only one other person had the motive to kill Dr. Grant, so far as I knew now.

"How do you know he gave a rip about being replaced?"

"Because people don't like to be rejected. Especially men."

"How do you know that applies to this Sam guy?"

"I'm surmising. How *else* would I know?"

"Honestly, Cat! For an intelligent person, sometimes you act so dumb. Plus stubborn. And opinionated."

"Well, thanks for boosting my confidence."

"I don't want to boost your confidence. Maybe I ought to boost your humility."

"Get to the point."

"Sure thing, kid. My point is: *Why don't you just ask him?*"

"*Ask* him! Hermione, all he's gonna do is give me some lame answer."

"How do you know what he's gonna say? Let me put this another way. He's kind to patients, you said."

"Yes."

"And does his work well, doesn't he?"

"Yes."

"In every other way he seems to be an honest person, doesn't he?"

"Yes."

"Well then, what gives you the right to decide that he couldn't possibly have a good reason why he didn't mind being replaced?"

"Because I can't think of a good reason."

"See? We need some humility training."

"Oh, all right!"

"By asking him, you aren't going to know any *less*."

◇ 12 ◇

I was out of Hermione's by one, feeling much better able to cope. There's something about her painfully honest attack on my jugular that leaves me feeling better.

I'd hit the day running this morning, and had made an appointment to see Dr. Jacob Coyne at his home between one and one-thirty. If I found a parking place, I'd be early. If not, I'd be late. This is Chicago for you.

Jacob Coyne lived in a regentrifying part of Old Town. This is an area less than two miles north of the Loop that has had many characters over the decades. The buildings are still mostly narrow-fronted brick structures three stories tall, counting the basements, with steeply peaked roofs and some gingerbreading. Originally they were fine family homes. The ones that found themselves on main streets as the city grew became rooming houses, then stores—grocery stores in the ground floor with tailors or seamstresses on the floors above. Then most recently they went into a decline, along with the area, and became currency exchanges and pawn shops and used clothing dealers. Now they were pricey again, and the whole area had become trendy.

I suspected Jacob Coyne of renting by the status of the address. But I had to admit it was convenient to U-Hosp by bus. There were no parking places, but I got into a nearby garage and was at his place by one-fifteen.

"Come in." He lived on the first floor, which was at least eight feet above the sidewalk level. A flight of ten or twelve steps led to the door. Another flight of six steps or so led down to the basement apartment. I'm told that in the old days, houses were built with the first floor several feet up because Chicago was founded on a swamp (no jokes about current politics, please) and so the downstairs was considered only good for cellars. Now they are called "garden apartments." The fact that the first floor is built so far above ground level means the windows are difficult for burglars to break into and therefore the windows aren't barred. Once inside, though, I noticed they had some heavy brass window locks.

"I'm not sure what you want from me," Coyne was saying.

"Like I told you, I'm interested in why people go into emergency room work. My intention in the article is to profile maybe eight people who do this work. Show how different they are from each other. But still they come together as a team to save lives." I left out the part about whether trauma units are worth the cost. I didn't want the staff to be bending over backwards to try to prove it to me.

"Well, that sounds very—" He couldn't think exactly what. I waited. Pauses can be revealing. "Very technical. Are you sure readers will care about it?"

"The story of my life. All I can do is hope."

He led me to a white sofa with a loosely fitting cover. A friend had told me recently that loose slipcovers were in these days. To me it looked like somebody had thrown a sheet over it. Two of the walls were old brick. This, too, was considered a selling point. It's another thing that has gone through changes of fashion—covering up the structural elements, uncovering them two decades later, covering up another two decades on. This place would rent for more money because of the exposed brick.

"I have two roommates," Jacob said. "That's Jim's room." He pointed at a doorway, "And that's Ollie's. Mine's back there."

"Well, it's a good way to cut costs," I said.

He almost groaned. "I have so much student loan money to pay back. You wouldn't believe!"

"I'd believe."

This place would rent for about ten times what Marveline's apartment would cost. So even with the roommates, he'd be paying at least three times what she did. Of course, she was just a nursing student, and he was a fully qualified graduate M.D. with a specialty. Still, I bet he owed more money than she had ever seen in her life. A hundred thousand dollars in debt was not unheard of in cases like Coyne's.

Jacob Coyne wasn't a particularly warm and cuddly guy. He was big, tall, and angular, not graceful. His bones were large, with big joints, as if he had been assembled from parts left over from a dinosaur skeleton.

His personality was not especially likable either. Repeatedly, I had seen him focus on patients as cases rather than people. He tended to leave the soothing and encouraging of a patient to the nurses.

But who was I to make these judgments anyway? The world was full of people who were not people-persons, and nobody objected. If you were an accountant, or bricklayer or landscape painter, who cared if you weren't congenial? There was really no good reason to believe, arrogantly, that Jacob Coyne was lacking in some way just because he hadn't majored in bedside manner. His job was to repair damaged people, and he did it well.

"So tell me," I said, "why emergency medicine? Why not dermatology or cardiology?"

"I ask myself that sometimes. Trauma's so hectic. It can be totally nonstop when you're on the floor."

"Yes?"

"But I guess that's why. To avoid boredom. I did all those other rotations. You know how they put a medical student through obstetrics, surgery, medicine, psychiatric, and all? Boring. Boooooring. And you have to remember that in the hospital it's more interesting than it's going to be in practice, because you have all these different cases on the floor, plus they're sicker than the ones who waltz into an office. In practice it's just case after case, one at a time."

"But even then, surely you have to deal with problems and crises."

"Not like in the emergency department. There it's always something new. You never know what will come through that door. You can be sitting there in a quiet moment eating your candy bar, and two minutes later you have a case that may demand every single skill you have or the patient will die."

"Yes, I can see how that would be challenging."

"And in the trauma center, they're not *malingering*. They're really in need of your help. Can you imagine being a specialist in internal medicine and seeing patient after patient whose troubles are nothing more than nerves and overeating and not having enough to do?"

"Well, okay. Yes, I have to agree with you."

"And the other reason I like it is, when you're off you're off."

"What do you mean?"

"When I leave my shift—say it's three P.M. to eleven P.M.—the eleven to seven staff takes over. I don't have to think about work after I walk out the door. The cases continue to be watched and treated, and by the time I get back the next afternoon, a whole new set of cases is coming in. I don't take patients home with me in my head, like you would if you had long-term patients. Like in private practice."

"Yes, that makes sense." It agreed with my assessment of him, too.

The apartment door was opened by someone with a key. A squarely built young man came in. Springy red-brown hair, a manner of walking on the balls of his feet like a boxer. Maybe just short of thirty years old. He carried a fistful of mail.

"Oh, sorry. Didn't know you had a guest. Hi!" he said in a rush.

"Ollie, this is Ms. Marsala—" Coyne said.

"Happy to meet you! I gotta get to bed. Been up thirty-six hours. Jake, you gotta take care of this. It was your turn. It can't wait forever. They'll turn off the gas. G'night all."

Coyne was left with the envelope in his hand. It was a bill, judging from its transparent window.

Slightly embarrassed, either about the bill or Ollie's abrupt manner, Coyne said, "He's a second-year resident in obstetrics. He gets a little freaky after a triple shift."

"Can't say I blame him."

The bill disappeared into Coyne's jacket pocket. I now noticed that his jacket looked like good-quality wool. And for that matter, his shirt said hundred percent cotton to me. I don't have the time or the money to keep up with fashion trends, but there's a crisp crinkliness to good cotton that you can't miss.

● ● ●

I'd spent half an hour with Jacob Coyne, and still found his character hard to pin down. If I wasn't mistaken, he was very cautious, and I suspected he was keeping something from me. However, pushing him wasn't likely to help, and besides, I had an appointment with Fern Butler at two.

The little creature in the back of my brain whose voice sometimes sounds a lot like my mother's said, "Are you putting off talking with Sam?"

My own voice said, "Can't rush sensitive discussions. Have to be centered, secure in yourself—"

Little Creature changed voices to someone less proper than my mother and said, "Bull."

But voices or not, interviewing was my work. By Saturday I needed a first draft of my story about people who work in trauma centers. The final copy had to be in on Wednesday. In my work, writer's block is what gets you fired. It's important to leave a dead day in the schedule somewhere for "back-burnering" a project, so you can reassess and revise it with a fresher eye. Two days would be even better. There was no time to lose.

Oak Park is a suburb nestled into the west side of Chicago, twenty minutes west of the Loop. It's a straight shot out the Eisenhower Expressway, and today there was no snow, sleet storm, multicar pileup, or wooden crossties burning on the Congress Street El—a situation that had happened once and tied up the Eisenhower for hours—so I got to Fern Butler's house on time, too. This was a good omen. On time twice in one day!

Oak Park, a flat urban/suburb is rectangular and laid out on a grid, so there's no trouble finding your way around. I got off the Eisenhower at Harlem, just west of Oak Park, and doubled back three blocks to the house. Fern had said, "It's a small brick and wood house."

She had said nothing to prepare me for that house, nor could anything she said ahead of time really prepare me.

"Gawd!"

It was a tiny bandbox. Even though this was the middle of a July heat wave and water was rationed, the lawn was bright green. The kind of green you get if you fertilize and water so frequently that you have to mow every three days. The front walk was short but spotless. There wasn't a leaf on it, nor even the scuff from the heel of a shoe. It ended at a flight of three steps up to the front porch. The steps and the porch were covered in indoor-outdoor carpeting that was as bright a green as the lawn.

On either side of the front steps, absolutely symmetrically spaced, were four bushes, eight altogether, clipped into perfectly conical shapes. In front of them, as a kind of border, were white-painted posts through which was strung a chain with big links. The chain was also painted white. On either side of the front door, up on the porch, were white square plastic planter boxes filled with pink plastic geraniums. The door was painted bright white with a sparkling golden brass doorknob. There were two small windows on either side of the door, and in each were perfectly symmetrical swags of lace curtains. The mailbox, next to the door, was a white wicker basket. I was sure that whoever had made the design decisions fervently wished there could be two mailboxes for symmetry, but knew that would be going just a bit too far.

The brick walls were painted brick red. I wondered for a few seconds why anybody would paint brick the same color it already was. It might have previously been painted some shade they didn't like, of course. Then I thought of the more likely answer. Bricks were too uneven in color for the person who lived here. The paint evened them up.

Fern had seen me coming and opened the door.

"Didn't describe it to you," she said softly. "Figured you might as well get the full effect." She stepped back and said more loudly, "Come in and meet my mother."

The inside was much like the outside. Gold and green wall-to-wall carpet covered the floors. Every table was glass-topped. China dogs, cats, shepherds, and ballerinas appeared to float in space, a few feet off the floor. The wallpaper was flowered, the rug was flowered, and all the patterns, combined with the lace curtains that let sun in as spots and dots, camouflaged the real shape of the room. I was disoriented and for several seconds didn't see Fern's mother.

My eye finally caught motion in a wing chair on the other side of the glass coffee table. A tiny woman, wearing a floral print dress, sat in the floral print chair, her face floating above the invisible body like the smile of the Cheshire cat. In fact, she looked quite a bit like a satisfied Siamese.

"Good afternoon, Mrs. Butler," I said in a way my mother would have approved.

"I am *not* Mrs. Butler."

"Oh, I'm sorry."

"I took back my own name when I got rid of Mr. Butler."

"I see." I was sure she meant legally, not murder.

"I am Mrs. Smerdlov."

"Oh. Thank you. I'm Catherine Marsala."

She didn't appear disposed to shake my hand, which I had held out only slightly. "Sit down," she said. "What do you want?"

Fern gasped, "Mother!"

"I'm a reporter. I'm doing a—a kind of essay about trauma centers, and I wanted to interview Fern."

"For what?"

"For what she thinks about the trauma center and how she likes working there, and so on."

"Why?"

"People are interested in places like that. They know that if they were in a serious auto accident, for instance, they'd probably be taken to one. But they don't know how they work. Trauma units are mysterious places. People are curious."

"People are altogether too curious. Curiosity killed the cat, I used to tell Fern when she was little."

There wasn't much to say to that. It may have been a mistake to ask Fern if I could interview her at home. Her mother wasn't going to discreetly slip away and let us talk.

I said, "Well, when you work as a reporter, you sort of have to have a degree of curiosity. If you—"

"Are you married?"

"No, ma'am."

"Well, don't."

"Ma'am?"

"Men aren't worth it. They take advantage of you, you know. Of your good nature. Then when you need them most, they leave."

"They may not all be equally inconsiderate—"

"Don't you be fooled! One or two came after Fern, when she was younger, but they were sleazy. They could see from the house that we had money. You have to look below the surface. You can't just go around taking people at their word."

Fern said, "Mother—"

"I'm talking, Fern. People will tell you anything they think you want to hear."

"That's very true, Mrs. Smerdlov."

"See? You understand. Did you hear that, Fern? This

young lady gets around. She interviews people. She hears them trying to deceive her."

"Mother, I see quite a few people myself. At work."

"I'm talking, Fern. You pay some attention to this young lady here. She'll cure you of some of your trusting notions."

"Mother, would you like some tea?"

"Are you serious? Not at this hour. I just had lunch."

Fern was obliquely cuing her mother to offer me some tea, but her mother wasn't taking the bait. And actually, I was eager to get out of here. This elderly woman was making me feel itchy from head to toe.

It was interesting that the authoritative charge nurse, Fern, was less than authoritative in her mother's presence. I guess that's true of most of us. But I didn't much like to watch it.

I stayed thirty minutes. A root canal would have been equally pleasant. As the clock moved toward two-thirty, Fern said she had to leave for work, like I did, of course. When she got up to go, I asked her if I could give her a ride, and she accepted.

As we walked toward my old Bronco, I said, "How do you usually get to work?"

"The Congress El line."

"So you get off work at eleven P.M. and out here about midnight and have to walk home from the El stop?"

"When I'm on this shift, yes. It's only five blocks."

"It takes guts to be on night shift."

"I carry Mace." She shrugged. My guess was, at any hour it was a delight for her to get out of that house.

As we pulled away from the house, Fern started laughing.

"What's so funny?"

"You should see your face."

"Why? What's wrong with my face?"

"Your thoughts are written all over it."

"Are you kidding? I have a professional, calm, poker face."

"Well, actually, that's the problem. You're trying so hard to be expressionless."

"Sorry."

"Look, Cat. I know my mother is bitchy."

"Hey, I didn't say anything."

"She may be a bitch, but she's my bitch."

At two forty-five, the afternoon westbound rush is just barely beginning on the Eisenhower. We zipped eastbound next to the El. I said, "Fern, why didn't anybody tell me that Sam Davidian had been the director before Dr. Grant?" I had put off asking anybody this. I was afraid if I mentioned it, they would start to think he could be guilty and they might tell Hightower. But Fern seemed kind of accessible.

She said, "You didn't know?"

"Not at first."

"Oh. I suppose nobody mentioned it because everybody thought everybody else knew about it."

As simple as that.

To change the subject, I said, "There are more women M.D.'s than I expected on the unit's staff—Zoe and Sonali—"

"Half the new med school class is women," Fern said.

"Well, that's wonderful."

"It may be wonderful, but it's making it hard to get great nursing students."

"Why?"

"In the old days, the girls who wanted to be doctors were discouraged from doing it. And there were a lot of them. So they became nurses instead."

"But that was very sad!"

"It may have been *sad*, but it sure got us some great nurses!"

"Well, yes, and I suppose it's part of your job to make sure the nurses are good."

"In the old days, girls needed a lot of support at home and at school to have any chance of being M.D.'s."

"Did you ever want to be a doctor?"

"Sort of. My mother wasn't in favor of it."

Probably med school would have taken Fern away from home too much. "My mother has been a bit of a problem, too," I said, understating the case quite a bit. "She thinks the work I do is extremely unladylike and extremely dangerous."

"Maybe it's the generation they're part of. If they'd been born thirty years later, they might have been doing the jobs we're doing."

"I don't know. My mother's personality is a lot different from mine."

"My mother and I are more alike than I want to admit, sometimes. But we apply it very differently."

"I don't see you as being very similar to your mother. Except—do you think maybe you carried over some of your mother's precision into nursing?"

She smiled. "I don't use nearly as much precision at home as I do at work. You should see my underwear drawer. Gives new meaning to the word *chaos*. But, yes, you may be right. You can't approximate dosages of medications. And I would say I'm quite strict with the student nurses."

"Speaking of student nurses, how is Marveline doing?"

"Well, Marveline is not one of our brightest stars."

"She's empathetic with patients."

"And loves the children."

"You're very good yourself with the children who come in. Have you ever wanted a child?"

"I'm not married."

"There are a lot of single parents."

"I know. I also work long hours. It just wouldn't be fair to the child."

"That reminds me, you remember DeeDee? The burned baby who came in the first night I was there?"

In a deep, grim voice, Fern said, "Vividly."

"Tell me—you and Dr. Grant exchanged a glance about her while Michelson was treating her."

Fern said cautiously, "Yes. That poor little thing."

"Fern, that child looked *boiled*."

She hesitated. "I'm not really supposed to talk about patients."

"Look, I know that you and she thought it was child abuse. Why?"

"Oh, well. I suppose if you already know. We called DCFS that night. You have to when you suspect child abuse."

"But what made you suspect it?"

"The burns were awfully severe, for bath water. Even hot bath water."

"And?"

"Did you notice there were no burns under her arms or in her armpits, or the sides of her chest? If she fell in hot water, she'd scramble to get out, and reach for the edge of the tub with her arms out. There would have been burns under her arms. The pattern of these burns is like—like she was protecting herself by holding her arms over her sides and chest. Somebody poured boiling water on that child."

We arrived at the U-Hosp trauma center with five minutes to spare. As we walked in, I saw Sam, standing and staring at me with his fists on his hips.

· 13 ·

He was blocking my way, not that I couldn't have walked around him, but it would have been exceedingly rude. Fern took one look at him, one look at me, and detoured rapidly around us both.

Sam continued to stare at me. I can play who-flinches-first as well as the next person, so I waited.

He said, "All right, Cat. What's wrong?"

"Well, I've been meaning to talk with you—"

"We were getting along so well, and then suddenly whammo! You're as cold as if I were an ax murderer."

"I had things to think about."

"You left here last night without saying a word. And this morning all I could get at your house was your machine."

"That's because I wasn't there."

"No doubt."

"I was out by nine-thirty."

"You have every right to dislike me if you want, but I think at least I deserve an explanation. Why the sudden change?"

The door beeped behind us, but we just stepped to one side.

I said, "Why didn't you tell me that Dr. Grant had replaced you as director?"

A gurney came in, pushed by two EMTs. The nurse from

the previous shift, the one we were just now replacing, met the cart. Slaby came, too. I don't know whether it was a man or a woman on the gurney, although it was small enough to probably be a woman. There was an endotracheal tube in the throat. But I was not quite sure it was the throat, because most of the face was gone. The patient was making horrible gurgling noises.

The EMT on the right, who stepped back to allow Slaby and the other nurse to take over, said laconically to them, "Shotgun."

Sam said to me, "Is *that* what this is all about?"

Slaby stepped between us and said to Sam, "You gotta take this case. I can't give it to one of the residents."

Sam followed the gurney.

I was left standing.

Sam's patient had facial trauma but apparently had not lost much blood. The problem was to keep an airway open while saving her eye, and stopping the slow ooze of blood. Then, unexpectedly, Slaby said, "The BP is climbing."

"Do we have any decent history?" Sam asked.

"No."

"Fern!"

She answered from the desk. "Yes?"

"Try to find somebody at home at the patient's address and get her medical history."

"Will do."

To Slaby he said, "Let's go for nitro paste."

Slaby left the operating room and returned with a little tube of stuff. She extruded a short line of it on the patient's shoulder and spread it around.

"What's that?" I asked her.

"Nitroglycerin paste. It works like the nitroglycerin tablets people put under their tongues."

"And the skin absorbs it? Oh, sure. Like those airsickness patches. Or nicotine patches."

"Yes. We measure by the inch. It's quick acting for emergencies like this."

"Why not just put some nitroglycerin in the IV?"

"We do sometimes. But nitroglycerin is absorbed by PVC tubing. You can lose thirty percent of it. You need special infusion equipment to do it right. This way we know what we're doing."

Sam totally ignored us, dealing with a patient in real crisis. The woman was gurgling. Sam decided to do a tracheotomy, and for some reason I just didn't feel like watching her throat slit open. It had to be done, but I didn't have to be there.

Five minutes later some cops brought in a man they'd found lying in the street. They weren't sure whether he'd been hit by a car or just fell down and stayed down. Fern talked with him first and then brought Billy Michelson to see him.

The man alternated between some odd form of sleep and sudden nonstop talking.

"Do you remember walking into the street?" Michelson said.

"LaSalle, yah, I go there a lot. Goes all the way down to the lawyers' offices, and all those big expensive lawyers offices, you know, LaSalle. Curbs and all. Lightposts. You got your sidewalk and then you got your curbs."

"Do you remember falling in the street?"

"Some places you can get food, too. Wrapper. You gotta watch out for those wrappers, though, 'cause they blow around like you wouldn't believe. Walk down a street at night and one of those wrappers'll come blowing right at you, catch you by the leg. They slither, like. You ever heard wrappers blowin' along the street at night? Nothin' sneakier, slither, slither. Wanta trip you up, is what. Slither."

The man was sitting up on a table while Michelson listened to his chest. I wondered how he could hear anything with the man talking a mile a minute. Fern, meanwhile, was taking his temperature with a gadget I'd seen them use on other patients. It takes temperatures in the ear. Since he couldn't stop talking, this was a good thing. Then Fern put on gloves to draw blood.

Michelson said, "We just need a blood sample, Mr.—"

But the man didn't say who he was. Michelson asked him to lie down, but he kept talking as if he didn't hear, and Michelson finally just took hold of his shoulders and eased him back. Then Michelson started pushing on the abdomen.

"Any pain here?" he said.

The man didn't answer. He had fallen asleep.

Michelson and Fern left Marveline watching the patient and stepped away.

"All the signs," Fern said. "Fever—"

"Germ smell," Michelson said.

I asked, "What are you talking about?"

"Germ smell. The man smells like he has pneumonia."

"But from the way he acts, he must be on some kind of drugs."

"No doubt. But he's got pneumonia, too." He turned to Fern. "Get me some chest films. But I bet they'll confirm."

Sam was in surgery a long time with the shotgun victim. I heard Slaby say Sam had saved her life but not her face. The patient would go from here to a bed in the hospital and, I supposed, would soon be seen by a plastic surgeon.

While this was going on, we had a woman from a traffic accident who claimed whiplash. She had screamed so much, she had convinced the EMTs to bring her here, instead of an emergency room. One of them told Fern, "Bet the X-rays don't show much."

Fern said, "Gotta take it seriously, now she's here."

They went through the usual routine, of course. Dr. Bachaan asked the woman, "Do you have any ongoing medical conditions?"

The woman was suspicious and combative. "Like what?"

"Well, do you have any health problems? We need to know that kind of thing if we're going to treat you. Diabetes? Hypertension?"

"What's hypertension?"

"High blood pressure."

"I have fireballs in the uterus."

Sonali blinked. Sonali had a little trouble with Americanisms anyway, and probably thought this was a peculiar idiom. Fowler, the student nurse, who was a native Chicagoan, said to Sonali, "She means fibroids."

Right about then, Sam came striding back from washing up. There was blood on his scrub pants and shoes.

"Okay," he said to me. "Coffee time."

We went to the lounge. Coyne was unwrapping a chocolate bar. He threw the wrapper in the wastebasket and wandered out. Sam poured coffee from the pot, plunked the cups on the table and said, "Sit."

We sat.

He said, "Tell me exactly why you have a problem with this."

"Why I have a problem? Why wouldn't I have a problem?

You hide the fact that you were director before Dr. Grant. She was put in to replace you."

"And?"

"And how am I supposed to know how much you resent that? Remember, you and I were talking and we were saying Marveline was the only one with a motive to kill Grant, and you have a motive that's probably bigger than hers was. She was only being cautioned by Grant, after all. And here I am, hiding your motive from the police!"

"That's a motive?"

"Of course! Your pride must have been hurt."

Sam put both hands over his face and groaned. When he took them away, he was half smiling. "What a stupid thing!" he said.

"Don't evade."

"I wouldn't think of it." He smiled more broadly. "So you hid this from the police?"

"Yeah. Well, yeah. At least temporarily."

"For my sake? Why?"

"Uh—"

"Cat, you may not realize it, but you're bigoted."

While I goggled at him in rising indignation, he added, "I mean that in the nicest possible way."

"Oh, thanks. You'd better be able to explain that."

"Look, you are assuming that I *wanted* to supervise the unit. That I wanted to be director. My guess is that a big part of why you think that is that I'm a man. Your assumption is that all men want to boss people around."

"Well, most men—"

"Don't even say it. My point is, you never asked *me* what my goals were, or what I liked doing. And the fact is, I don't like bossing people around."

"You could have said so."

"I probably implied it. You weren't listening or you weren't believing. As a matter of fact, I've known all along that Hannah Grant felt the same way as you do. She *believed* I resented her. I actually told her I didn't, but she thought I was just being polite. When people are prejudiced, they're blind. You, too."

"You didn't make it clear."

"I guess not. Did I have to?"

"Oh, hell."

"Anyhow, let me make it clear now. I don't want to run the unit. I'm a doctor, not an administrator. Besides not wanting to do it, I'm not very good at it."

"Oh, come on. You're probably very good—"

"You're making the same mistake again. You think I *could* be good at it and maybe even that I *should* be good at it because I'm a man and men should give orders. That's sexist. Plus it's not true. What I like is saving lives."

"That's certainly admirable."

"Sure, sure. But what I'm trying to say is that I don't do it because it's admirable or so that people will praise me. I really like it. And I'm good at it. I don't have to be good at everything in the world. I'm crummy at basketball but not bad at baseball. I can't play a musical instrument. I'm very good at woodworking. And I'm very good at seeing a patient come in, totally chopped up, and getting quickly to the most serious thing that's wrong with him. It's almost an instinct. Or an art. I'm really, really good at that."

"Ahhh." Sometimes there's not much you can say. He was right. I hated to admit it, but he was. Come to think of it, I should admit it. "Okay. You're right. And I'm sorry."

He smiled. "You were a little strangle-voiced when you said that. But thanks."

"But why did you hide it from me? That Grant had replaced you?"

"I never even thought of it. Never crossed my mind one way or the other. I thought everybody knew."

"Oh."

"You thought I'd been kicked out of the job, right?"

"Well, I was led to believe that."

"Did whoever told you about this mention that I had asked to get out of the job?"

"No. They said you'd been replaced."

"I asked to be replaced."

"Oh."

"I had only agreed to do it temporarily, when the previous director moved to Pittsburgh. Temporarily had stretched out to eighteen months. I was spending more time on paperwork than in surgery. And I was also being a policeman."

"Like what?"

"Oh, drug thefts quite some time ago. Then a year or so ago we had some complaints from patients or relatives that items were missing from their pockets. Or wallets. I started watching. I got an old wallet from home and left it peeping out of a patient's raincoat pocket. Turned out the janitor was taking them."

"Not Lester Smalley!"

"No, no. Lester is a sweetheart. Another guy."

"And you got rid of him."

"Sure."

"Good."

"Good. Right. He was sixty-two years old. His wife has Alzheimer's. One of his daughters is retarded and lives with him. He has a son, but the kid doesn't help the family financially. Sure, I fired him. I got rid of him."

"But you can't let somebody steal from the patients!"

"Of course you can't. That's why I fired him."

"So you agree somebody had to fire him."

"Yes! But I hated it. I didn't enjoy finding out it was him, and I don't have to do that particular job."

"But if somebody has to do it—"

"Look, I don't want to be a politician either. And I don't have to. I don't want to be a housepainter. Or even a fire-fighter, even though somebody has to do it. I want to be a trauma surgeon, and by God, that's what I am."

He was called to a case, leaving me to contemplate this question: Was I stupid or just arrogant?

The tempo in the rotunda had quickened again, as it did every couple of hours in some random, mysterious way. As it had done when Dr. Grant was killed.

That thought made me feel very uneasy, although there was no special reason to be.

The rotunda was perfectly normal, in a bloody, chaos-on-the-surface way. Dr. Michelson and Slaby, the nurse, worked on a patient in treatment bay three, Davidian and Fowler in five, Coyne and Marveline and a nurse I didn't know in six, Peters and Fern and a med student in the OR. Sonali Bachaan was just seeing somebody off to X-ray.

Out of sheer, foolish nerves, I walked down to the lounge and looked in. It was silly. What did I think I'd find, a dead body? And I felt even sillier when I saw that the lounge was peaceful. One of the cooling motors in one of the food ma-chines kicked in and hummed, and one of the fluorescent lights flickered like distant lightning, but nothing else moved and nothing was out of place.

I went back to the rotunda.

Sam Davidian was sending his patient out, talking to the nurse in the intensive care unit on the phone. Peters came out while he was doing it and said, "Is that the ICU?"

He nodded.

"Tell her to hold. I've got one going up, too."

Lester Smalley came past, mopping, mopping, mopping.

All normal.

About seven, it cleared out again.

I realized how much I had grown to understand the rhythms of the place. It was obvious why whoever had killed Dr. Grant had chosen a moment when the unit was very busy. Traffic up and down the corridor was lighter then. And except for the students, whom everybody kept watch on, staff didn't notice where other staff was. Also, when it was busy, staff members didn't hang around in the lounge the way they did in slow periods. They'd go get coffee, sure, but they brought it back in here.

Sam wasn't the killer, thank God. He'd convinced me. And it was not Marveline either, I was quite sure.

In the midst of the quiet period, Hightower walked in. He was carrying a paper bag. Seeing the rotunda empty of patients, he strode right up to the desk.

"Miss Kruse, we'd like just another short chat."

Marveline stared at him. The whole staff crowded around.

"We can do it here, if you want. Out in the police room, maybe?"

Marveline nodded. Maybe he was trying to break her down slowly. I said, "What about her lawyer?"

Hightower cast up his eyes. "We'll let her call and ask him, if she wants." Now I was sure he was just trying to wear her down. Anyway, it was six P.M. Would she be able to get hold of the man?

"By the way," Hightower said, "we've identified most of

the stuff we took from the lounge for testing. Except this."
He pulled the clipboard out of his paper bag. "Who owns this
clipboard?"

Zoe Peters said, "Oh, hell! You had it all along."

"Yes. Obviously." Hightower studied her suspiciously.

"That's outrageous! I've been accusing Fowler of stealing
it!"

"It was found in the lounge when Dr. Grant was killed."

"Well, I didn't kill her! I would think you people would at
least have the ordinary decency to *tell* us when you take
something!"

Poor Marveline. She was caught up in a crime she didn't understand any better than I did. Only she was bearing the
brunt of the pain. I went out through the double doors into
the anteroom. Through the glass window of the police cubi-
cle I could see her shaking her head, and Hightower talking
to her.

I went back to the rotunda. Marveline was an adult. She
knew she should ask for her lawyer. Maybe she was talking or
maybe she was waiting for the lawyer. What more could I do?

But if the killer wasn't Marveline, and it certainly wasn't
Dr. Sam Davidian, then who? Of all the people in here on
Monday, who faced an immediate, distinct threat from Dr.
Grant? None of the doctors seemed to. And none of the nurses. None of the baby docs—residents or med students—although I thought Dr. Grant may have considered Zoe Peters
less than a stellar performer. Other than Marveline, none of
the student nurses was under threat from Dr. Grant. And
none of the patients, of course.

None of the patients?

What was I saying?

Tanya Williams, DeeDee's mother, was at serious risk from Dr. Grant.

Child abuse was a felony. Hannah Grant was preparing to call DCFS. Fern had told me they always notified DCFS immediately.

But would Tanya Williams know that Dr. Grant was suspicious of her? Grant hadn't stated her suspicion in words. She'd just exchanged a glance with Fern, which I intercepted.

Would Tanya Williams have caught that glance?

I thought of Tanya Williams, overweight, and not assertive overweight like Hermione, but waxen fat. Tanya Williams, responding to questions as if she were not all there mentally. But my great-aunt used to quote: "The wicked flee where no man pursueth." How much more so is it true that the wicked are always on the lookout for being caught. That day, she must have known she had to take DeeDee to the hospital. If the child died at home, and she hadn't tried to get medical help, she'd be in big trouble. And she may have regretted burning the child after she did it, in the way a lot of child abusers do. But the hospital would have represented danger to her. She must have been very much on the alert for the slightest glance of suspicion.

She must have seen it in Dr. Grant's face.

Would Tanya be foolish enough to think if she got rid of Dr. Grant nobody else would notice?

Possibly. She might have thought that once you got past the admitting doctor, the hospital would just treat the child. It wasn't smart thinking, but Tanya Williams wasn't smart either.

Speaking of smart, the way Dr. Grant was killed was very smart. It was true that the sponges and tongue depressors were on every side cabinet near every examination table. So

Tanya Williams certainly could get hold of the weapon of death. But would she have the smarts to realize that a sponge pushed down the throat would stick and be hard to dislodge? More than that, the fact that the murder had actually worked, that it had been hard to solve, was a result of the fact that when the unit was busy, the lounge was rarely in use. Could she possibly guess that?

Certainly not. Not even if she were a lot smarter than she seemed. You had to work here to know it. Not even Hightower really understood.

But she may have been desperate. Not thinking, just acting instinctively to protect herself, doing the first thing that crossed her mind. Grabbing the first weapon she saw. Tanya Williams may have taken a big risk and simply lucked out. One thing I've learned about life. It's just fine to think and plan ahead and try to be smart, but sheer damn dumb luck, if it's on your side, works every time.

· 14 ·

When did Tanya, DeeDee, and the med student leave the trauma center? DeeDee had been released to the burn unit. But at what time? Before or after Dr. Grant had been killed? Hannah Grant had not been seen after five past four, and I found her body at four twenty-nine. Was Tanya Williams still in the trauma unit then?

I looked for somebody to ask. Sonali Bachaan was the first person I saw as I crossed the rotunda. She was walking toward the corridor. I grabbed her sleeve.

"Do you remember when DeeDee Williams went up to the burn unit?"

"Who?"

"DeeDee Williams. Monday afternoon. The child who was supposedly burned in the bath."

"I don't remember her."

No, I guess she wouldn't. She hadn't treated her. Dr. Michelson had treated her. He was leaning over the central desk, trying to find the specific form he needed in a long vertical file of twenty or more different formsets. He pulled out one headed "Nuclear Medicine." I touched his shoulder.

He said, "Hi. Hi, Cat."

"Hi. Do you remember what time DeeDee Williams and her mother left the unit Monday afternoon?"

"Why do you—"

"I'm trying to help Marveline. DeeDee was the child who was—"

"Who was burned in the bath. According to her mother. I remember that. I think they went to the burn unit with an orderly and Brunniger about four-fifteen or four-thirty."

"Okay. Thanks." Right on the borderline. It didn't leave her in or out.

Fern was showing Fowler how to replace supplies in the cast room. I grabbed her and repeated the question.

"Uh—well, by four-thirty, I would say, Cat."

I was disappointed. "Isn't it possible to be more exact than that?"

"Of course it is."

"How?"

"Cat, we don't just fling patients around hither and yon. She'd have been signed out of here at a specific time."

"How can I find out?"

"We'll just look it up. You finish that," she said to Fowler.

We went to the bank of files behind the central desk. "This should have the whole week," she said. "It's probably on the computer, too. Going to computerize the whole thing soon, but I'm quicker at finding it this way."

I waited. The double doors beeped.

"Mm-mm. There it is." She showed me.

Four-twenty. That certainly didn't eliminate Tanya Williams.

The radio buzzer sounded. Fern left to check it, and within five minutes we were in a crunch again. It must be like cars on a highway. There'll be a bunch of half a dozen or a dozen, then a big gap before another bunch. The EMTs brought in, of all things, a toxic pharmacist. He owned a small, one-man pharmacy on the near West Side. For some reason known only to young boys, his son had the idea that setting off three illegal M-80s in his dad's shop would be a fun way to end the day. Apparently, the result was drugs and chemicals and fluids of unknown toxicity all over everywhere. The man's hair was two colors, brass and green. One hand was slightly burned. One eye watered continuously. But what everybody was most afraid of was the wild mix of drugs he must have inhaled, a toxic cocktail whose potentially lethal ingredients could not be specified.

Sam muttered to Fowler, "—treat for symptoms, and Fowler, get me about a hundred test tubes with stoppers."

She said, "Yes, Dr. Davidian."

"Slaby, notify poison control and get a specialist down here ASAP."

The man's son, by the way, had thrown the firecrackers from outside the storage room door and was unhurt.

While this was going on, we had a single-car accident arrive. Even I could diagnose the cause of the crash. I could smell the odor of alcohol on the patient without even getting near him.

Then we had three children from a school bus that overturned going around a corner and rolled down an embankment. The thirty or so less-injured children had been taken to various emergency rooms. We got the three serious injuries.

Again, the trauma unit was busy.

Sam had switched to one of the children, who needed immediate surgery. A nurse I didn't know was readying the OR. Fern gave her some instructions and left to look at the other patients. Zoe Peters, with Slaby the nurse, was caring for the pharmacist, who was currently being closely examined by an elderly man with a fuzzy gray beard and no hair on top of his head. The environmental contaminant specialist, no doubt. Brunniger looked on with great interest. Michelson was caring for one of the other children. Jacob Coyne sutured the arm of the third child. The drunk driver lay on a table under the watchful eye of the med student Perkins. A portable X-ray stood nearby, and the tech held the film cassettes ready to slip under the patient. The resident, Qualley, came from the back somewhere and bent over the man. Michelson went off with some specimens. Coyne went to make a phone call. The nurse, Natasha Horne, came back from taking a radio call at the desk, looked in on Sam, decided he didn't need additional help, and went back to the desk. Then Michelson said, "Horne, can you lend us a hand?"

Suddenly I was uneasy again.

I went out to see whether Hightower had finished questioning Marveline. He hadn't. It looked to me as if Marveline was crying.

I went back into the rotunda. Partly I was feeling like a fifth wheel, and that made me uncomfortable. I wondered why I felt so apprehensive. It was the fact that we were busy again, like we were when Hannah Grant was murdered.

I walked down the corridor and looked in the lounge. Nobody was there. Good.

I walked back down the corridor. I saw a hard candy on the floor, but that was all.

Back into the rotunda. I looked in the OR window; Sam was beginning the operation on the child.

I asked Fern, "Is Marveline back yet?"

She said, "I don't think so."

"I suppose she's still out there with Hightower."

Fern was assembling paperwork at the central desk.

Some cases take longer, some shorter, of course. After a time, the doctor gets his or her patient stabilized, and then makes calls to other parts of the hospital, talking with people there about taking the patient and what to do for him. Peters and the specialist in toxic stuff chatted with the medicine floor about admitting and keeping an eye on the pharmacist. One of the children went off to X-ray. The staff started taking breaks. Michelson went to get coffee. Coyne came back with one of his everlasting chocolate bars. This man was addicted. Sam was still with his patient, but I went and looked in the window and he was doing what they call "closing," sewing up the surgical field from the bottom up.

The tempo was winding down again. I was still uneasy.

Looking around, I had a sudden realization. Somebody was missing. I said, "Where's Sonali?"

Fern said, "Here someplace."

"Not in the rotunda."

"Bathroom, maybe. She won't be long. She knows she's not supposed to hang out in there."

I walked rapidly back down the corridor to the women's rest room. Sonali was not in there. Feeling even more uneasy, I tried the men's rest room. There is such a strong habitual resistance to entering the men's room that I knocked twice first, then opened the door an inch and called in, but nobody was there. Not even Sonali.

I glanced in the lounge again. I was certainly getting spooky and weird.

But she wasn't there or back in the rotunda either. Sam couldn't get away from his patient yet. Fern said, "Was she in the bathroom?"

"No."

She went to the central desk. "Now, that is odd. I often beep people who are probably in the unit, if I don't see them. I'm going to beep her."

She sat and swiveled her chair to the beeper equipment and punched in Sonali's number. We waited a minute or two, while Peters at the adjacent phone called for an orderly to take the pharmacist to medical.

Finally Fern said, "Beepers don't always work."

"No. Hers may not be charged."

"Still—" She pulled over the mike for the PA system. "Dr. Bachaan to the trauma unit," she said. She repeated it twice. We waited again. "That only pages our section of the hospital." After a few seconds' more thought, she called the central U-Hosp desk and asked for a universal page.

By now pretty much all the staff knew there was trouble. Michelson, Slaby, Peters, Brunniger, and finally Sam, as he got out of the OR, all crowded around the desk. They made all the same suggestions, of course: Look in the rest rooms, try the lounge, try the cafeteria. I said I'd already looked in the rest rooms and lounge, but Michelson went anyway. Sam sent Brunniger to the cafeteria. Fern said, "The universal page works in the cafeteria."

Sam said, "Sure, but maybe she's asleep with her head on the table."

This was so common an occurrence in a teaching hospital that everybody just nodded.

Sam walked over to look in our mini-lab, but she wasn't there either.

Brunniger came back and reported that she wasn't in the cafeteria. Fern checked the last couple of hours of patient records, just in case Sonali had gone someplace with a patient, but she hadn't, and we all knew she hadn't.

I said, "Listen, group. We've got the cops here. We have to tell them."

Hightower stood with his hands on his hips, his face registering the belief that we were all incompetent. "Did you look in the rest rooms?"

Fern said, "Of course."

Marveline had come back with Hightower and the other cop and now looked more confused than ever.

Hightower said, "Did you beep her?"

Fern said, "Of course!"

I said, "We've done all the usual things."

"Did you call her home?"

Fern said, "She doesn't go home in the middle of a shift. And she's certainly not supposed to go home without telling anybody."

"'Supposed to' doesn't mean people never do it."

Well, he was right, of course. Slaby called Sonali's dormitory number. Nobody answered.

"Okay," he said, taking charge. "Who saw her last and where?"

They talked about it, but nobody could remember seeing her in quite a while. Michelson said, "She was in the group right here when you came in to ask whose clipboard that was."

"Okay. Did anybody else see her after that?"

Brunniger said, "I saw her a minute later as the group broke up."

"Where was she going?"

"She went to the desk there. She used to sit and study when we had a lull."

"Anybody else?"

But nobody else remembered anything.

"Then I guess I may have seen her last," I said. "I'd gone to the—well, to be honest I walked out to see whether you were done with Marveline. Then I went to the rest room and lounge and came back in here and saw her and spoke with her. After that I talked with a couple of other people, and right then we got a new patient. And then three new patients, and it got really busy."

"During this busy period, did she work on any of the patients?"

The two specialists, Dr. Davidian and Dr. Coyne, exchanged glances and shook their heads. Coyne said, "Not with me." Fern Butler, the charge nurse, and Slaby, the other senior nurse, both said no. The residents, student nurses, and med students shrugged or shook their heads.

"Well," Hightower said, "she's been missing more than an hour. I'm afraid we've got a problem."

I almost felt sorry for Hightower. It wasn't his fault, but at the same time it didn't look good for him to have a missing person, one who had vanished right under his watchful eye.

Sam, as acting head of the unit, said to Hightower, "What do you intend to do?"

"Call some uniforms in from the district. Get a search going."

"Yeah, fine. But meanwhile she could be in danger or dying someplace."

"You have another suggestion?"

I said, "I have."

"What?"

"Try her beeper."

"Are you nuts?" Hightower said. "You already did that. She's out of the building or unconscious or dead."

"We haven't looked everyplace here yet. There are closets, spaces under cabinets, and bins of soiled linen and big bins of hazardous waste trash. And she's a tiny woman. She could be anywhere. But she should have her beeper clipped to her pocket, like everybody else around here. What I'm suggesting is you beep and keep beeping her beeper and we'll just walk around and see if we hear it."

A patient came in then, a closed-head injury, unconscious. Jacob Coyne and Fern Butler took it on, while Slaby started beeping Sonali and the rest of us all walked the unit.

I paced softly through the cast room, which had deep shelves filled with boxes of flexible wrist supports, plaster-impregnated gauze, metal elbow protectors, and so on. The boxes were stacked three deep on floor-to-ceiling shelves on two walls of the room. It would take half an hour to lift all the boxes down and look behind them.

I cocked my head, standing first in the front of the room, then in the back, listening for a beep. The room was bright in the fluorescent glare, but even with no shadows whatsoever, it seemed ominous. The equipment that hung on the wall— finger splints, pink plastic molds that looked like half a hand, L-shaped metal pieces pierced with holes—resembled instruments of torture.

Even the cabinets under the examination table would be big enough to hold a little person like Sonali, if she were folded up.

But there was no sound of her beeper.

As I was turning to go into the next room, the medication storeroom, I heard shouting.

I ran back toward the central desk. The shouting was coming from the corridor that led to the lounge.

Somebody screamed.

In the corridor, Sam and Hightower stood stock-still, the door of the linen storage room open in front of them. Marveline leaned against the farther wall, her hands over her eyes. She was weeping quietly now, but she must have been the person who screamed.

I pushed in front of Sam and looked.

Sonali Bachaan lay on her side on the floor of the closet, a couple of sheets spilled behind her. Her beeper went off once more, and then quieted. Her thin brown arms were folded in front of her chest, and both legs, visible under a white skirt, were bent at the knees. There were a couple of pieces of red candy on the floor near her.

She was so slender that folded up this way she reminded me of a fossil of one of those long- and light-boned prehistoric birds found pressed in rock. Bones as light as soda straws and long dead.

• 15 •

The next few hours were ghastly. Work had to go on in the trauma center, of course. Sam called in another doctor, a specialist in emergency medicine, from his backup list, and Michelson called a second-year resident who was supposed to be on vacation. Fern called in another nurse and a nursing student. These four additional people were not needed just to fill in for Sonali. They were needed to cover for staff members who were being questioned by cops, and for Marveline, who was so distraught that both Sam and Fern agreed she'd better go home for the rest of the evening.

I am not much given to tears, but it seemed like every time I watched one of the staff suture a cut or close an incision, I thought of Sonali and her tiny, embroidery-like stitches, put in so intently, and my eyes would grow teary.

With those tiny, scar-erasing stitches, she really should have become a plastic surgeon. I wondered what life events had made her want to do emergency work. I'd never know, now.

Sam had pronounced her dead, so there was no need to pull her body out and try to resuscitate her; therefore the crime scene was undisturbed. The evidence techs got their photos and their samples in pristine condition.

Hightower was satisfied with that. It was the only thing
that did satisfy him, however. He was extremely annoyed that
we did not all know where we had been every minute of
the last hour and a half. He was annoyed that Sonali had
vanished from the floor so long before we realized she was
gone.

She had been killed with a scalpel, thrust into the back of
her neck between the upper vertebra and the base of the
skull. Quick, efficient, practically painless, and as Hightower
said, "Something you'd have to know how to do."

Unfortunately, everybody here knew enough to know how
to do it. Even the student nurses.

I said to Hightower at one point, when he was questioning
me, "At least now you realize Marveline couldn't be guilty.
She was with you when Sonali was murdered."

"You could have more than one killer here."

"Oh, please! Do you really believe that?"

He must not have, because he changed the subject.

So much for the idea that Marveline killed Dr. Grant. And
then I realized that DeeDee's mother, Tanya Williams, was
also out of the running. Tanya Williams was either at home
now, in the burn unit with her daughter, or maybe in jail for
child abuse. She certainly hadn't been in the trauma center
today. And what would she have against poor little Sonali
Bachaan, anyway?

One thing for sure: I'd better interview Zoe Peters and
Billy Michelson.

The press howled outside the double doors. If the murder
of one doctor on the premises of a major teaching hospital was
big news, two murders was stop-press material. In Chicago the

major networks run weekday news starting early. Channel 7
starts at four, Channels 2 and 5 at four-thirty. At five-thirty, all
three break for the national news, and then come back on at
six. Channels 9 and 32 run news at nine, and Channels 2, 5,
and 7 again at ten. Sonali Bachaan's death came too late for the
four o'clock news, but they could make the six P.M.

They were rapacious. You'd have thought we had thrown
raw meat outside into a land of wolves.

Then there was the radio. Chicago has dozens of radio
stations, and all of them seemed to be reporting live from
U-Hosp.

And the print media! There are three major papers in
town, *The Chicago Tribune, Chicago Today,* and the *Chicago
Sun-Times,* several smaller dailies, hundreds of really small
presses, and dozens of magazines.

There were videocams, press cameras, audio recorders.
Trucks clogged the streets outside and a pair of traffic cops had
to be assigned at opposite ends of the block to make sure the
ambulances could still get through. One van with a roof-
mounted satellite gun refused to move out of the way and
was towed away by the cops, with the reporters running
alongside screaming. It was a good object lesson to the others.

Patients continued to arrive. At five, the ambulance
brought in a young man who was holding his head and
screaming. He had a longish shallow cut on his head, which
bled freely. He'd been found wandering blindly outside,
about a block away. He kept saying, "I'm dizzy!"

Sam washed down the cut, asked a few questions, flashed
a light in his eyes, and finally said, "What is your occupation,
Mr. Rooney?"

"Writer."

"What do you write?"

"Oh, a lot of different things."

"Look at me, Mr. Rooney."

"It's hard," he said weakly. "My eyes don't focus."

"Let me ask you this, Mr. Rooney. Would your eyes focus a lot better if I introduced you to a personal friend of the dead woman?"

"What do you mean?"

"Are you here for what you people call an 'exclusive,' Mr. Rooney?"

"Absolutely not!"

"Ah! That put a little vigor in your voice."

"You've got the wrong idea about this! I was hurt."

Sam turned to me. "Cat, in a minute, if this young man doesn't cooperate, I will ask you to go get one of the police officers."

I said, "Okay."

"Mr. Rooney, I will then ask that policeman to search you. If he should find—oh, let's speculate—some identification in your pocket or wallet to the effect that you are employed by television or the press, I will instruct him to arrest you."

"Arrest me for what?"

"Between us, we'll think of something. Medical insurance fraud? Entering the protected scene of a crime under false pretenses?"

"There isn't any such law."

"Tried it before, have you? Do you believe me when I say we'll think of something? Theft of services, maybe. That sounds promising. I think if you spend a couple of hours in the police station explaining why they should let you go, it will set your reporting back a bit, even if you finally get out."

"Oh, shit!"

Rooney hung his feet over the examining table and started to get off.

"Hold it," Sam said. "I'd better put a few stitches in that

cut. I'll say one thing for you, Rooney. You go to great lengths for a story."

When he finished with Rooney, Sam said to me, "Let's talk a minute."

"Sure," I said, wondering what was coming now.

We sat in treatment bay one, which was empty.

"Cat, you know I trust you," Sam said.

"What on earth—"

"But you're a reporter, too. I'm going to have to ask you to make a decision. Are you planning to do a story on the murders?"

"No!"

"Why not?"

That stumped me. I couldn't give him a flip answer, not for something as important as this.

"Sam, about four years ago I decided to go freelance. I knew it would be hand to mouth financially. I did it because I was frequently being forced by the paper to do one of two things: put a lot of time into stories I believed were trivial, or treat stories superficially that I thought were really important. In other words, when I went freelance, by making sacrifices I became my own boss. Sort of. Now and then I have to take on a stupid assignment in order to be able to eat. But I don't have to do anything I object to."

"Why would you object to doing a story on the murders?"

"That's hard to answer. It just doesn't feel right. Dr. Grant was nice to me and Sonali Bachaan was a good person. I don't want to *use* their deaths to—to feather my nest."

"Are you saying that there's nothing that could be written on their deaths that would be respectable?"

"No. Depending on why they were killed. I can't know that yet. I'm just saying that just supplying a sensational ac-

count of what happened here for current headlines isn't what
I would do."

"Let me push this a little further, then. I'm sorry, but I
have to."

"Go ahead."

"I'm acting administrator, like it or not. I can't let you stay
here and have inside access to people who are trying to get
their work done, if you plan to write about it."

He knew, of course, that I could write a story on the basis
of what I knew already. He was risking that I'd just walk out.
For a moment, I also was angry that he'd put our new and
fragile relationship at risk. I might walk out and never come
back. "Are you protecting the trauma unit, or the hospital, or
yourself, Sam?"

"All three, I'm afraid. But mainly the people. The staff.
They see you as a colleague now. They talk to you as a
friend."

I was angry. But he was right, from his point of view.
There were privacies to protect. "How about this? I'll do just
the article I came to do, no different. But if we find out who
killed Grant and Bachaan, and it's something I want to write
about, I'll clear it with you first."

"Done."

Now all I had to do was explain this to Hal Briskman. He
would be after me as soon as he heard about the second
death.

I said to Sam, "You know, not all of us reporters are like
Rooney."

He chuckled and said, "Prove it."

What got lost in all the furor was the fact that a young
woman was dead. And she had been a person of great
promise, I thought—sensitive, skillful, smart. The media

wanted to talk with people who knew her. They wanted tear-
ful memories. They wanted "human interest." Neither I nor
any of the staff had any desire to talk with them.

They thronged outside the doors. We could see them,
pressed up against the glass, looking at us as if we were on
display. I made a point of staying at the far end of the rotunda, out of their sight behind the intervening central desk.
Jacob Coyne picked up on this.

"You hiding from your peers in the media, Cat?"

"Well, some of them know me. If they see me, they'll think
you guys gave me special treatment."

"I suppose you're going to keep your exclusive on this story all to yourself."

"What?" His assumption that I'd surely do it was a lot
more insulting than Sam's simple question. "That isn't the
kind of story I came here to do."

"It's like a lotta dollars just fell in your lap, though. Isn't
it?"

"No. I wouldn't feel right using Hannah's and Sonali's
deaths like that."

"Suit yourself. But I bet you will. Time will tell, won't it?"

It was lucky I caught Hightower in the corridor where nobody else could hear. Lucky for him. I would have spoken
wherever we were.

"This has gone far enough, Sergeant."

"It certainly has—"

"I want to ask you a few questions."

Maybe he was feeling hassled. He was just as perfectly
dressed as ever, but there were tension lines around his eyes.
Being twenty feet away when a murder was committed probably wasn't going to be a positive career credit.

"How is it going to hurt to talk with me?" I demanded.

He thought it over, no doubt processing the fact that I was acquainted with his boss's boss's boss, which could have unpredictable implications.

"I suppose it couldn't hurt."

He walked me down the corridor, where the scene-of-crime people were still working. I went a few steps farther, to look in the linen closet. With Sonali's body removed, the little closet, filled with towels, sheets, and gowns, looked peaceful enough to remind me of a hope chest. Which it certainly was not.

While Hightower worked the key in the lock on Dr. Grant's door, the detectives began removing the linens. They were taking them all out, hoping someplace inside the closet there'd be usable evidence. My guess was there wouldn't be.

Hightower said, "We can go in here."

Hightower closed the door of Hannah Grant's office behind us. He took her seat behind the desk and I was left to pull out the only other chair, a metal folding thing that was wedged into a space between two bookcases. The office was very small and cramped.

"Look, Ms. Marsala," Hightower said, "I don't think we need to be enemies."

"Neither do I." I assumed he wanted something from me, even if it was only a good word to Harold McCoo. But if you're dealt the hand, play it. "Let me ask you just a few things."

"Go ahead. I don't think we have many secrets."

"First: The pathologist must have taken scrapings from under Grant's fingernails, since she'd been in fairly close contact with her killer. What turned up?"

"There were traces of skin and blood. But they were her own skin and blood."

I sighed, picturing her death agony again. "Yes, I noticed scratches on her cheeks and lips. Trying to get the sponge out of her throat."

He nodded.

"All right. Number two: There was a blood smear on the floor of the corridor just outside the lounge. Whose blood type was it?"

"What blood smear?"

"Near the entry to the lounge. Brownish, old blood."

"Oh. That wasn't blood. That was chocolate." He smiled, feeling one up on me with this answer.

"Chocolate? Chocolate! No kidding. Okay, number three: There was some red crushed stuff in the corridor today that looked like candy."

"It was candy. Part of a cherry LifeSaver."

"Sonali's, then. She loved hard candy. Number four: I don't suppose you've had a chance to make a list of exactly where everybody was today while Sonali was being killed."

"Not entirely. But it's going to be even less exact than when Dr. Grant was killed. The possible time frame is twice as long. Whoever killed her put her in the closet because in there she wouldn't be discovered soon. That way, the killer could be almost anybody. He improved his technique a bit this time."

"On the other hand, this time he or she took the risk of carrying a scalpel around."

"Okay. Desperate. But clever."

I said, "And no fingerprints on the scalpel?"

"No. But frankly, I'd hardly expect it. At any given moment half the people around here are wearing gloves."

"All right. Number five and last: I've always thought that Hannah Grant was killed because of something that came up that day, something she discovered and decided to tackle somebody about. She might have made notes or looked up records or something. Can you let me see exactly what papers or notes or whatever was on her desk when she was killed?"

He smiled smugly. "As a matter of fact, I can. Not only can I show you what was on her desk, but exactly which items were in what piles."

"That's absolutely wonderful!" I actually thought it was pretty basic, but what the hell? Give the guy some help, huh?

He took papers out of his briefcase. There were three separate piles of several sheets, each set held by a paper clip.

"These are copies, not the originals," he said. He put them down in a row on the desk.

"There you are, Ms. Marsala. Have at it. If you're satisfied, I think I'll get to work now."

I almost said, "Please do."

My satisfaction at being left alone with Dr. Grant's papers soon turned to mystification. They were case reports—all three piles, except for the smaller sheet from a memo pad on the top, which was the one that had made the police suspicious of Marveline. "Warn Kruse. Again!"

The three piles contained different numbers of case reports.

Pile number one was the largest. There were about thirty case files in it. I read through them as well as a layman could, and found that most of the medical terms were incomprehensible. For the time being I put the medical stuff, both diagnostic terms and treatments, out of my mind and searched the sheets for anything that was common to all of them. It didn't take long. The reports listed who was involved in the treatment of each patient—the doctor in charge, the nurse, the assistants, even the student nurses and residents and medical students when there were any. The only thing common to all these patients was that the attending physician was Sam Davidian.

This gave me a very nasty feeling. It suggested that she had been keeping track of Sam for some reason and might give him a whole new motive for killing her. However, I pride myself on facing facts. I can always run away screaming later.

My horror at finding this made me look much closer at all the other data in these cases. The kinds of patients varied— black and white and Asian, old and young, badly hurt and not so badly, head injuries, legs, everything. After quite some time, I found one other similarity. In all cases Sam had sutured a cut. Back and forth I went through the papers, and eventually proved to myself that in every case he had used the local anesthetic Tegucaine before doing the stitching.

What the hell?

I read it all again, including his notes, and discovered that in many of the cases he noted swelling around the cut when he used Tegucaine.

By now my head was aching. I turned to the second pile. This was just two sheets, which made me feel better. One was the case of a sixty-eight-year-old woman who had caught her hand in a wringer, a device that's used to squeeze water out of clothing. She had what they apparently called a "degloving" injury. This was very nasty, stripping the skin entirely off the hand. The accident had happened at home, and the EMTs thought it had taken the woman a while to get to a phone. By the time they got her here, she had lost quite a bit of blood. The woman also had some sort of kidney disease, and when she died in the trauma center of some sort of heart thing involving fibrillation, it apparently wasn't unexpected. There were terms I didn't understand, such as hyperkalemia. I made a note of them to ask somebody. The doctor on the case was Zoe Peters, the nurse was Fern Butler, and assisting was Brunniger. The case was dated five weeks ago.

The second was a freak restaurant accident that had taken place a month ago. A car apparently went out of control on State Street and slammed into a restaurant full of people. Among those hit was an eighty-year-old great-grandmother celebrating her granddaughter's graduation. She had been blasted by flying glass and bruised by the chairs that hurtled forward in front of the car, and she'd died here in the trauma unit. The doctors were Zoe Peters and Sonali Bachaan, the nurse was Fern Butler, and student nurse Fowler assisted.

Again—what the hell?

The last pile was almost as big as the first. I went through it carefully, a little better able now to read the forms. There was the case of a young man who had borrowed his brother's motorcycle. However, he had never ridden a motorcycle before. He drove it down Northwest Highway, went straight where the road curved, and ran right through a Walgreen's window into the cosmetics department. While he was not gravely injured, the EMTs had brought him here because of the sheer number of cuts from window glass and the resulting blood loss. There was a teenager who thought it would be interesting to climb into the high school gymnasium at night and fell through the skylight. Altogether there were twenty-seven cases. All different kinds of accidents. All different kinds of people. All involved, among other forms of treatment, cuts that were sutured by a doctor here. All were stitched by Dr. Jacob Coyne. In all cases he used Tegucaine as a local anesthetic. In no case did he report unusual swelling around the cut.

• • •

About ten P.M., a man entered the rotunda through the U-Hosp doors. He was of medium height, and despite the hot weather wore a three-piece gray glen plaid suit with the buttons of the vest just slightly straining at the buttonholes. He was shaved so smoothly that his cheeks looked varnished.

He stood in the U-Hosp side of the rotunda, swiveling his head on his neck. The two patients he saw, one in bay four and one in bay nine, were the only outsiders present. He held up his hand with the index finger pointing up and hissed, "Staff! Staff! Come here."

Then he stood right there and waited, expecting everybody to go over to him.

Dr. Zoe Peters marched over and said, "What do you want?"

"Get the staff."

Peters put her hands on her hips, about to blow him away, but both Sam and Fern Butler got there before she could create a scene. Michelson followed, telling Brunniger to stay with his patent. Slowly everybody drifted over, including Lester Smalley, Sue Slaby, Natasha Horne, and me. Marveline Kruse was home sick.

"I am Henry DeKooning, Associate Director of University Hospitals."

Nobody responded.

He waited a couple of seconds for somebody to express amazement that he would condescend to visit us, but when no one did, his anger got the better of him and he said, "What the hell do you people think you're doing down here?"

Sam said smoothly, "Did you want to say something specific?"

"Two doctors killed! Do you have any idea what this does to the U-Hosp reputation? What's the *matter* with you people?"

Sam said quietly, "The only thing wrong with us is that we've lost two good friends and two good doctors."

Subtlety wasn't DeKooning's long suit, however. "How can this killer get away with doing this? Don't you people watch what's going on? Do you just let somebody come in and stab somebody else right here in front of you?"

Sam passed his hand over his forehead. "We were working. The murder took place in that corridor." He pointed. "Shall I show you where?"

DeKooning looked across the rotunda and shook his head. "I've had to stay five hours overtime tonight to deal with the police and the media. This is terrible. If you people can't police yourselves down here, I'll have to put security officers in with you. Or maybe I need a different staff here."

Sam said, "Mr. DeKooning, I know you're upset. We're upset, too, but we're working. I think maybe you'd better reflect on the fact that several of the people here are students, to whom you owe help and continued education. The rest of us, the M.D.'s and the nurses, are professional people who could get a job anywhere—by that I mean anywhere *else*—tomorrow if we wanted to. And if you are sufficiently foolish, we will."

From Peters, Coyne, and Michelson:

"You bet!"

"In a second!"

"Well put, Sam!"

"Oh." DeKooning hadn't anticipated a rebellion. Out of sight of DeKooning, I raised a thumb to Sam. The administrator said, "I'm going to station security in that corridor and over here by the U-Hosp door. We can't let another killing happen."

"That's an excellent idea," Sam said.

• • •

Forty-five minutes later the eleven-to-seven shift started to arrive. The first thing they said when they came in was "I could hardly shove through the press out there! All the reporters wanted me to come back out with a story."

The second was "What the hell are you people up to here?"

Tonight we all trooped out of the trauma unit in a bunch, exited the back way, down the corridor into the hospital rather than out the trauma center entrance, avoided the press by sneaking past the cafeteria and out a food delivery door on the north side, then dragged ourselves to the corner near the parking garage. For a few seconds we stood under the sickly light of a sodium lamp, not knowing what to say to each other. I had whispered to Sam on the way out, "I haven't been fair to you." He'd asked me to go out to a late dinner tonight, but I was too sad and exhausted and conflicted, and I think he actually was, too.

"Dinner Saturday night?" he said.

"I'd like that." Time would tell.

Now we all nodded at each other—Jacob Coyne, Sam Davidian, Fern Butler, Zoe Peters, Qualley, whose first name I still didn't know, Sue Slaby, Natasha Horne, Belinda Fowler, Lester Smalley, and the med student, Brunniger. Most of us must have realized by now that the killer stood among us. Finally, Zoe Peters said furiously, "God damn it! Sonali never did one damn thing to hurt anybody!"

We all nodded.

We headed to our cars, the bus, or the El.

When I got home, I found that LJ had amused himself by unwinding the entire roll of toilet paper. He does this by flying at it, claws extended, and then "walking" up the side of the roll. I said to him, "People tell me southern fried parrot is no good to eat, LJ. But I'll never know if I don't try it."

Of course, he ignored me.

The answering machine was blinking. The first message said, "This is Hal Briskman. I want you to do an exclusive on the murders at U-Hosp."

I stopped my machine and called him. This was one of the few times I'd ever got his machine, instead of him, but of course it was very late. I said, "Hal, I can't do it. Somebody can cover the murders from the outside. I think ultimately my story on the people who do trauma work will be more interesting to the public as a result of the murders. But I can't cover the murders from the inside. I've got too many friends there now."

When I finished, I drew a breath. It would be a shame if he was angry with me. I needed his support.

The second message said, "Cat? Please don't give up on me! Let's just have coffee and talk." It was Mike, of course.

The third message was from Mike. It said, "Cat, call me anytime. Even if it's late."

The fourth message was from Mike. It said, "Cat, don't shut me out. Please? Please?"

• 16 •

Zoe Peters said, "We can talk while I'm jogging."

"Jogging!" I said, dismayed. "I don't jog."

"If you don't, you should."

"Don't joggers develop knee problems?"

"Sometimes they do. You can't give in to your knees. You just keep jogging and eventually the knees adapt."

I was beginning to think that the world was supposed to adapt to Zoe Peters, not Zoe to the world. She had said she'd meet me here at her apartment this morning, but as soon as I'd knocked on the door, she'd come out bouncing on the balls of her feet. She was dressed in cerise stretch pants and tank top, purple headband, no makeup as usual. Zoe lived in a building owned by the university and rented to graduate students, med students, residents, and very junior professors. I said, "Listen, I get a lot of exercise. I'm on the go every minute."

"It's not the same. It's not aerobic." She was already running in place. She jogged away down the hall. "Follow me."

"I don't think I can do an interview on the run."

"Hey! I agreed to talk with you! I didn't agree to disrupt my whole schedule."

She jog-bounced down the stairs. She jogged out the front

door, where the heat hit us like dragon's breath. "Are you going to run in these exhaust fumes?"

"Of course I am. Follow me."

She jogged east. I was sweating in twenty steps, gasping for breath in a block. Then I realized how lucky it was that I don't go to interviews wearing high heels, stockings, and a tight skirt. This thought supported me for another two or three minutes.

She led me east for three blocks and then we were at the lake. We jogged down an underpass under Lake Shore Drive near Northwestern Law School and back up steps on the other side. My lungs were screaming for mercy.

The lakefront is cooler than the city if the wind is east, off the lake. Today the wind was only a slight drift of air, and it was from the west, from the city. "This is just an illusion of fresh air," I gasped. We were running now on the part of the beach that is paved.

"Well, it's not an illusion of exercise."

She was right about that. "Why do you have such a tight schedule?" I gasped.

"Sixty hours at the hospital. Studying for the exam. Meetings. Some political involvement."

She wasn't even breathing hard. Sweat was running down the back of my neck and my breathing was developing a weird musical note on each intake. A note that sounded like middle C played on an oboe. This must be bad. I consoled myself that I had a doctor with me. If I went into cardiac arrest, surely she knew what to do. Then I reflected that of all the staff, she was the one in whom I had the least confidence.

"So do you—aaahh—like working in the trauma—aarrh— center?" I puffed.

"Not too much. Liking it isn't the point."

"Then why—?" I couldn't get any more words out.

"It was either that or surgery. They're not going to get me into any shitty women's specialty."

"Whhhhhat—"

"Like ob-gyn. Or pediatrics. Gimme a break! Not this kid!"

We jogged. She said, "I mean, I've had enough to cope with. It's time I got some respect."

We jogged. She said, "People will take advantage of you. You have to be able to stun people with how you're a seriously strong person. Tough. In control. I'm going to love being the boss of a trauma unit someplace."

We jogged on the cement esplanade a block or so, then hit the sandy beach. Sand is very hard to run in. "Ahhhhh!" I flopped down on the beach near where Lake Shore Drive curves past some landmark Mies van der Rohe buildings.

She stopped but jogged in place. "What's the matter with you?" she demanded.

"Tired!"

"Well, you shouldn't be! We've gone about half a mile, tops. That's disgraceful!"

"I'll bet I can type faster than you."

She had absolutely no sense of humor. "Finger muscles don't consume much oxygen," she said.

"Can we talk here?"

"Can't. I'm behind schedule. You've held me up too much already."

"But—"

"Catch me at U-Hosp, if you absolutely have to."

As she jogged away I heard her call back, "You'd better work on your cardiovascular adequacy."

• • •

The address that Billy Michelson had given me was on South Constance, not far from Jesse Jackson's house. I had heard Jackson didn't spend much time there. The neighborhood was just south of the Museum of Science and Industry and the University of Chicago, an area that was largely black. Michelson had said he lived with his parents. The street was tree-lined and the house—thank heavens!—looked cool. I had still not recovered from my stupid jog.

"This is my mother. Mom, this is Cat Marsala."

"I'm happy to meet you, Mrs. Michelson."

"Well, I'm just delighted to meet you, dear. Billy says you're a reporter."

"Yes, ma'am." Mrs. Michelson was tallish and very erect. This was definitely a person you addressed as "ma'am." She wore a white lace blouse with lace at the cuffs and a black cotton skirt. Her hair was white. She looked cool despite the hot day.

She said, "I always wanted to be a reporter myself."

"Did you really?"

"But somehow or other, I became a kindergarten teacher."

"You probably do more good for people—"

"Now, you don't have to butter me up, dear. Teachers do good, no doubt about it. But it isn't glamorous. However, you came to talk with Billy. Sit right down. I'll just get you a cool drink."

"Don't trouble yourself," I said, but she had left the room.

Billy laughed. "Let her do it, Cat. My mother *always* has a cool drink in the refrigerator in the summer. And after all, somebody has to drink it. She always has hot drinks on the stove in the winter. Hot cider with allspice, cloves, cinnamon, and nutmeg, usually."

"She's lovely."

"She is, actually. She's great."

"I have just one question. What does she do when it isn't cold enough for the hot drinks or warm enough for the cold drinks?"

"Peanut butter cookies."

"Oh."

Mrs. Michelson came in with two tall ice-filled glasses on a tray, along with a giant pitcher of lemonade in which slices of real lemons floated.

"Oh, gee, I'm never going home," I said.

She laughed. "And now I'll leave you two alone."

I was so comfortable it took me another couple of minutes to remember I was looking for a double murderer. Billy Michelson was likable, but that didn't mean he was innocent.

"Dr. Michelson—"

"Billy."

"Billy, why the trauma center? Why didn't you go into cardiology? Or dermatology?"

"Oddly enough, when I was in med school, it never occurred to me to do emergency medicine. When I started, I didn't even know there was such a specialty. I wanted to be a psychiatrist."

"That *does* surprise me. Why?"

"Well, you know the old joke—a psychiatrist is a doctor who's afraid of blood. When I first started med school, I wasn't real keen on blood."

"I see. But why the change?"

"I got used to blood. Seriously, two reasons, I guess. The first is that you make a real difference. You make a real change for the better in a person's life right away. Right there. Right then. You save a life, or you prevent lasting damage. It's satisfying because you don't have to wait to see results."

"That makes sense."

"And second, the longer I was in med school, the more I realized I didn't want to have an office."

"I don't get what you mean."

"Like in a regular medical practice. You know, you'd have an office, and office hours, and a secretary, and an office nurse, and billing, and overdue bills, and finding a doctor to cover when you took a vacation. You get a roof leak, and you spend the next three weeks seeing patients in somebody else's spare room. Your office nurse quits, and you have six weeks of temps who don't know your procedures. And then there's tax forms, and insurance forms, and fire inspections. And your office furniture wearing out. And on and on. The more I thought about it, the more I realized I'd hate it."

"Yeah, it sounds horrible!"

"See? Now, in the trauma center, I don't have any of that. The hospital does the billing and sends in the insurance forms; the nurses actually do most of the filling in of the patients' charts. The building and the furniture and the equipment and the medications and the hot water are all there ready for you. I get to do what I like and what I'm good at *practically all the time*, which is take care of patients."

"You strike me as a person—um, who attaches a lot of importance to being good at what he does."

"Right. Why not? It's more satisfying, being good at what you do. I mean, what's the fun in just slopping along your whole life?"

There was no answer to that. I'm moderately perfectionistic myself.

He said, "There's another thing."

"Go on."

"It's the work schedule. I'm there eight hours. With travel

to and from, maybe nine and a half hours. If there's a major disaster it can be more, of course, but that's rare."

"Yes?" This sounded like what Jacob Coyne had been saying about leaving the job and not having to think about it between shifts.

"Someday I want to marry and have children. I don't want to be the kind of husband or father who's always away. Always putting the job first, which means putting the family second. I want to be a father to my children."

Not quite like Jacob Coyne, then. "Slight change of subject," I said. "You believe the trauma center is valuable?"

"Good God, yes! We save lives."

"You do more than an emergency department could?"

"Absolutely. Not because we're better doctors, but because we have the high-tech equipment and specific specialties all in one place. We have basically all the same equipment as an ICU, all the intensive care stuff. We can measure oxygenation of the blood on a continuous basis, and the gadget will sound an alarm if the figure goes below a certain point. Same with heart rate. We have high-speed warm infusion units so we can get fluids into people at the right temperature quickly. We do what we specialize in, which is stop the dying process during what we call the "golden hour" when there's still a chance. Stabilize them. When we get them to a point where they can be nursed back to health, they go to another part of the hospital. It doesn't make sense to have all this expensive equipment at every small neighborhood hospital, but it sure saves lives to have it within reach. If I were in a serious accident, I hope I'd be taken to a trauma unit. They're not only effective, they're efficient."

• • •

We had a couple of crazies that Friday afternoon in the trauma center. Fern told me crazies were a pretty constant problem. "We've had an unusually easy week, as far as nuts go," she said. "Of course, we've had an unusually difficult—" She stopped right there. No need to describe what we'd been dealing with.

Our first nut walked in through the double doors at about two minutes after three. Walk-ins are supposed to go to the triage room. If the nurse decides they're desperately ill or hurt, she sends them right on to us. If it's a head cold or nothing much more, she sends them to the emergency department.

This guy walked through without stopping at the triage desk. The guard should have intercepted him, but in fact only followed him in. Sam went forward and said, "What's going on?"

The guard said, "Well, he sure ain't a reporter."

By this time Sue Slaby, the nurse, had approached the man. He was shabbily dressed in layers of dirty clothing. A street person. She said, "Are you sick?"

He said, "You gotta take me in."

"Are you sick? If you're not, we can get you a bed in a shelter."

"You gotta take me in *here*."

"But we only treat serious injuries—" she began.

He pulled out a short-bladed knife. She jumped back. "I can get serious!" he said. "Take me in or I'll stab myself!"

"Don't do it!"

He rammed the knife into his abdomen. Slaby reached forward. The guard and Sam seized the knife and threw it to one side. Sam immediately turned back to the patient. Slaby ripped open the clothes over the man's abdomen.

"Nothing!" she said.

Sam said, "Too many layers of clothes. It's *real* hard to push a knife through layers of cloth."

He sedated the man, who said as he was falling asleep, "That's what I wanted in the first place."

The guard had him wheeled out in a wheelchair, guarded by two orderlies. I think he went to psychiatric.

The next was a woman who walked in carrying a baby. This time the guard came in with her and stayed close. Fern said, "Is the baby sick?"

"Well, I think she was."

"Can I see her?" Fern held out her arms, but the woman still held the baby. The child was wrapped in a yellow blanket, and what I could see of the back of her head didn't look right. The skin seemed bluish, but I was no expert.

"She was sick," the woman said.

"When was that?"

"Last week. She was coughing and all."

"And then what happened?"

"She got worse, I think, because she stopped coughing, and I thought that was good, but she stopped breathing, too, and I knew that wasn't right."

"May I hold her—"

The woman backed away from Fern. Fern said, "Then what happened?"

"Well, after she wasn't breathing for a while, I thought I should fix it, so I put her in the freezer. That's good for keeping things, isn't it?"

Fern said, "How long ago was that?"

"Uh—I think Tuesday. No, that can't be right. I think it was last Sunday. Yeah, I heard the church bells down the block. Sunday."

"And now you've brought her here for us to try to help,"

Fern said, slowly and soothingly. "That was the right thing to do. I think you should let us see her."

"I took her out today, you know? But she didn't seem to be any better."

She gave the baby to Fern, finally. The child, of course, was dead. Sam called the police. The woman went away with two women police officers and a social worker. I found Fern in the cast room, crying.

"That beautiful little child. Did you see how perfect that little girl was?"

"I saw."

Tears ran over Fern's cheeks and she wiped at them with her hand. "Some people would give anything to have a beautiful little girl like that."

"I know."

"The world just isn't—isn't *right!*"

The media crowd had thinned out, since there was no fresh news coming out of our unit. They took themselves over to Area Two Police Headquarters, which was a relief to all of us. At six, just as I was ready for a caffeine fix, the doors opened to another walk-in.

Mike.

I glanced around, hoping nobody was watching, grabbed Mike, and sidled over toward Lester Smalley's cleaning closet.

"Mike, I'm working. They don't want people having company here."

"I'm not company."

"Look, this isn't a good time."

"But there aren't any good times, as far as you're concerned, are there, Cat?"

"People have broken up relationships before us. Why are you making this so difficult?"

"*Because I don't want to break up!* We're suited to each other. We're right. I just don't understand what's the matter with you."

"Mike—" For a second I thought of taking him to the lounge and talking there, but every time I so much as had a cup of coffee with him, he thought we were right back together. Even sitting down would be a mistake. "Mike, we've been over and over this. Can we just be—" No, hold it. If I said, "Let's be friends," that would lead to the same problems. I'd tried that half a dozen times in the past.

"Mike, we have to just end it."

"No, Cat. Don't do this to me."

"You're making it harder."

"I want to make it harder."

"It's over, Mike. Please go."

"*I don't want to go!*"

His voice carried, even though I was keeping mine quiet. Sam turned to look, but had the sense to keep out of it. Michelson was working in the treatment bay closest to us, but he had a teenager from a drive-by shooting who was in critical condition, and he didn't even glance up. Slaby, Marveline, and Brunniger were working with him, and were also too busy to look.

"Mike, I want you to leave."

He spread his arms out. "I'll die without you."

"Don't be absurd!"

"All right. I'm leaving. This is the end."

He was so foolishly dramatic, I studied him to see if he'd been drinking, but he showed no signs of it. It would be safe to let him drive.

"Yes, Mike. This is the end."

• • •

Sam had the sensitivity to keep away from me after Mike stalked out. A couple of the others seemed to be avoiding my eye, which was just as well. Fern raised her eyebrows and looked away. She seemed sympathetic. Zoe Peters, always rather self-involved, didn't appear to have noticed any problem.

And Billy Michelson, I was suddenly aware, was having trouble with his patient.

Michelson was usually somewhere in the running for the Mr. Calm of the Year Award, so when I noticed Marveline waving at Sam from treatment bay five where Billy was working to save the teenager, I was surprised.

Sue Slaby was assisting, and she put her hand on Billy's arm just as I arrived, saying, "Come on. You can't do anything more for him."

But he threw her off so hard she reeled back against the instrument stand. The jar of swabs, jar of tongue depressors, jar of Betadine, and several boxes of supplies slid off onto the floor. The jars shattered with several loud cracks. Slaby said, "Ow!" Betadine splattered everywhere. Lester Smalley, who was working around the desk, raised his head, grasped his cart handle, and started toward the mess.

Marveline burst into tears and ran out.

Sam said, "Get back in there, Kruse! Act like a nurse, damn it!"

And she did come back. She took over the spot where Slaby had been. Sam ignored Billy for the moment, studying the patient. In ten short, efficient seconds, he checked the pupils of his eyes with the flashlight, glanced at Slaby's recording of the blood pressure, felt his carotid pulse, then pinched hard on the web of flesh between the patient's thumb and index finger. Meanwhile, paying no attention to Sam, Billy readied the patient for another jolt from the defibrillator.

The patient was a young white boy, maybe twelve or thirteen years old. I could see a patched wound in his neck. It looked to me like a bullet wound.

Billy said, "Clear!"

The electricity jolted the body, but the monitor showed no heart action. Sam said, "That's it, Billy. You've done this how many—"

"Twenty times," Slaby said.

"No! Get back!"

"It's over. You can't save them all."

"Get out of my way! Clear!"

Michelson's eyes were wild. His breath was coming in gasps, and there was sweat running down from his hair over his forehead.

"Quit it, Michelson!" Sam yelled.

"He's too young to die! Can't you see this is just a kid? He's too young!"

Sam went behind Billy, grabbed him from the back, threw his arms around Billy's chest, and locked his hands in front of Billy's waist. He held on tight.

"You can't help him. He's dead. He's dead! You can't help him."

Michelson didn't try to throw Sam off. He froze where he was and started crying. Sam just hung on for a while until Michelson finally calmed down. Finally Billy said, "I'm sorry."

"It's all right," Sam said.

"I'm sorry. I kind of lost it."

"You kind of did."

"I'm sorry, Sue," he said to Slaby.

Slaby rubbed her back. "No problem," she said. "I know how you feel."

Since we were in a temporary lull, Sam sent Slaby to the lounge to sit down and stretch out for a few minutes "or until

Fern pages you." Then he said to Billy, "Go immediately to the cafeteria. Take a dose of complex carbos, caffeine, and chocolate and call me in half an hour."

"Okay."

"And include something with an unhealthful amount of fat and salt, too."

"You're not mad at me?"

"Billy, everybody is stressed out in this job. Even without what's happened this week. You stressed out the right way, in my book. You wanted to save somebody who was beyond the reach of help. That's a lot better than the guy who starts giving up when the patient still might be salvageable."

"I've never behaved this way before."

"Probably never will again either. Now go to the cafeteria. I don't want to see you for at least thirty minutes."

I sat and brooded, disheartened. The killer of Hannah Grant and Sonali Bachaan should be punished. But to me it didn't seem like any progress was being made. By Hightower or by me.

Lester Smalley washed the floor in front of me, smiling at me in a self-deprecating manner as he went by, while I raised my feet for him to wash under them. This is always extremely awkward. You feel like Louis XIV or something, sitting down while somebody else washes the floor under your feet.

Smalley washed, then squeezed the water out of his mop and returned, drying the floor. The air around him smelled of bleach.

"Mr. Smalley, don't you ever take a break?" I said.

He didn't answer, and for a few seconds I thought he was ignoring me, until I realized with a pang that his mind didn't think that any statement beginning with "Mr.—" meant him.

"Lester?" I said.

"Oh, yes? Ma'am?"

"Don't you ever take a break?"

"Lunch break."

"You see a lot, don't you?"

"Well, I don't know what you mean, Ms. Marsala."

"Cat, please. I mean you pass by and people hardly notice and go about their work, so you must see what they're doing and how they're doing it."

"Mmm. I surely do."

"Have you noticed anything going on around here that struck you as odd?"

To my surprise, he instantly said, "Yes indeed."

"What, Mr. Smalley? What is it?"

He glanced around. He rested both hands on the mop handle and shook his head. "There's evil here."

I didn't know whether he was slightly unbalanced, or trying to make an impression, or actually knew about a real wrong. It didn't much matter. His words sent cold chills down my back.

"Evil like what?"

"People dying."

"Who? You mean Hannah Grant and Sonali Bachaan?"

"Ah, don't listen to me. I probably imagine it all. I am not the man I used to be, you know."

"What did you used to be?"

"I was an economist. Third year of grad school. Writing my thesis. Went into the war."

"The war—?"

"Viet Nam. See, I wasn't prepared for that."

"Nobody was prepared."

"They weren't. Indeed they weren't. Lost a lot of friends.

Blood all over, don't you know? It always bothered me. It bothers me when the young die."

"When the young die?"

"We were all kids. Eighteen, nineteen, twenty. Lot of them dead. I got to taking some drugs, you know. Over there you needed it. People don't want to admit it, but it's true. I got so I was stoned all the time. But it was mainly the war. When I got home I couldn't ever quite concentrate my mind. Something was wrong in my head. You know."

"I see. It's a sad story, Mr. Smalley."

"Oh, I don't know. There's a lot of stories like that. The war. You know. I didn't die."

"No."

"Of course, it's no better when the old die. If they shouldn't."

I had been thinking of him as an old man. But if he was twenty in 1968, say, he couldn't be much over forty-five now. How astonishing. He stood in front of me holding the mop, a scrawny man with large knees and large elbow joints, never quite properly shaved, always a little stubble somewhere. A part of the trauma center staff, but never really part of it . . .

. . . a man who could go anywhere and not be noticed.

"See you," he said. The doors had opened and he had spied some blood to mop.

The blood was dripping from a gurney, just coming in the door, pushed by the EMTs. A little trail of blood followed their path. Fern moved in to take the place of the EMT nearest me. The EMT stopped, letting them go on past. He bent over to stretch his back and sighed. "Long day. Although this was the easiest one we've had in a while," he said. "Just two blocks down here at the stoplight."

"Somebody run a stoplight and hit him? Or her?"

"Him. Neither. He ran his car into the stoplight pole. It was so close to here, we coulda pushed the gurney from there to here, except it's SOP to put 'em in the ambulance."

"Oh."

"Actually took longer that way." He headed toward the corridor. "I'm gonna go get a Coke."

I walked over to see what patient the gods of chance had brought us now.

The face was bloody. Sam was getting the stats from the other EMT, while Sue wiped the blood from the man's face. He looked familiar. She wiped away the blood that was pooled across his eyes.

It was Mike.

· 17 ·

"Mike, what happened? What did you do?"

I knew enough not to grab Mike and shake him, but I wanted to. There was a cervical collar around his neck. He might have a spinal injury. Mike either didn't or couldn't answer. But I shouted at him until Sam pulled me away.

"Is this who I think it is?" he asked.

"It's Mike. It's my—my ex—"

Sam turned around and yelled "Jacob!"

"Aye-aye?"

"Take this case, please."

I said, "Why are you giving him the case?"

"I'm not going to make life-and-death decisions on somebody I know, not if I can help it."

"But—" I lowered my voice and whispered to him. "You don't know him. And I want you to take the case. I have more confidence in you."

"Listen, Cat. I wish this guy was out of your life. Don't put me in that position."

"Please? I trust your judgment."

"I'll hang around." He smiled. "I'll give Coyne the benefit of my wisdom."

Coyne moved in fast. Sam told him the EMT's findings. Coyne said, "Marveline, page the X-ray tech."

Fern had already wheeled in the suture cart, and I noticed that Mike had a lot of small cuts on the scalp and head. I'd been here long enough now to recognize windshield cuts. He must have crashed into the light pole and gone flying through the windshield. Which meant he wasn't wearing a seat belt. Which meant he was behaving foolishly.

Foolishly or suicidally?

I went to the desk and grabbed one of the EMTs who had come in with Mike. He was drinking a Coke and finishing some paperwork, but I could already hear a call coming in on his partner's radio.

"Can I ask you something?"

"Sure." He'd gotten used to seeing me around here, and didn't think a question from me was odd.

"He skidded into a light pole?" I gestured at Mike.

"Well, I wouldn't say skidded."

"Were there any skid marks at all?"

"Uh, no. Not really."

"So he *drove* into the light pole."

"It'd be my guess."

"And wasn't wearing a seat belt."

"Nope. Went right through the windshield."

His partner said, "Hey! Let's go. We got an LOL-squared."

"What's an LOL-squared?" I asked.

The partner said, "Little old lady lying on linoleum."

The other EMT said to me, "Now, don't take that wrong. We sympathize with our patients. It's just—"

"It's just a stress-reducer," I said.

"Yeah. Keeps the job bearable."

"We have a few in reporting, too."

"Such as?"

"Well, 'if it bleeds it leads.'"

They left. For a minute I couldn't stand to go back to Mike, or even turn around and look at him.

I heard Dr. Coyne tell Fern to call a neurosurgeon. That meant he suspected either brain damage or spinal cord damage. I waited in a chair at the other end of the rotunda while they worked, watching everything they did, but from a distance. In some illogical way, distance made it easier to take. I felt guilty for driving Mike away, guilty for not understanding how desperate he was. And I felt furiously angry at him for doing this. It was an intentional kick in the face to me. He'd driven into that light pole to show me.

To show me what? To show me I was a horrible person, selfish for wanting to go my own way? To show me he didn't want to live without me? To show me he really loved me?

The neurosurgeon came and consulted. He didn't think the trauma-unit X-rays were adequate. He left, saying he would talk to radiology about what he needed, but they'd better get the OR ready, too.

Finally, Sam came over to me.

"He's pretty much out of it, but you can try to talk to him if you want to."

"Tell me what shape he's in, before I do."

"He's not in danger of dying."

"Thank God."

"We're afraid of spinal cord damage."

"Better that than brain damage."

"Well, maybe."

"Maybe? Sam, tell me exactly what you mean."

"The fractured vertebra is pretty high up. The higher the spinal cord damage, the more of the body is affected."

He stopped. I said, "Tell me all of it."

"Well, he could be paralyzed from the upper chest on down."

I felt cold. Sam asked whether I was going to faint, so there must have been some change in my color.

"No. I think I should talk with him now."

"They'll be here to take him to X-ray in a couple of minutes."

"And after that?"

"Dr. Eddington is probably going to have to operate tonight. He thinks there's a piece of fractured veterbra pressing on the spinal cord."

"All right."

Mike was lying utterly still. It made the usual Mike, the "real Mike" all the more vivid in my mind—his nervous energy, bouncing on his feet, constantly in motion, his curiosity, his irreverent humor. There hadn't been much of that in recent weeks.

I said, "Mike? Open your eyes."

He did. "Cat? Is that you? I'm in a mess." His eyes filled with tears.

"You are. But these doctors are the best."

"I'm sorry. I can't quite remember—I don't know what this was all about, in a funny—"

"Come on. You don't need to remember everything. Concentrate on getting better."

"Well, yeah. I guess. Cat, I can't feel anything. I think I'm paralyzed. They won't admit it, but I know I am."

"No. If they don't admit it, that means they think you may not be."

"I don't believe you."

"Mike, look at me. I always tell you the truth."

"Yeah. Yeah, Cat. You do. Even when it hurts." He started

to laugh and the tears ran down the sides of his head into his ears.

"The orderlies are here to go to X-ray," I said.

"And then what will happen?"

"Surgery, I think. To remove the—the whatever is pressing on the spinal cord."

"When I get out of surgery, will you come and see me?"

"Yes, I will, Mike."

"Promise."

"I promise."

Unbelievably, it was only ten P.M. It seemed like four weeks had gone by. I tried to remember whether I had eaten dinner, but I just couldn't think. I went to the lounge and bought candy. I took my candy to the rotunda and sat in a chair in the empty treatment bay four.

Bright fluorescent lights poured a brilliant blue-white glow over everything. I stared dazedly at the big room. Michelson was back at work. Sue Slaby was back at work.

I felt stunned. There was no real pain anyplace, but I felt like I had been beaten, beaten softly, as if I had been hit a thousand times with sacks of something yielding, like flour, that had left me puffy and numb. I had bought a candy bar from the machine, then thought two would be better, and got another. Now I ate them both in less than two minutes.

I closed my eyes. Faces and questions flashed at me in the dark.

The lounge floor the day of Hannah Grant's murder. Dr. Jacob Coyne had said he lost a quarter and therefore didn't have enough coins for the candy machine. But didn't somebody tell me they saw him come back to the rotunda with a chocolate bar?

Dr. Billy Michelson was capable of freaking out. Could he have been going a little nuts for some time, unnoticed by the staff? Could he have killed Dr. Grant?

Would the killer have counted on listening for the alarm being given when somebody found Dr. Grant's body, then running in to "help" and obscuring some of the evidence? And if so, should I be most suspicious of the people who ran in first, Sam Davidian, Jacob Coyne, and Marveline Kruse?

Also, the people who ran in first were able to touch some of the stuff—the tongue depressor and sponge—and that would explain away traces, if there were any, like fingerprints or hairs or whatever, that might be found on the objects later.

If Sam had killed Hannah Grant, it would have gone like this: She would have stopped by while he was treating Colczyk and asked to see him when he was done. He would have left Colczyk and gone to the lounge. Maybe he got coffee while Grant was talking. When he found out that she knew he had done something wrong, possibly with Tegucaine, he would say, "Let me get something to prove my innocence," returned to the rotunda for the tongue depressor and sponge, then gone to the lounge and killed Grant, knocking his coffee over in the process.

Then why go back later, the time Fern beeped him? Had he left something incriminating, something he picked up later when he ran in to start the resuscitation efforts?

If Fern killed Grant, she could have met with Grant the first time right between treating DeeDee Williams and moving on to Georgia Holyrood. Or when she went for medication for Georgia Holyrood, she might have stopped in to see what Grant wanted. She could have returned to Grant while

Zoe Peters was working on Georgia Holyrood, and killed her then. Or right after finishing with the woman.

Zoe Peters could have done it the other way around. When she went to get the suture cart and left Fern with Georgia Holyrood, she could have gone to the lounge to see what Grant wanted. Then, saying she had to take care of the patient, she could have returned to the rotunda. After Georgia Holyrood died, she could have left Fern with the body, returned to the lounge, then peeled and ate an orange as a cover while she begged Grant to believe that she would do better on the job. Then she killed Grant and left, forgetting her clipboard in her panic.

Billy Michelson could have taken a break from Shirley Holyrood while the X-ray tech was developing pictures of her back and neck. Like the others, just when he slipped out of the rotunda wasn't clear. We didn't really know whether Grant was killed at four-ten or four twenty-five. But Michelson had a stable patient and therefore more time than most of the others to get away.

Jacob Coyne, of course, had a critical patient, but also a hopeless patient. And his case ended—in death—before the others. He could easily have left the body of John Holyrood to Fowler by four-fifteen. He could have gone to the lounge, talked with Grant, returned to the lounge, bought a chocolate bar as a cover (lying about it later), killed Grant, dropped the quarter in his haste, dropped some chocolate in the corridor in his haste, and been back in the rotunda by four-twenty.

But why?

Had Coyne fallen in love with Marveline, and would he have killed Dr. Grant on Marveline's behalf? Ridiculous.

Could two people have worked together? Sam Davidian and Jacob Coyne? It would certainly confuse the detectives.

Could Coyne have killed Dr. Grant, because clearly he had more time, and could Sam have killed Sonali Bachaan? Even more ridiculous.

Little, delicate Sonali—could she have seen the killing of Dr. Grant? Why wouldn't she tell? Could she have been blackmailing the killer?

What about Lester Smalley? He was the unseen man who went everywhere.

Fern Butler was also able to go everywhere. She circulated more than any of the doctors, because she was the one over-seeing the practical workings of the unit. She usually an-swered the radio-call buzzer when it sounded, but she didn't have to. Whoever was nearest when it went off picked up the call.

And what about Zoe Peters? How far would her anger and determination take her? Did Dr. Grant have serious doubts about her competence? What would she do if she were thwarted?

• 18 •

For the last four days I had been straining my mind to think who could have killed Dr. Grant, and then Sonali Bachaan. Now I was simply too exhausted to think anymore. I tried to lean back in the treatment bay chair. It was built to be un-comfortable. I tucked my feet up under me, which was bet-ter. If brain cells could feel numb, mine did. A kind of half-sleep came over me.

Maybe when you really stop using your rational side, something else takes over. I have friends who say this is the artistic, intuitive right side of the brain taking over from the rational left side. The left side, they say, takes longer to get to some conclusions because it has to dot all the *i*'s and cross the *t*'s. The right side is willing to leap. To a certain extent, though, I believe that the right side works better when the left side has collected some facts for it to leap around on. For half an hour or so I was either in a daze or half asleep.

Suddenly I sat up.

I knew who had killed Hannah Grant and Sonali Bachaan. And I knew how everything fitted in.

Tegucaine. And the chocolate smear on the corridor floor. The Kleenex, Zoe's and Fern's patients, and Jacob Coyne's odd behavior.

I felt cold.

• • •

Everybody was still here, moving around, doing their work. Lester Smalley, still mopping. Brunniger, the med student, Fowler and Kruse, the student nurses. The nurses Sue Slaby, Natasha Horne, and Fern Butler. Dr. Zoe Peters, the resident. Dr. Billy Michelson, the fourth-year resident and Qualley, the second-year resident, whom I hardly knew. Dr. Sam Davidian and Dr. Jacob Coyne. I looked for Sergeant Hightower, but he and the rest of the detectives had left. I'd have to put in a call to him, but not from here where I might be overheard. I was going to tell him who killed Grant and Bachaan and let him deal with it. It was his job, not mine.

Jacob Coyne had just sent a patient to the burn unit. It was five of eleven. The eleven to seven staff was starting to arrive. I followed Coyne to his locker, and before he could get his regular clothes out, I said, "Let's go get some coffee in the cafeteria, where we won't be bothered. At least by anybody from here."

"Hey, I'm in kind of a hurry. It's been a long day."

"It's gonna be a long life, if you lose your job."

"What are you talking about? Are you nuts?"

"No. I'm completely sane on this. Let's go talk about Tegucaine."

He immediately stood straight up, left his street clothes in place, and slammed the locker door. I led the way across the rotunda to the door into the rest of the hospital. I led the way down another corridor—left turn, right turn, past the gift shop—and into the cafeteria. The whole way, he never said a word. At this time of night there was no staff on in the cafeteria, but several people were at various tables eating and chatting. There was a far greater range of food machines here than in the trauma center lounge for the late-night crowd—

machines that served hot stew, macaroni and cheese, tacos, burritos, even several kinds of soup.

We each took a cup from the cup rack, a spoon from the spoon bin, then put quarters in the voluntary contribution box and poured coffee. Silently, we walked to a table on the far side of the room and sat down.

Dr. Jacob Coyne looked at me with his eyes wide. "What's your problem?" he asked belligerently. He could be as belligerent as he liked; the fact that he'd come with me immediately made it perfectly clear he knew what I was talking about.

"Tegucaine is a local anesthetic that's been approved by the FDA for human use."

"Obviously."

"It's just been approved. It's brand new. Beckmann Laboratories would like its new anesthetic to sell widely. They want favorable physician reports to come in."

"Of course they do."

"It means big money to them. They have decided it was worth paying for. Paying bribes for, that is."

"I don't know what you mean."

"Swelling around a cut can stretch the stitches. Tegucaine causes undesirable swelling where it's injected. Except when *you* use it. You give it favorable reports."

"It's worked well for me."

"I don't think so. I think they've been paying you off."

He considered this a couple of seconds. "You can't prove it."

"Well, I'm not so sure. I think a bit of a survey by the FDA might turn up the fact that most senior physicians haven't been very impressed by Tegucaine. But a lot of hungry young doctors, doctors with a big accumulated debt, mysteriously think it's great stuff."

He stared at me with huge, terrified eyes. "What are you going to do?"

"That's up to you." He continued to stare. "It isn't as if you fudged something that could actually kill people."

"No, no it isn't!"

"Don't be so eager to excuse yourself."

I saw Fern Butler come into the cafeteria. She must have wondered where we'd gone. Coyne saw her, too.

"I don't want Fern to hear this," he said.

"Everybody may hear, eventually. Maybe you can make restitution."

"How?"

"Give back the money. And blow the whistle on Beckmann. You were under a lot of financial pressure, but you were also spending money you shouldn't have. Marveline has faith in you. I'd kind of like to think she's right."

Fern saw us, waved, and went to one of the hot water pots. Fern had no need to hear this accusation, so I hurried it up.

"I'm serious about this, Coyne. I want you to discuss with Sam how you're going to make up for it. I want you to convince me that you deserve to be a doctor. Ethically. Or I'll blow the whistle myself."

He started to take in a breath. Maybe he intended to bluster. If so, a second or two of studying my face convinced him not to.

"Okay," he said. "I understand you're giving me a chance, and I appreciate it."

My eyebrows rose. I was skeptical.

"I didn't say I *liked* it," he said, "but I do appreciate it."

"You have years of training and real skills. You're a person of value to society. But you have to use your training right."

He made a move to get up. I said, "Uh—Coyne?"

He had a "what now?" look on his face, but he had the

sense not to say it. I asked, "When I found Hannah Grant's body, there was a chocolate smear in the corridor outside. And people said you came back into the rotunda with a Snickers bar. But you told me when you lost your quarter, you couldn't get any candy out of the machine. Did you go back later, or lie, or what?"

"Neither one. I got a Snickers from my emergency stash."

"Where's that?"

"My locker. It's in the corridor, near the lounge door."

Fern approached our table. She carried a banana wrapped in plastic—why wrap a banana?—a mug of tea, some sugar in a paper envelope, a paper napkin, and a spoon. The mug, like ours, was actually china, not plastic, and the spoon was metal. This is as elegant as it gets in a hospital.

"Well, I'll be going," Jacob said.

He nodded at Fern and left. She said, "What was that all about?"

"What was what all about?"

"He looked sort of funny. Like he'd lost a pint of blood."

"Oh, a personal problem. I think we should leave it to him to work it out."

Coyne disappeared out the doors. I would have to check at some point later and find out what he'd done. For that matter, I would have to ask Sam specifically and confirm that Coyne had told him the whole truth. Sam was acting director, however much he didn't want to be, and it was his baby now.

The group in white coats at the table in the middle of the cafeteria got up, took their trays to the tray return slot, and left.

Fern ate half her banana. She tore the corner off her sugar packet, poured it in her tea. Then she reached for the spoon to stir it.

"Yuck!" she said. She dropped the spoon. It had a purplish smear down the handle.

I said, "That looks like grape jelly to me."

"Don't you think a *hospital* could clean its silverware?"

"Maybe it was clean when they put it out. Maybe somebody with sticky hands reached into the silverware bin."

"Maybe. It's still disgusting."

She wet her fingertips in a little tea, then wiped her fingers on her napkin. Then she picked up the napkin and wrapped it around the spoon handle and stirred the tea.

Inadvertently, I gasped.

Her eyes flicked up at me.

I wiped all expression from my face, but it was too late.

"You know," she said.

"Know what?"

"Don't act innocent. I suspected an hour ago that you knew. It was in your face. How did you know?"

Were there any other people left in the cafeteria? I tried to take in the area without moving my eyes, tried to keep looking directly at her. I didn't see anybody, and I didn't hear any voices.

This was no place for a confrontation.

"How did you know? The tissue?" She put her hand in her pocket, fingered something, then relaxed. I was utterly certain that she had checked to see whether some weapon was there.

Maybe the best thing was to keep her talking until somebody walked in. If she was smart, she would attack me now. If I was smart, I could keep her focused on what I was saying long enough.

"There weren't any fingerprints on the tongue depressor," I said. "It could have been held by a killer wearing gloves. God knows there are enough gloves in the unit. But Hannah Grant would have been suspicious. People don't wear gloves to the lounge. She wouldn't have allowed anybody wearing gloves to approach her without a fight. It would be too obvious. You took what looked like a Kleenex out of your pocket. Maybe pretending to cry and wipe your eyes. The Kleenex concealed a tongue depressor. Then you pulled out the sponge with your left hand, stuck it in her mouth, and rammed it down with the tongue depressor."

"You're right."

"Whoever killed Grant had to use something to conceal the tongue depressor for an instant. Otherwise, Grant wouldn't let it get that close without fighting back. The only likely thing in the whole room was a Kleenex Hightower found in the wastebasket. A Kleenex with your color of mascara on it. Grant and Peters don't use makeup and Horne and Bachaan use brown mascara. And a Kleenex is perfect camouflage, because you could use it to simulate remorse."

"Uh-huh. So that's how I gave myself away." Her tone was calm, paced and low. She was planning something. I kept talking.

"No. At least it isn't why I thought it was you."

"Oh?" She slipped her hand in her pocket again and left it there.

"I had narrowed the possibilities down to you, Davidian, Coyne, Michelson, and somewhat less likely, Bachaan and Peters. You and the three men could get away from the rotunda most easily."

"Of course. So?"

"But I thought it would be very unlikely that any of the three men could approach Hannah Grant without starting a struggle. They're big. Coyne and Davidian are tall and Michelson is wide-shouldered and seems big. And they're men. If Dr. Grant had been accusing any of them of wrongdoing, she wouldn't have let them get right up close to her without fighting back. You're not small, but people view women differently. You, she might let get close to her, especially if you were holding a tissue to your eyes and weeping."

"And so you knew."

I took a sip of my coffee, which gave me an excuse to half turn. There was absolutely no one else in the cafeteria. The huge room stretched away in three directions. We were sitting at a table against the west wall, far from the door.

"No, those were probabilities. I'll tell you when I really knew."

"Tell me then. Since you're so smart."

"Dr. Grant was already worried that you were killing older women. But she didn't have any proof. When she saw Georgia Holyrood die, she thought you had killed her. Since she suspected this before the body was released, she could have it tested for a whole range of drugs. She asked you to meet her in the lounge. When you did, she told you what she thought. You claimed you could prove it wasn't true, and left her to go get the tonge depressor and sponge. Meanwhile, Sam discovered that he'd misplaced his coffee. You saw him heading to the corridor, and you couldn't allow him in there, because you had to go back and kill Dr. Grant. So you beeped him to go look at the Holyrood child."

"Mmm? So what? How could my beeping him make you suspicious?"

"There was nothing wrong with the Holyrood child."

"A cut."

"You didn't need a trauma surgeon to stitch that cut. Two stitches! Zoe could have done it perfectly well."

Still nobody came into the cafeteria. There were just the two of us in a space the size of a basketball gymnasium. If worse came to worst, I was going to jump up and run for the door. It

was too bad I had brought Jacob Coyne over here to the far
side of the room, away from the exit. At the time, I had no
idea of speaking to Fern at all, and just figured that Coyne
and I needed privacy.

It was eleven o'clock exactly, right between shifts, which
probably explained why nobody was coming in for food yet.

Fern was taller than I was—well, most people were taller
than I am. Usually I counted on being sneakier, but in her
case I had my doubts.

Keep her talking.

"But I was finally certain you were the killer," I said,
"when I realized I had seen the murder."

Fern said slyly, "But nobody saw Dr. Grant's death."

"Not Dr. Grant. I saw you kill Georgia Holyrood, the old
lady whose family was in the automobile accident. You
spread nitro paste on her as if it were salve, and her blood
pressure plunged and she died."

Fern jumped from her seat, tipping the heavy table into
my stomach. In one hand she held a scalpel and in the other
a syringe.

· 19 ·

I had known it was coming, but I was stunned by the suddenness of her attack. What an idiot I am sometimes! The table hit me square and hard, right below the rib cage. With the breath knocked out of me, I rolled away from the table, but I was lying on the floor, and rolling over, I saw Fern right above me. The scalpel was sweeping down at me.

I kicked up, caught her elbow with my heel, and flipped over again. Rising to hands and knees, I scuttled away from the table. I didn't know where she was, and I jumped to my feet, just as the scalpel slashed through the back of my sleeve. I felt the fabric rip and heat pierced the back of my arm.

Fern was practically on top of me. I didn't know what was in the syringe, and I didn't want to find out the hard way. I backpedaled, facing her.

She was between me and the door and we were at the side of the cafeteria farthest from the exit. I looked desperately around the room for some kind of weapon, but the knives, forks, spoons, and trays were near the door. How I'd love a tray, at least, to use as a shield!

She took a pace forward. I took a pace backward, toward the kitchen. She was stalking me. The only place I could find a weapon was right behind me. The kitchen.

I turned and ran at top speed, blasting through the kitchen door, and when she followed, I tried to slam the swinging door into her face. But she was too smart and jumped back out of the way.

I was in a gigantic room, but a gigantic room without any open floor space. Rows of sinks stretched away on my right. On my left was a long bank of metal wire shelves, tier upon tier, containing colanders, sieves, and strainers for washing vegetables. Nothing here was heavy enough for a weapon.

I ran down the narrow aisle. Fern was close behind me. I wasn't as big as she was, not as tall and not as heavy, but I ran faster.

At the far wall were doors to coolers. They didn't lead out of the kitchen, so I made a U-turn up into the next aisle. On one side of me was a long line of gas-fired cooktops, rank after rank of burners. But on my other side was a long line of tables with chopping-block tops, and underneath them were shelves filled with skillets.

I grabbed two large skillets, one for each hand, and turned to face her. She stabbed out with the syringe, and I swung the skillet in my right hand with all my might. She yelped. The syringe went sailing up over the chopping-table aisle and vanished into the distance, where I heard it fall. I was swinging down the other skillet at Fern's head, but she had snatched up a pan from the floor and it met mine in midair with a clang.

I bashed at her with the other one, and caught the side of her head. But she was smart. She leaned aside with the blow and the pan grazed her ear hard, splitting the top, but didn't knock her down.

Now we were both bleeding, me from the scalpel cut in my arm and Fern from her ear. I hoped it hurt like hell. She took a step toward me. I took a step back.

"Wait a minute," she said. "All we're doing is damaging each other."

"No kidding."

"Maybe this isn't necessary. Maybe we could just go our separate ways. Fighting isn't any way to solve things."

"Give yourself up, then."

"I don't think that's necessary either. We should discuss this and come to some kind of mutual understanding."

She sounded perfectly rational. More rational than I did, for that matter. At least, if you didn't know the circumstances. But of course she was trying to lull me into letting her get close.

"Fern, you're a murderer. A multiple killer. I don't even know how many times over."

"Oh, now. Don't be so excitable." Her voice was sweet and soothing, just as soothing as it was when she consoled badly injured patients, just as soothing as it was when she talked to frightened children in the trauma center. "I don't see why you're taking this so badly. Really, I've been helping people, you see. Those old women are like tumors on their families. They suck the life juices out of people, and they don't die until it's too late for the families to start a life of their own. Did you know that the average woman lives to be seventy-eight? That means the probability is that her sons and daughters are well over fifty before they get rid of her."

I thought of saying not all old women were like her mother, but there wasn't much point in trying to reason with her. There was a lot of point in keeping her talking until I located the knives. I kept retreating, being very careful where I put my feet, feeling behind me each time I put one down. To slip now meant death.

"How many old women have you killed?"

"Oh, I don't know."

"You've forgotten?"

"Well, it's been quite a lot, you see? I would think eighteen or nineteen. I'm not keeping score. It's not—uh—like notches on a gun. It's more like housekeeping."

I said, "If you attack me, the police will know you're guilty."

"No. They won't know any more than they do now."

"Jacob Coyne knows you and I are here together."

"I'll tell them Zoe came in to talk with you so I left you alone."

"They'll know that isn't true."

"No they won't. The shift is over. Zoe always takes longer to change clothes than anybody else. Nobody'll see her leave. Everybody's going home. With the time it takes people to get home, by tomorrow morning nobody will know to the minute where anybody was."

"They'll know it was you."

"They'll suspect me. And that's all. They're welcome to have all the suspicions they want."

Knives! A wall full of knives to my right and Fern's left. I lunged and grabbed a heavy cleaver. Fern was right-handed, so she had to turn her side to me if she wanted to grab one.

She backhanded the skillet at the cleaver, as if she were trying to backhand a tennis ball a mile into the air. The cleaver rang and twisted in my hand. A shock ran all the way up my arm. A stinging pain hit my elbow and shoulder.

By the time I had brought the cleaver back to fighting position, Fern had a foot-long knife.

Fern had dropped her scalpel when she grabbed the knife, but she kept the skillet in her left hand. I had the cleaver in my right and a skillet in my left.

She slashed at me, and she had both more reach and a longer knife. She missed my body. I didn't realize it until a few seconds later, but she'd cut the side of my right hand. Blood was oozing onto the cleaver handle, making it slippery.

Furious, I crashed the cleaver down at her, again and again, hitting the skillet and the knife, and once, grazing her left arm and opening a cut there.

We forced each other up and down the aisle near the chopping tables. There wasn't much room to maneuver in, and we staggered, crashed back against the table edges, tripped and righted ourselves, and finally, when I was fed up and desperate, I hit out at her so hard that her long knife broke in half.

But my hand, slick with blood, couldn't hold the handle of the cleaver after such a hard blow, and the cleaver spun up into the air, fell, and bounced under the tables.

Fern, shrieking with pain and fury, threw her skillet and knife away and grabbed me. She got hold of my skillet, wrenched it out of my hand, and threw it away. Then she went with both hands for my neck.

The movies fool people about this, about smaller but quicker fighters overcoming larger opponents, David killing Goliath. But in fact, if David doesn't drop Goliath in the first minute or so, Goliath is going to win. Unless the larger fighter is extremely slow, extremely stupid, or extremely timid, in a long fight, height and sheer mass will eventually prevail.

Fern was smart, fast, determined, and had the courage of madness.

When I realized how much stronger she was, I was appalled. It wasn't only her larger size, it was training, of a sort. Now that I thought back, I remembered her lifting patients to turn them on the examining tables. Somebody had told me once that nurses had to be very strong, but the words hadn't really registered. Now I remembered Fern singlehandedly lifting that construction worker onto the table. I was completely outclassed.

I wrenched myself away from her, but I was weakening. The next time might be my last.

I ran behind a metal-screen tier of shelves of saucepans. As she followed me, I pushed the shelves over on her. She wasn't hurt, but it took her two or three seconds to untangle herself from the pans that rained around her and bounced all over the floor. Meanwhile, I looked desperately for someplace to run, a door to get out of here, or someplace to hide.

The only door nearby was not an exit. I could tell by the fact that it had no glass panel. There wasn't any other choice, and even if it led to a storeroom, I could lock it or wedge it from inside and keep her out.

I tore the door open, rushed inside, and slammed the door. Then I leaned my shoulder against it while I felt around for a light switch. It was right next to the doorjamb and I flipped it up. I was in a cold room, from the temperature. A walk-in refrigerator. Not a freezer, thank God. Shelves of broad, flat cooling pans were ranged on all three sides and in a large bank down the middle. I had just a glimpse of what looked like Jell-O and maybe vanilla pudding in pans near me when Fern hit the outside of the door with a crash.

There was no inside lock. Why would there be, in what amounted to a huge refrigerator?

Fern must have thrown her whole body weight against the door, because the frame trembled. The door was built to open inward, unfortunately. Possibly that made it easier to carry in loaded trays of unjelled pudding and Jell-O. The latch was a simple L-shaped handle that you pushed down. I looked around for something to push against it to wedge under the latch.

I tried to stretch over and grab some of the trays off the racks. Fern hit the door again, but I managed to hold it shut, bruising my left shoulder. In the instant while I thought she was backing up for another run at the door, I let go of the door, lurched for the rack, got one tray—and the door burst open.

Fern came in like an avalanche, throwing the whole weight of her body against me. I fell onto my back, then kicked up at her with both legs. The kick must have caught her in the chin. She reared up with blood coming from her tongue. I grabbed a tray again, planning to sidearm it into her head. But she slammed both fists into the bottom of it, blasting it upward out of my hands and into the light bulb in the ceiling.

Everything went black.

I felt Fern's hands, grasping for my neck. She missed, clawing at my shoulder in the pitch dark. I pushed her, then reeled back into the racks and fell onto the floor. One of the tiers of racks fell over behind me. I heard Fern grunt with effort as she threw a fist toward where she thought I was. The blow only grazed my lower back because I was jumping up.

I turned and butted my head into her stomach, catching her squarely. We both fell against the door with a thud, but it opened inward and didn't move. She grabbed for my neck again, dragging her nails all the way down my cheek as I spun away. We were both slipping in spilled Jell-O and pudding.

I sidestepped in the black dark, felt her nearby, even heard the rustle of her clothes as she jumped to where she thought I was.

I leaped directly at the sound and landed on her back. She was standing, but my weight dragged her to the floor. I seized her hair in both my fists and held her down. She struggled, making strange, bubbling noises. Her hands reached back to try to grab my hands and she clawed skin off the backs, but I held on. If I let her go now, I would surely die. It was cold and dank and smelled of vanilla pudding.

It should have been funny, I thought, fighting in pudding, but it wasn't. My eyes must have been wild, wide open, and fierce. I held her hair, held her head down, and when I finally realized that she had stopped clawing at me and that the peculiar bubbling noises she was making was because she was breathing in pudding or Jell-O, I just held on harder.

It could be a trick. She was tricky, all right. With my knee I felt forward, trying to figure out what she was lying in without letting go of her. My knee touched the rim of a metal pan. The best I could remember of what these pans had looked like, in the few seconds I had to see them, was that they were only four or five inches deep, but quite long. Maybe two feet wide and three feet long, each filled with enough pudding for a hundred patients. I pictured her neck caught over the sharp rim of the pan, her face in whatever the pan contained. And I was glad.

I waited and waited. I knew perfectly well that by now she was probably dead, but my terror and anger were so great I just held on. My clothes were clammy and sticky. I shivered.

Finally, I sat back. Then I was overcome with fear that she would instantly jump up and grab me and kill me, so I seized her hair again and held on.

But she did not move.

Keeping one hand gripped tightly in her hair, with the other I felt for the carotid pulse in her neck. There was none; but I was no expert. I held on a while longer.

Gradually, I faced the fact that, for the first time in my life, I had killed a person.

I wasn't as sorry as I should have been.

· · ·

I was covered with slimy, slippery, sticky, cold stuff. It was dark and icy in here. But where was the door? No light whatsoever came in around it, which made sense; there would be a good seal around a refrigerator door to hold in the cold. There were no visual cues at all.

The room as I remembered it was about ten by twenty feet, so there would be no problem finding my way out. All I had to do was start anywhere, find any wall and go feeling along it, all the way around if necessary, until I got to the door.

I walked two or three careful steps, slipping over slimy stuff underfoot, hitting my shin against pans, until I reached a wall. I felt along it only a foot or so before I was blocked by a rack of trays. No problem. There had been racks along both walls as well as down the middle, so I'd just keep feeling along. I went slowly for a while, counting my footsteps, and in about twenty feet came to a place where the racks ended. The end wall, farthest from the door probably.

I froze. I thought I had heard a sound.

Fern was alive. She was after me.

No, that wasn't possible. My ears strained and my eyes were wide open, as if they could help my ears to hear.

There was a plopping. Pudding or Jell-O, falling from some spilled tray.

I went on and came to another right angle. Now I worked my way along another bank of trays in racks. As I got closer to the front, some of the racks were empty where we'd crashed into them. And then my foot hit something soft.

I screamed.

Then there was silence. It was Fern, lying on the floor.

I couldn't bring myself to move, to step over her or around her. I was just too frightened.

But I had to. I had to get out of here before the cold killed me.

I made up my mind, shut my eyes—yes, I know this was idiotic, since it was pitch black anyhow, but the mind is a strange thing—and took a long step over her with my left foot. It worked. I lifted my right foot over without my foot hitting her, and then felt my way to the corner.

Now it would be just a couple of feet to the door. There it was. I felt the edge of it. What joy!

I felt across it to the handle.

Which wasn't there!

I'd heard about refrigerators without inside handles, but this couldn't be one! The cooks would be in and out of here all day and anybody might get stuck in here. It would be completely unsafe to have a walk-in refrigerator with no escape.

Shaking, I felt the door again. Here were the hinges. The latch had to be on the other side. Here was the edge, and back a little—was a hole. I stuck my finger in the hole and felt something metal. Now more terrified than ever, I crouched down to feel around on the floor.

The handle lay next to the door with its metal shank snapped off.

We had crashed into it while we were fighting.

I had no idea of the time. Midnight? One A.M.? Nobody would look for me. I had left the trauma center at the end of the shift, and they would think I'd just gone home. Sam might wonder why I didn't say goodbye, but I hadn't said goodbye when I'd been so angry with him, and maybe he'd figure I'd gone to check on Mike, anyhow.

Oh, my God.

What was the temperature in here? It wasn't a freezer, but still, the temperature couldn't be over forty-five. You could develop hypothermia in warmer places than that.

I was dressed in light summer clothing. That was bad. And the clothing was wet and cold. That would make it worse. I had lost some blood because of the scalpel cut in my arm and the knife cut on my hand. That would make it still worse.

When would the morning cooking staff arrive? Not much before five A.M., I guessed.

Fern had been wearing a white cotton jacket over her scrubs. I was going to have to take it off her. Maybe the scrubs, too. No, that would be impossible. I couldn't bear it.

I went over and touched her, very gingerly. Her face was cold. Her eyes felt like they were open. She was really dead.

For the rest of my life, I never want to think again about getting that jacket off her. Then, when I put it on, it was wet, and thin cotton, and not much help. I retreated to a corner near the door, folded myself down into a sitting position, and shivered.

I could easily die here.

Doesn't eating keep up body temperature? There was a pan lying on the floor, tilted and half empty. I scooped up some of the sticky, cold contents and put it in my mouth. Vanilla pudding. Ugh! Pudding ought to be chocolate, if it's going to be any good at all, but even chocolate pudding would have gagged me now. My throat wouldn't accept it. I forced a swallow. I got a little down, and finally a little more. Then I gagged again and I knew that if I took in any more I'd be sick. I wrapped my arms around my legs and put my head down on my knees.

For a while, as I crouched there, shivering, wondering whether I was warmer in the corner because of the reduced air flow or colder because my back was against a cold wall, all I could hear was the dripping and plopping of pudding or Jell-O from containers that had been tipped. And the cycling on of the refrigerator motor every so often. I didn't know how often. I had no sense of time. Each time the motor went on, I would cringe, knowing that a few seconds after the motor noise started, an icy wind would blow through the darkness.

Then, quite a long time later, I began to notice that I was dozing off and wakening, then dozing off again. Someplace I had heard that falling asleep when you're chilled was danger-ous. But it was just so tempting. I got up, once, and jogged in place for half a minute, but it was too painful. My eyes ached with every bounce, and my knees ached after a few steps. It didn't seem to make me any warmer either.

So I sank back down and let lethargy take over.

And then Fern Butler started to move. I heard her shift first, just a little, and groan. Then there were unmistakable sounds of her sitting up. Then I saw her slowly start to rise to her feet. She was wearing her green surgical scrubs. She stretched and rose taller, right before my eyes. Her hands were fists. Slowly she uncoiled her fingers, and I noticed for the first time how sharp her fingernails were. She had paint-ed them silver. They were little, tiny scalpels.

Something far back in my mind said that there was no light in this icy prison and I couldn't possibly see Fern. But it made no difference to me. I did see her.

I knew that if I became totally unconscious, she would not be able to find me. So I gave in, and fell asleep.

· 20 ·

I guess the kitchen cleaning crew, who came in around four A.M., discovered the mess in the kitchen, but it was another forty-five minutes before anybody thought to look in the refrigerator. Actually, there were many refrigerators, including three just for milk, one for meat, one for vegetables, and so on, all kept at different temperatures and humidities. Plus, there were several freezers. The cleaning crew called security when they found the mess. Then security looked around to see whether anything had been stolen. Finally, they realized that some of the blood they were seeing on the floor might be human, not beef, and then they did a thorough check of the whole kitchen complex.

When they found me, I was unconscious. I know now that I was given oxygen, packed with heating pads, and whisked into emergency, not the trauma unit. I don't remember any of this.

Sometime after that, I was placed in a bath of 105-degree water until my "core temperature" came up near normal. The first thing I remember was wondering why I was taking a bath in what I believed to be the middle of the night.

People drew blood. Then people drew more blood.

Then an extremely crabby face appeared in my line of sight. Chief of Detectives Harold McCoo stood just inside the door of my hospital room, so furious he was all puffed up. His forehead was corrugated with frown lines. His eyebrows almost met in the middle.

"Cat, I would *never* have believed you'd do anything like this again! How stupid can you get?"

"What? I didn't do anything!"

"Try to confront a murderer." He pulled over a chair, turned it around, and sat on it backward, leaning aggressively toward me over the top. "After everything I told you the last time!"

"I didn't."

"Oh, sure. She chased you into a refrigerator with a knife for no particular reason."

"I did *not* tell her that I suspected her. Really, McCoo! I didn't. I went to the cafeteria to talk with—uh, with one of the other staff members about a problem he might be able to fix. She saw us leave the rotunda and followed us there. I don't know why."

"You knew she was guilty before that?"

"Yes. But I was going to tell Hightower as soon as I got home."

"You didn't speak to her?"

"No."

"You didn't telegraph your suspicion? By a look? By body language?"

"No!" I thought about it. I may have studied her, wondering how a person who was such an experienced nurse, so good with children, so skilled, could also be a killer. I *did* remember looking at her. "Oh, McCoo. I certainly didn't intend to. But who knows what you can convey, inadvertently? Especially to somebody who's already watching every glance anybody makes."

He studied me a moment, then he sat up, more relaxed. "All right. I believe you."

"Well, thanks a whole lot! That's very generous of you! Why don't we just remember that without my help Hightower would never have figured out who committed the murders."

McCoo sighed. "Well, you had an inside track."

"One I constantly offered to share with High—oh, never mind." Hightower was a good detective. There was no point in trying to belittle him.

I said, "Actually, I've wondered—in the dark of the night last night, feeling sick—the look I gave Fern, if I did, wasn't much. It wasn't even enough for me to remember."

"So?"

"Suppose that's what happened to Sonali? She was watching Fern for some innocent reason, to learn some medical technique, and Fern thought she was giving her a 'suspecting' look."

"Oh, my God."

"That's how I felt. I felt chilled."

"Lord!"

"I know. At the same time—you know, Fern herself was a very damaged person."

"Who damaged a lot of other people. She just went out there and decided who ought to die, and killed them!"

"Not randomly, though. She was dominated by symbolism, did you notice? To her, everything represented something else. The older women she killed were stand-ins for her mother. When she wanted to keep Dr. Grant from telling about the murders, she stopped her throat with a sponge."

"What about Dr. Bachaan?"

"She was afraid Sonali would go on thinking about whatever worried her, and finally figure out that Fern had killed the old women. So she stopped her thinking with a knife at the base of the brain."

"She was a nightmare nurse. My opinion is you've saved the state money by killing her."

I said, "McCoo, have you ever thought about, when we're in a hospital, how totally we rely on the nurse's being sane?"

"Now I do. I didn't before."

"They bring medication, shoot it into our IV line while we're lying there unconscious. It could be anything!"

"Being conscious wouldn't help either. You never know what stuff they're using."

"Exactly."

"Which," McCoo added, "is quite a compliment to all the nurses in the world. Hundreds of thousands of them, with immense power. And doing their jobs professionally and with empathy."

I reached out a hand and touched his arm. "Will I get into trouble for, well, you know, killing her?"

"There won't be any charges, if that's what you mean. We found extra nitro paste in her locker. The case is locked up. How do you feel about killing somebody, though?"

"I was shaking when I first realized it today. And then I thought about all those—those—Dr. Grant and Sonali and the women. It may catch up with me again later, but I don't feel all that bad."

"Why did she kill Dr. Bachaan?"

"Either Sonali was blackmailing her, or she'd noticed something. The little I knew of Sonali, I suspect she noticed something about the deaths of the elderly women and she hadn't put it all together. She was from India, you know. She was having a few language-barrier problems and she may not have been clear on hospital procedure and other things. I think her instinct when puzzled would be to assume it was her fault. She probably got worried and simply asked Fern to explain it."

"Not a good idea."

"No. A deadly idea."

While he was sitting there, shaking his head, an aide came in and said, "This is your lunch tray. I know it's one o'clock, but you weren't allowed it before." She was all smiles, putting the plastic tray on my table and swinging the table over the bed.

She whisked off the plastic cover and left.

I stared at the meager offering. Some hot chicken soup that looked like glue. Hot tea. And vanilla pudding.

"Vanilla pudding! Oh, no! Oh, no!" I pushed the whole table back so fast the tea slopped onto the blanket.

McCoo picked up the pudding dish and went charging out into the hall. I heard him at the desk, saying, "Look at this! Doesn't anybody around here have any common sense?"

He gets mad at me, but he gets mad *for* me, too.

By two-thirty in the afternoon, as a result of my constant nagging, begging, demanding, and finally almost incessant whining, I got the staff to put me in a wheelchair and take me to see Mike, over in Loeschner Neurologic Services Center. To get there, we crossed a glassed-in bridge at the sixth-floor level and covered a dozen corridors.

Mike was lying in bed with a metal ring around the top of his head. It was held up by several rods that ran down to a kind of saddle thing over his shoulders. The nurse who had intercepted me and then permitted me to visit had said it was called a halo.

Apt in form only. For Mike I imagined it was more like a torture device, and not at all heavenly.

"Hi, Mike."

"Cat. You came. I thought you'd given up on me."

"How are you feeling?"

"Oh, not so good."

"What do the doctors say?"

"They say we'll wait and see. I don't know what that means. It's very scary, Cat." His lips trembled, but he didn't cry. Maybe he was too weak to cry.

"You had the surgery last night?"

"I guess it was last night. I wasn't really sure what time of day it was, or anything."

"It must be disorienting. First the accident, then the anesthetics and all."

"I just don't know what's going to become of me."

"Mike, how did the accident happen?"

He looked away for just a second. "I don't really remember."

"Are you sure, Mike? Think."

"I can't think! I don't know!"

I didn't believe him. But he was a sick man, and I let it go.

"Cat—"

"What?"

"I've been thinking. I'll be here for a while, in this hospital, I mean. And I won't have any alcohol while I'm here. If I go to AA regularly after I get out—if I ever get out—would you come back to me?"

"Can we wait and talk about it as time goes on?"

"No, I need to know. I need to have something to live for."

"You're not dying."

"If I'm paralyzed, it's almost like dying."

"Anyway, people shouldn't live *for* other people. People should live for themselves."

"Cat, don't be so cold to me. I need you. Please tell me you will."

"Maybe, Mike."

"That's more than you've said in months. I'm going to believe that means yes."

I got back to my hospital bed about three, in a precarious mental condition. Sam was waiting there. Apparently he'd checked on Mike by phone and then come up to see me.

"He's okay, Cat."

"He doesn't think so."

"Well, he's been told that with a few weeks' rehab he'll be walking."

"He really doesn't think so."

"Are you so sure? Maybe he doesn't want *you* to think so. Maybe he wants your sympathy."

"Well, he has it. I feel like a monster."

"What do you mean?"

"I think I should stay with him. He really can't handle life without me."

"Cat, listen to what you're saying. Are you telling me that you'd marry and settle down with Mike, even though you don't care for him?"

"I do care for him."

"Do you love him?"

"Well, no."

"See?"

"But I wouldn't have to marry him either."

"So you're going to live with him, even though you don't want to?"

"Maybe just long enough to straighten him out."

"Do you really believe you'll be able to straighten him out?"

"How do I know! Dammit, all I know is I don't feel good about myself this way, and don't people say if you don't feel good about what you're doing, you're probably doing something wrong?"

Sam pushed his hand back and forth across his eyebrows. "Look, what are you suggesting? Living with him? Suppose you did live with him a couple of years. Would you feel good about that?"

I shook my head. How could I know? "Maybe I would if it put him on his feet."

"Cat, I don't want to say much one way or the other. I don't want to do more than ask questions, because I'm personally involved here."

"I appreciate that. I don't want you to feel like you're walking on eggs either, though."

"You know about what the substance abuse counselors call an 'enabler.'"

"Sure. A person who covers for the drug user or alcoholic. Like a wife who calls the boss in the morning and says he's sick when he's really hung over."

"The idea is that enablers don't help and they may even be perpetuating the problem."

"Well, that 'enabler' business has always bothered me. There's a whiff of blaming the victim about it. The alcoholic husband may be a victim of his disease but his wife is a victim, too, and it's just not fair to imply that by trying to help she's really in some way trying to keep him sick. I mean, maybe she's misguided, but no sympathetic person sees somebody screwing up his life and doesn't try to help."

Sam said, "I agree. But supposing helping doesn't help?"

"Yeah, well, mostly it doesn't. That's true."

"Al-Anon, you know, the AA group for people close to alcoholics, talks about detachment."

"Detachment," I said, "is easier said than done."

"There's a kind of tyranny that people who have a problem can hold over you. You feel guilty that they have a problem that you don't, so you start to compensate."

"Sure, but am I my brother's keeper?"

"Maybe for your brother. But you're not everybody's keeper every minute of the day."

We sat there, me in my bed with the back angled up, Sam in his plastic chair. We didn't know what else to talk about. Obviously he didn't want to ask me anything about Fern just yet. Suddenly a thought hit me. He saw it in my face.

"What?"

"I just remembered something about my visit to Mike."

"What?"

"The orderly wheeled me in to see him—in a wheelchair. And he never asked why."

Hal Briskman wasn't annoyed with me. What he said was, "If you were an employee, I'd fire you."

But then he said, "Of course, you're not. I need your article as soon as you get home."

I just purely love Chicago weather. This strikes some people as odd, but then, there are a lot of people living in Chicago besides me, so they must not be too turned off by it either.

I love the winds off the lake, and sleet. But most of all, I love walking in falling snow. Well, maybe not most of all. What I love most of all about Chicago weather is that it's always changing. It's the opposite of San Francisco. Different parts of San Francisco are known for their different—and consistent—weather. In San Francisco you can be in warm sunshine, and walk six blocks and find cold fog. In Chicago you stand still, wait half an hour, and the new weather comes to you.

My friends think I'm being Pollyanna when I say I love snow and sleet. Not so. There's one mood of Chicago weather I don't like. That's very muggy, very humid, very hot days we often get in July. I still have to work, get places, walk to interviews, and I arrive feeling like I have all the energy of a sea slug.

Somehow, a case of hypothermia cast summer weather in a new light for me.

They let me go Sunday morning, and as I left the hospital, the heat hit me hard, but it felt good.

I'd had time in the hospital to plan my article. The idea of trauma centers, whatever the financial costs, is one that won't die. The human costs of not having them is too high. It's not that there's anything wrong with emergency departments. It's the extras in a trauma center that are so necessary—the on-call anesthesiologist, the twenty-four-hour trauma surgeon, and the equipment. It's hard to imagine the public agreeing to do without treatment that has been developed and is there to be used. We're going to have automobile accidents, fires, air crashes, and construction accidents as long as civilization is anything like it is now. I don't think the public will stand for knowing that, in case of an accident, less will be done for them than might be. It's the manner of paying for trauma centers that's going to need work. Certainly billing all the loss to the individual hospital is not working.

In the article I would describe the people who work in trauma units. And with some fudging of the causes and data about the patients I saw, I would describe the lives saved. I do facts. Let the public make policy.

Sam drove me home. We were still quite tentative with each other. Someday I might write a character study of Fern and why she was the way she was. But not right now. It was a sensitive subject for me. As for Sam's telling me I had to leave the unit if I were planning to write an inside story, I respected him for that. Anyhow, you can hardly say that you want to meet an independent man and then become furious when he behaves independently.

I had explained to him about Coyne and Tegucaine. And I had asked him to take a look at the case reports about the two elderly women that had been on Dr. Grant's desk at the time she died. "There were others Dr. Grant didn't suspect."

Sam said, "We'll probably never know how many women Fern killed."

"How did she get away with it so long? Wouldn't autopsies show too much of some drug or other?"

"Autopsies aren't magic. There's a 'drug screen' that's done in suspicious deaths, but it's limited to a few of the most common things. If you tested for thousands of drugs, it would cost hundreds of thousands of dollars. And besides, when somebody dies after a serious accident, it isn't usually considered suspicious."

"Whenever she saw an elderly woman patient whose blood pressure was falling, she spread nitro paste on them and dropped the blood pressure further?"

"In the other case report you told me about, the elderly woman who was injured when the car drove into the restaurant, Fern must have injected extra potassium. That's hyperkalemia. Easiest thing in the world to do. We keep potassium around to correct low potassium situations. And she knew from the woman's history that she had a kidney problem. Even if an autopsy had been done, they'd lay the death off to kidney trouble."

"And she killed when she was working with an inexperienced doctor? Like Sonali or Zoe?"

"I guess."

"And I suppose that's what Sonali noticed."

Sam said, "I guess. You knew there was some chicanery going on. I didn't. I blame myself."

"You shouldn't."

"Yeah, maybe I should. I might have saved several lives. My mind doesn't work that way."

"Now you're saying I have a suspicious mind."

"Of course! Why not? It's a good thing to have, and in your job it's essential. In mine it's not. Usually."

"Not if you don't want to look at things squarely."

"But it's unpleasant to be constantly suspicious. You look into everybody's possible motives all the time. All that nastiness."

"Somebody has to do it."

"Wait a minute. Didn't we already have this discussion?"

I said, "Did we? No."

"Yes we did. But it was the other way around. Weren't you asking me how I could stand my job? All that unpleasantness and sadness day after day?"

That stumped me. He was right.

He said, "Maybe we're more alike than it seems at first glance."

"Well, it's possible that maybe we could get along."

"You're very cautious."

"And I hope very honest."

"I'll buy that."

"Did you know," I said, "that Coyne was disparaging you?"

"Yes. But I didn't know why."

"He knew you were recording swelling with Tegucaine, and he wasn't. Anything he could do to partially discredit you would make that look less suspicious."

"Well, I'll deal with him on Monday."

"I figured out why the trauma center was disturbing to me."

"Oh? Why?"

"Chance. It makes it so obvious how much we're all just playthings of random luck. The Holyroods didn't know they were going to be hit by a truck. If they'd left home two seconds later, they'd probably all be alive. Nhu Duc Tran was literally struck by lightning! Colczyk was just playing on the school playground. Hit by a stray bullet. It shows me how we can all be hit, metaphorically speaking, by a stray bullet."

"Does it make it any better when it's the consequence of some considered action? Like Hannah Grant. She knew Fern might be dangerous, but she confronted her anyway."

"Grant was courageous."

"Yes. She was."

I said, "Who did you think killed Dr. Grant?"

"I never decided. I was suspicious about Lester Smalley, but I felt sorry for him at the same time."

"I knew Lester Smalley didn't kill Hannah Grant."

"How?"

"He would have had to mop his way toward the lounge to make it look reasonable, and mop his way back. And if he had, he'd have mopped up the chocolate smear on the floor."